THE MISSING CLIENT

Krystal Powers

ISBN-13: 9798990616608 (ebook)
ISBN-13: 9798990616615 (paperback)

Book cover designed by RockingBookCovers.com

Printed in the United States of America

DECEMBER 8, 2006

Mikey slouched in his 1979 black Pontiac Bonneville. It had two enormous doors and a carmine velvet interior. The odometer had turned over twice, which meant the car had clocked over two hundred thousand miles. Clothes and toiletries were strewn all over the vehicle's interior.

He held a black cell phone he'd just bought from a drugstore in Lake Arrowhead. He was trying to get the thing to work, because he had to make three calls. The crappy instructions sure weren't helpful. He grabbed his list of numbers and went for it, dialing the first one. To his surprise, it worked; it was ringing.

But no one answered. Not even an answering machine picked up, just an endless string of rings. One after the other. Mikey called back twice, but it was the same thing. He tossed the phone on the passenger seat and slid his hands around the smooth steering wheel.

He didn't know what that meant. Rather than waste time, he moved on to the second call. A man answered and Mikey rattled off the name of the person he was looking for.

"No one by that name lives here," the person on the other end said, sounding grumpy and put out.

Mikey rubbed a hand around his head, feeling the rough stubble of his buzz cut. "Are you sure?"

"Yes, I'm sure."

The man ended the call, not giving Mikey a chance to follow up. He was sure the man was lying, but what could he do? Well, he could try again in case he dialed the wrong number. This time, the same man answered, so Mikey hung up rather than get into a whole thing with the guy.

He made his third and final call. The person answered after several rings; this time, he hit the jackpot. The voice sounded like he remembered. After all these years.

Mikey gripped the phone. He didn't need to introduce himself. "It's me."

The phone went dead. He knew this might happen, but he figured he would get further into the conversation. Especially after all this time. But no, just straight to a hang-up. So much for a fresh start.

A wave of frustration rolled across Mikey's body. Screw this! He flung the phone onto the passenger seat. It bounced and landed on the floor.

He was still in the parking lot of the store in Lake Arrowhead, putting him one hundred miles from where he needed to be. With no traffic, the drive would take over an hour and a half. But with rush hour starting, who knew how long it could stretch?

He was out of luck for tonight.

He needed to gain control of this situation. He thought of the letter he received. It contained the stupid line about money not being the key to happiness. It was a threat. A threat disguised as a platitude.

Well, he'd get what was his. Sooner rather than later.

They could ignore his calls, but what would they do when he showed up in person?

PART 1

GETTING MY FOOT IN THE DOOR

CHAPTER 1

Client Number One sat across from me at my kitchen table. Len Zobak. My landlord. It was Saturday, December 9, 2006. Was this what I envisioned when I started my forensic accounting business? I wasn't quite sure.

Len was taller than me, with a full head of dark blonde hair and pale blue eyes. He was trim, in shape, and around seventy years old. Despite the temperature being in the high seventies, Len wore a collared shirt, sweater, and blazer. I felt hot looking at him. I dressed in a short-sleeve shirt, jeans, and sandals. My living room's sliding doors were open, a slight breeze wafting through the apartment.

Len clasped his hands together. "Jocelyn Bennett, can you tell me about yourself? You've been my tenant for a while now, but I don't know much about you. Except that you're an accountant."

I lived in Brentwood, a Los Angeles Westside neighborhood. It was known for being an enclave of wealthy and famous people. I resided in a lesser-known area containing a swath of condos and apartments where young professionals flocked after college. Nearby San Vicente Boulevard was home to trendy restaurants and shops.

My building on Montana Avenue was from the 1970s and had an open-air courtyard with palm trees and green landscaping. I had a unit on the third floor with white walls, woodwork, and carpet. The furniture was from an earlier life when I owned a tenth-floor condo on Wilshire Boulevard near Beverly Hills. That place, and my life back then, felt like ages ago.

I looked across at Len. He had asked me a question. Whether I could tell him something about myself.

I straightened up in my chair. "How about the condensed version? I'm from Omaha, Nebraska, and an only child. I came to California to attend Stauffer University in Claremont. After graduating, I moved to Los Angeles."

I stopped there and didn't mention that I had long blonde hair, green eyes, and stood five feet, six inches tall, since those things were obvious to Len. I assumed Len knew I was young, though I wasn't sure if he would guess I was twenty-six.

Len smiled. "That was good. I feel like we're old friends." He ran a hand along the buttons on his blazer's sleeve. "And you studied accounting at Stauffer?"

"Yes. After I graduated, I studied for the CPA exam."

"That stands for certified public accountant,

right?"

"That's correct."

Len furrowed his eyebrows. "That's a challenging test. Isn't it?"

I nodded. "Back when I took it, the pass rate was below fifty percent."

Len leaned forward in his chair. "Then what?"

"Then I started working for Harman & Haskell, a public accounting firm. Most of the time, it's just called Harman."

"They're a Big Four, right?"

The Big Four were the four largest accounting firms in the world. At one point, it was the Big Eight. Through mergers, it was reduced to five. After the Enron fraud, one of the Big Five, Arthur Andersen, ceased to exist, so four remained.

I shook my head. "No, they're considered second tier. Harman is fifth or sixth in the rankings, depending on the year."

"And what did you do after you left?"

"I worked as the chief financial officer of a real estate company."

Len raised his eyebrows. "You were the CFO?"

"Yes, that's correct."

"What company?"

"ADWR. Adam Davis Westside Realty. Have you heard of it?"

Len frowned. "I think so. Can you refresh my memory?"

"Well, the company's gone now. My boss, Adam Davis, the owner of the company, is in prison for fraud."

CHAPTER 2

Len's eyes grew wide. "Your boss went to jail for fraud?"

"Yes. Adam Davis was running a mortgage fraud through the company."

"All by himself?"

"No, there were others involved."

"And they're in prison too?"

I pushed away a few stray hairs that had crossed into my eyes. "One is. The other's not."

Len looked like he was doing calculations in his head. "Who is the other one in prison?"

"Greg West. Harman & Haskell, my old firm, were the auditors for ADWR. Greg was the partner on the ADWR audit. In fact, I used to work with him. It was pretty shocking that he ended up being involved."

"No kidding. You said one person wasn't in prison. How did he or she get away with it?"

I shrugged. "I guess he was clever enough to get out. Tom Anderson left the United States shortly after everything was discovered."

"Do you think they'll ever find him?"

I wasn't sure what would happen to Tom, but I figured he was gone for good, which gave me a measure of peace. "I don't know. Tom had a home and business in Brentwood. He left all that behind."

Len frowned. "I'm sure the authorities are on the lookout for him. He would be arrested if he ever arrived back in the United States."

The thought of Tom slipping back into the country made me shiver, even though I knew it was unlikely. "I think you're right."

Len waved. "He's never coming back. If he's smart. How did the fraud get discovered?"

I blushed. "I was the one who figured it out."

"And all of this cost you your job, I take it."

"Yes. Once Adam was arrested, that was it for ADWR. Although he shut things down well before that. On the positive side, it prompted me to start my company."

Len clasped his hands together. "It's always wise to work for yourself."

Len surprised me. Everyone I had talked to about starting my business said the opposite, inundating me with stories of catastrophe. They threw around statistics about the failure rate for small companies like rice at a wedding.

I pulled myself from my muddled thoughts. "I hope you're right."

"Tell me. Do you miss it? Your old life?"

I thought about Len's question. My trajectory since leaving college had been up, up, up. After ADWR imploded, it went down, down, down. And now? Well, my life felt unrecognizable. If I thought about that too much, I became overwhelmed with doubt and believed the naysayers in my life.

I tried to avoid getting sucked into the negativity. And I couldn't unload my woes on my first client. I smiled. "I'm looking forward to new opportunities."

Len snapped his fingers. "Wait a minute! Adam Davis. He's the one who came here looking for you."

Len had helped me out when I first moved into this building, and I would always be thankful for that. "Yes, that was him."

Len shook his head. "What a bum."

I laughed and Len smiled.

He pulled a small notepad from his blazer pocket. "Sorry for all the questions. I like to get to know the people that I hire. I don't mean to pry."

"It's okay. I don't mind. Is there anything else you want to know?"

His face grew serious. "Not right now. But I have a problem. And I'm hoping you can help."

CHAPTER 3

My stomach filled with butterflies and uncertainty washed over me. This was the moment I had been waiting for: finding out what Len wanted me to help him with. I hoped he didn't stump me.

I grabbed my spiral notebook and a blue Pilot G-2 pen. "What can I do for you?"

Len lifted his right index finger. "First, let's discuss payment. And do you need me to sign anything?"

I felt uncomfortable taking Len's money because he had helped me out with Adam Davis. But I knew that if I wanted to make a living at this, eventually I must accept payment. I also planned to have my clients sign a contract, also called a client engagement letter. I didn't yet know what Len needed help with, so I hadn't drafted one for our meeting.

"There's no charge," I said, my words coming out quicker than expected. "And right now, I don't need you to sign anything."

Len shook his head. "That's nonsense. What's

your hourly rate?"

I was planning to charge two hundred dollars an hour. But I couldn't bill Len that much. So I tossed out a lowball figure. "How about twenty dollars an hour?"

"We both know that's not your actual rate."

I smiled. "It's a discount, you know, for Christmas."

"Come on, now. Just spill it. What do you charge?"

I wondered if doubling my proposed rate might satisfy him. "How about forty dollars?"

Len nodded and smiled. "That's better."

Having arrived at an agreement on the fees, I could get to work. "What is it that you need help with?"

"I need some tax advice."

"What specifically?"

"I want to give some gifts, and I would like to know what I can deduct."

I felt relieved. This was an area that I was knowledgeable about. I wasn't a tax expert, but I knew the basics. "The current amount, for two thousand six, is twelve thousand dollars."

"And this twelve thousand dollars, it's total?"

"Per person."

Len raised his eyebrows. "Let me make sure I understand. Let's say I give money to two people. Are you saying that I can give each person twelve thousand dollars, for a total of twenty-four thousand dollars?"

"Yes, that's correct."

Len held his pen. "That's great."

He jotted a few things on his small notepad. While he wrote, I remained silent. He looked like he was thinking hard about something.

He looked up. "And what about the other person?"

"You mean the person you gave the gift to?"

"Yes. Does the person have to report this money as income on his or her taxes?"

"No," I said. "They don't."

He smiled. "You're making my day, you know that?"

He continued taking notes. Then he looked at me, and his smile vanished. "I heard the bank creates a report if you deposit a large amount of money. Is that true?"

"Yes. It's part of the Bank Secrecy Act."

"I see."

"The bank generates what's called a currency transaction report for all deposits over ten thousand dollars."

"And this goes to the government?"

"Yes."

Len wrote in his notebook. "Why's that?"

"Well, the Bank Secrecy Act was passed with the purpose of catching and preventing money laundering."

After several more questions, we wrapped up our meeting. Len pulled out two crisp twenty-dollar bills from his wallet. He placed them on the table. "I have a few more questions for you. Can we set up another time to talk?"

I was pleasantly surprised. I figured that today would be our only meeting. "Of course. Did you have a day and time in mind?"

"How about tomorrow at four?"

Len was my first client. And my only client. My schedule wasn't exactly packed. "That sounds great."

Len was now staring off, and I wondered if he had even heard me. I tapped my pen on the table, hoping the prompt would get his attention. He continued to look zoned out.

I cleared my throat. "Would you like to meet here? In my apartment?"

Len still appeared lost in thought, but then he slowly turned to face me. "I'm sorry, what did you say?"

I reiterated what I said before, unsure what Len had heard. "Tomorrow at four works for me. How about we meet here in my apartment?"

"Yes, that would be great."

"Is everything okay?"

He looked away again. "I hope so."

CHAPTER 4

I returned to my parking garage after dinner with two friends from college. We ate at an Italian restaurant at The Grove, an outdoor mall ten miles from my apartment. The mall was decked out for Christmas, including a giant tree.

I wore an apple-red cashmere sweater, dark jeans, and gold heels, the closest thing to festive holiday attire in my closet.

The Christmas music pumping through the mall put me in the holiday spirit. I still had the refrain of a song running through my head. Something about a tree and mistletoe.

I was also in a good mood because I had landed my first client. Yes, technically, it was an hour of my time. But I still made some money. And Len had scheduled a follow-up appointment for tomorrow. I felt more confident after today that I could answer his questions, but I still worried I wouldn't be able to help him. I wouldn't focus on that now. I had more work lined up. It was a start. And that was all that mattered.

I climbed the stairs from the underground parking garage and entered my building's enclosed outdoor courtyard. The complex had green Christmas lights draped over the bushes outside the entrance, and the three palm trees in the courtyard had white lights wrapped around the trunks.

Len had a first-floor unit right next to the front gate. I walked past his apartment on the way to check my mail. I grabbed the few letters in my box and stuck them in my purse.

Len's patio had a string of multi-colored lights. His blinds were closed, so I could no longer see the small tree in the picture window. It looked wrong. But why? I wasn't out most evenings and couldn't recall whether Len closed his blinds at night.

I opened my apartment door and trampled on a yellow envelope, my high heels almost puncturing holes into it. What in the world was this? Not wanting to touch it, I slid it to the side with the toes of my shoes.

I tossed my purse on the couch, slipped off my heels, and stared at the envelope like I do when I discover a spider in my shower. What should I do about this?

I bent over, still refusing to touch it. I had only been gone for a few hours, which meant there was a small window for when this was placed here.

The envelope was too thick to have been slid under the door. But the envelope itself wasn't what worried me most. It was that the envelope was *inside* my apartment. And someone had been in here while

I was gone.

CHAPTER 5

I made a beeline to my bedroom, reached under my bed, and retrieved a heavy-duty flashlight that I bought years ago for utility and self-defense. If the power went out, it could light up my entire apartment. If I had a home invasion, I could blind the person and then whack him over the head.

Not that I expected to use it on any bad guys, but you could never be too careful living alone. For example, I might come home one night from dinner and find that someone had been in my apartment. Oh, wait.

Gripping the flashlight, I moved through my apartment, checking every room and closet and looking behind and under every piece of furniture. The doors and windows were still locked. No one was in my apartment.

Feeling confident I was safe, I picked up the envelope and turned it over. There was no label, front or back. The metal clasp was closed, but it hadn't been sealed.

I walked over to my sizeable rectangular kitchen

table. My office, where I kept my files and business things, was my guest bedroom. As much as possible, I preferred working in the open space of the kitchen and living room areas.

I opened the envelope. Inside was a letter from Len. I understood how the package got inside my apartment in the first place; he had used his key.

I read Len's letter.

Dear Ms. Bennett,

Could you deliver these checks for me? All are local.

I wouldn't ask such a favor, especially after you were so nice to help me today. However, something has come up.

For your trouble, I have included payment. Please see the smaller envelope.

Sincerely,

Len Zobak

At the bottom of the letter was a list of five addresses. Attached to the letter with a paper clip were five checks, each made out for the same amount: $9,000. The smaller envelope contained a stack of hundred-dollar bills. Ten of them.

I set the checks, cash, and letter on the kitchen table and stared at the Christmas tree next to my patio doors. It was a ten-foot artificial tree with white lights and tinsel.

I did not want to deliver the checks for Len, but I felt terrible for feeling that way. I would love to help Len; that wasn't the problem. It was what he was asking for help with that made me uncomfortable. Stopping by unannounced at random houses? I barely felt like going to places where I was invited.

I didn't understand why he didn't mail the checks instead of hand-delivering them. Did he believe there wasn't enough time before year's end? Today was December 9; the post office could deliver the checks in at most a few days. Since they were local, they might even arrive the next day.

The checks were made out to such individuals as A. Baker. Len had not used the recipients' full names. The addresses were scattered throughout Los Angeles, including Sherman Oaks, Thousand Oaks, Torrance, Pasadena, and Diamond Bar. Sherman Oaks was the closest to me. Thousand Oaks was farther north of Sherman Oaks and might even be in Ventura County. Torrance was in the South Bay. Pasadena was east. Diamond Bar was even farther east, near my alma mater, Stauffer University.

These addresses were local, but it could take half a day to get from one end of Los Angeles to the other. I read the letter again and shook my head.

What had Len gotten me into?

CHAPTER 6

I shoved Len's letter, along with everything else, back into the envelope. Then I stepped into my high heels, locked my apartment, and went to see Len.

I arrived at his apartment, my keys in one hand and the envelope in the other. I knocked on his door, but he didn't answer. I felt like he was always home, but obviously he left from time to time.

I knocked again but still got no answer. I stood at the door, not knowing what to do. I felt uncomfortable holding onto $46,000: forty-five in checks and one in cash.

The door next to Len's apartment opened. The tenant, Betty Smith, a skinny woman with impeccable makeup and a silver bob, came out onto her patio. She wore dark slacks, a sweater, and leather moccasins. Supposedly, Betty was the first tenant back when the building was built. I had heard a rumor that she owned her unit, unlike the rest of us who rented.

Betty frowned. "What's all that banging going on out here?"

"Hi, Betty."

She crossed her arms. "Oh, it's you. The Numbers Gal."

Betty had called me by that nickname ever since she discovered I was a CPA.

Suddenly, Betty's attention was diverted. I turned to look at what Betty was staring at. Tara, another tenant, was lugging a basketful of clothes toward the laundry room. My unit had a washer and dryer, but I wasn't sure about the rest. Either way, there were on-site laundry facilities.

Betty walked off in Tara's direction. "Hey, you, wait a second. You can't do laundry past eight."

Tara froze, basket in hand, but didn't say anything. Betty was far enough away by then that I couldn't hear more of the conversation. I was sure Tara was receiving an earful about trying to sneak in a late-night load of laundry. It was a big no-no, which Betty helped enforce every chance she got.

I knocked again on Len's door and waited. He still didn't answer. I looked at his patio but saw nothing amiss. Since his blinds were closed, I couldn't see into the apartment.

Betty came back. I turned, but I didn't see Tara.

Her eyes widened. "That's a bright sweater."

That was a compliment, wasn't it? "Thanks," I said, hedging my bets.

She shook her head. "It's blinding, but it works on you."

So it wasn't a compliment? Or maybe? "Well, it is almost Christmas."

Betty sighed. "I suppose you're right."

I was eager to change the subject from my clothing. "Have you seen Len?"

Betty looked at me as if taking a police report. "What's this concerning? You aren't late on your rent, are you?"

"No. I was just wondering if you've seen him."

She narrowed her eyes as though scanning my body language for signs of deception. "I haven't seen him. I'm sure he'll be back. I'll give him a message for you."

"That's okay. I'll come back later."

She tilted her head, staring at what was in my hands. "What's with the envelope?"

I twisted the envelope around until it was behind my back. "Just some papers."

"You'd better get some postage on that. A mailing address would be helpful, if you plan to send that out."

I wanted to tell her to buzz off, but I always had the fear that the second she turned against a person, that individual was dead meat. I still wanted to live here without taking a long, convoluted way in and out of my apartment to avoid her. "Thanks, I hadn't considered that."

She attempted to smile, but it looked more like a grimace.

I tapped the envelope against my leg. "Well, I should get going. I'll catch Len later."

I turned around, headed toward my apartment, and swore I could feel Betty staring at me as I walked away.

CHAPTER 7

I locked my apartment door. I felt surprised at what had to be the fastest getaway I'd ever had from Betty. Usually, it took a force majeure to escape.

I slipped off my shoes and headed to my office. I had a small safe where I stored documents and valuables. The thing was so small and lightweight that a thief could stroll out with it tucked under one arm. My stuff would be gone forever. But it was all I had at the moment. I locked the envelope in the safe, where I would keep it for now.

I pondered my options. One was to keep the envelope until Len returned. A second was to return it to his apartment. In that case, I could write Len a note explaining that I couldn't deliver the checks. And then slip the message and envelope under his door. But because he had given me cash for my payment, the envelope was too bulky.

Even without the cash, just the checks, I still wasn't sure I could get the envelope to fit under the door. And I didn't feel comfortable placing $46,000 under Len's welcome mat.

My best bet was to keep everything in my safe and talk to Len when he returned. I was sure he would be back by tomorrow, and I could deal with this mess then.

I heard a knock on my door. Maybe it was Len, and I could get this all over with tonight, which would be the best solution.

I walked to my door and looked through the peephole. Betty stood on the other side. Not Len. My hopes were dashed. It looked like my quick getaway had been too good to be true. I should've figured.

Betty knew I was home, so there was no use hiding. I opened the door.

She was wringing her hands and chewing her lower lip. Her eyes were watery. "Something's wrong."

Maybe five minutes had passed since I last talked to her. "What happened?"

"Well, after talking to you, it got me thinking about Len."

"What specifically?"

"I saw him not that long ago. Right before I went to the market to pick up a few things. But you were looking for him, and he wasn't home. And I realized I hadn't seen him since the market. And I got to thinking."

"About what?"

"Well, his place looks different."

"Different, how?"

Betty sighed. Long and loud. "Does that matter? What *does* matter is that something is wrong."

27

"With Len?"

She kept wringing her hands. "Yes."

"What makes you say that?"

"Instinct."

I wasn't sure I wanted to work myself into a panic based on Betty's intuition. "Besides that."

"My gut is always right. I know there's something wrong."

Betty still hadn't convinced me to get worked up. "Okay, but there has to be something else."

"Well, how about this? He's not in his apartment. And some of his things are missing!"

CHAPTER 8

I stared at Betty. She continued wringing her hands, but she stopped chewing her lip. I didn't know what to think, let alone say.

"Hello? Jocelyn, are you listening? I said his things are missing."

I was confused. "What do you mean Len's things are missing?"

Betty rubbed her hands on her slacks. "Len's apartment. There are things missing."

"I got that much. But his blinds are closed. You can't see in, so how can you know anything is missing?"

"Because I looked inside. How else would I know?"

Her voice was getting louder and echoing off the stucco walls. The entire building could hear our conversation. Well, Betty's half. The start of a headache worked its way across my forehead, and I blinked several times, hoping to ward it off. "Did Len leave his apartment unlocked?"

"No, of course not. I know where Len keeps his spare."

"You used his key?"

"Yes, I did. He told me I could." Betty wagged her finger. "Don't take that tone."

Was this the first time, or had she done this before? Len had keys to all the apartments in the building. Had Betty been in my apartment when I wasn't home?

I put my arms behind my back. "What made you do that?"

"Do what?"

"Go in Len's apartment."

"He never closes those blinds, not even at night."

I thought the closed blinds looked different, but that didn't mean something terrible had happened, and it didn't seem like a valid enough reason for Betty to enter Len's apartment. "I close my blinds all the time."

She clapped her hands together. "How nice for you but Len doesn't. He sticks to a routine. And he never closes his front blinds."

Even though I disagreed with her decision to enter his apartment, I had no doubt she knew Len's habits forward and backward. "What things are gone?"

Betty leaned her head toward me as if she was sharing a secret. "A suitcase, some clothes."

"How do you know those items are actually missing?"

"I've been in his apartment a thousand times. He has two suitcases that he keeps in his closet. One is missing. There are also many empty hangers.

Something has happened, I'm telling you."

Was there anything to what Betty was saying? All I knew was that I talked with Len earlier today; we scheduled a meeting for tomorrow afternoon. Then a couple of hours later, he left me a note which said that something had come up. The letter, however, mentioned nothing about canceling our meeting. I assumed that wherever Len went, he would be back by tomorrow at four.

Since Len was my client and had a right to confidentiality, I wouldn't bring up the letter or checks with Betty. "Do you think there could be a simple explanation? Like maybe he had to go somewhere at the last minute?"

Betty shook her head, and her silver bob swished. "No."

"How can you be sure?"

"When Len leaves, he plans far in advance. He has me look after things."

"I don't mean a long trip."

"No. He still would have told me."

I found all this hard to believe. "Even for a few hours, he talks to you first?"

Betty fell silent and stared at me. I wondered what she was thinking.

It seemed likely that if Len left, he had done so in a hurry. "Maybe it was an emergency. And Len didn't have time to talk to you."

Betty shook her head again. "Len didn't have an emergency. Something's not right. I know it."

I didn't know what to make of all of this, but I

hoped that whatever had happened, Len would be back soon. The faster I could get these checks out of my possession, the better.

CHAPTER 9

I couldn't say for certain that everything was fine with Len, and I really needed to give the checks back to him. But standing here and talking with Betty wasn't helping. I wanted to move on. "Let's wait until tomorrow."

Betty glared at me. "Here are the facts. Len is gone. His blinds are closed. He mentioned not one word to me, even though I saw him earlier today. It's not an emergency. Something's wrong."

I didn't want to split hairs, but I had to say the obvious. "An emergency means something is wrong."

"Yes, I know that, but to me, an emergency implies an accident or something. I don't think it was a sprained ankle. Do you understand what I'm saying?"

Going around in circles with her and getting into a semantics debate was pointless. "Yes, I understand."

She smiled and smoothed her hair, apparently satisfied that I saw things her way. "Like I said, I talked to Len earlier today. He said nothing to me."

It still felt premature to assume the worst. "I know, but I'm sure whatever's going on, he's all right."

Betty's shoulders slouched. "What do I know? Maybe I'm overreacting."

"He'll be back."

Betty placed her hands on her hips; any hint of defeat I noticed moments ago was gone. "I need to know what you wanted to talk to him about."

"It was nothing."

She stared at me, narrowing her eyes into slits. "Did Len ever come and see you?"

I wondered how Betty knew about my meeting with Len. "See me about what?"

"He needed tax advice."

She knew the topic of our meeting too. "Len asked me some questions, yes."

Betty's hands were still on her hips. "Well?"

I raised my eyebrows. "Well, what?"

"What did he talk to you about?"

"I can't say."

She smirked. "Do you think you're an attorney or something?"

Irritation washed over me. Unless Len requested I do so, I could keep what he and I talked about private. Exceptions existed, of course, like everything. If a court or law enforcement agency requested information, I could be forced to turn it over. But for Betty Smith, Certified Nosy Neighbor? I didn't have to say anything. "Not exactly like an attorney, but what Len and I discussed is between him and me."

"You know, I told him to talk to you," Betty said.

"You did?"

"Absolutely. Len told me he had to talk to someone about taxes, and I told him he should go see The Numbers Gal, who lives up on the third floor."

So good old Betty was the one who referred my first client to me? I would've never guessed in a million years. I supposed I should be grateful and thank her.

This first client, however, had left me with an uncomfortable task, which complicated my life. My thanks to Betty for her recommendation would have to wait until I resolved things.

Betty waved. "Come on. I want to show you what I'm talking about."

CHAPTER 10

Despite feeling uncomfortable, I found it easier to follow Betty. Besides, I had a vested interest in Len's whereabouts. If something was wrong, I should know.

Together, we walked down the stairs and over to Len's apartment. Betty pulled a key from her slacks and unlocked the door. She stepped inside. "Len? Are you home? It's Betty and Jocelyn. We're checking to see if you're all right."

No one responded to her inquiry, so she walked farther into the entryway and turned back to me. "See? Len's not here."

So far, Betty was right.

Since Len always had his courtyard-facing blinds open, I knew what his apartment looked like. It was orderly with no clutter and nothing extraneous. His furniture was ornate with lots of dark wood. The pieces were in excellent condition.

Nothing in the living room or kitchen gave me the impression that something was amiss. No dirty dishes sat on the counters or in the sink. No food was out waiting to spoil. Everything was in its place.

A calendar hung on the kitchen wall. I moved closer to examine Len's appointments. Today and tomorrow had the same note: Jocelyn 302. Except for that, the only upcoming appointments that Len had marked off were Christmas Eve and Christmas Day. The other items for December, which looked to be routine doctor's appointments, had already occurred.

Betty caught me staring. "Come on. Move it, girl." She said it as though we were on the Oregon Trail, and if I fell behind, I'd be left for dead.

I followed Betty to the back of the apartment, where there were two bedrooms. Betty went into one and flipped on the light. The blinds were closed, which gave the room a claustrophobic feel. Like the living room and kitchen, the space was sparse but neat, containing a large dresser and mirror, a queen-sized bed, an armchair, and two nightstands.

Covering one wall was a collage of framed photos. Many were in black and white. A gold rosary hung from the right corner of a framed photograph of Pope John Paul II. Next to the pope was a replica of *The Last Supper* by Leonardo da Vinci.

Betty again noticed me staring. I felt like I was in grade school and just got caught chewing gum.

"Jocelyn, I said I wanted to show you something."

Betty opened a closet door and spread her hands like a game show host unveiling the grand prize. The problem was that I didn't know what I was looking at. I saw a closet similar to the one in my unit with mirrored sliding doors. Behind the doors were, wait for it, clothes, shoes, and small boxes.

Betty huffed. "Don't you see?"

"No, I don't."

Betty grabbed at a set of three loose hangers. "These had clothes on them. And look down here." She pointed to the floor. "There used to be another suitcase."

Betty and Len were closer than I thought. They had to be for her to know what was missing from his closet. I doubted they were more than friends. But what did I know? They were around the same age. Could there be something between them? Nah. It couldn't be. I just couldn't see Len tolerating Betty's personality.

I scanned the closet again in case anything popped out to me but nothing did. "You're sure that he used these hangers? How long ago was that?"

Betty faced me, but her hands still had a tight grip on the hangers. "Very recently."

"Is it possible that Len got rid of some clothes or donated them? Same with the suitcase. I don't think this means he's gone."

Betty shook the hangers. "He didn't just throw out these clothes. Believe me. Something's wrong."

I looked around the bedroom, hoping for something that might stick out, showing me that maybe Betty was right. But everything looked okay. "What could be wrong? Didn't you say you saw Len earlier today?"

Betty nodded. "Several times."

"And you didn't notice anything wrong?"

Betty pursed her lips. "No. Well, not really."

I didn't know how to respond. All I knew was that Len's letter said something came up; it didn't say anything was wrong. Could Betty know something that I wasn't aware of? "What do you mean, not really?"

"Well, I sensed something was wrong. I asked him, but he said he was okay. But then…" She let go of the hangers and shook her head.

I pushed Betty for more information. "Then what?"

"Never mind. I'd rather not discuss it with you."

I frowned. Betty didn't want to talk now? "Why won't you say what else Len said, Betty?"

She waved her hand in dismissal. "It was nothing. I'm sorry I brought it up."

I wondered what made her clam up. "How can you be sure it's nothing? You brought me in here because you were sure something was wrong."

"Well, Len and I talk a lot and I wouldn't want him blabbing about me." She smiled. "See, I can have private conversations too. Like an attorney. Or a CPA."

I sighed. It was too late at night to play games. Especially when I was standing in my client's apartment without his permission, all because I allowed my neighbor to get me worked up.

Betty cleared her throat. "But I know something happened to him."

How ridiculous was this whole situation? One

minute, Betty's talking my ear off. The next, she's withholding information. And she was escalating things. It wasn't just that something was wrong with Len, now it was that something had happened to him.

I walked to the entryway of Len's room. "What do you think could have happened?"

"I don't know, maybe someone took him or something?"

"Are you serious?"

Betty nodded, and her hair swished. "Yes. I'm very serious."

CHAPTER 11

I returned to my apartment. I convinced Betty that we couldn't do much about Len tonight; we should wait until tomorrow. Correction. I hoped I had convinced her to wait until then.

Despite Betty's protests, nothing looked off to me in Len's apartment. A few missing hangers and a suitcase did not mean something had happened. And it wasn't a good enough reason to spend an entire night panicking or sending out a search crew.

Of course, I could be in denial. Maybe I didn't want to face the fact that Len was missing. Because admitting as much meant that I was in a tough situation.

Despite my assurances to Betty that everything was okay with Len, now that I was alone, something about Len being gone frightened me. Because he had met with me this afternoon and was gone when I returned from dinner with my friends. Where had he gone? And why? And why leave me with the checks? What came up that prevented him from delivering them?

If this was the trouble that I would get into while working for myself, then maybe I should get a job sitting in a cubicle. When I started my business, I hadn't envisioned taking small-time jobs filled with ethical dilemmas that ended up being bigger headaches than they were worth. Not that I didn't have my share of headaches in the corporate world, but at least I had a guaranteed paycheck every two weeks.

Maybe I needed sleep, and I would feel better in the morning. Maybe the solution would come to me then. Maybe Len would only be gone overnight.

Maybe, maybe, maybe.

I thought of the various laws dealing with mail and money, some of which I had talked with Len about. Buzzwords popped into my mind, most of which I had learned about in college and in my extensive accounting training. Mail fraud, money laundering, interstate this or that.

Len could write off up to $12,000 per person per year. But he had written the checks for $9,000 each.

Did Len keep the checks to $9,000 instead of the tax-deductible limit of $12,000 to prevent the currency transaction report from being triggered? So what? That wasn't illegal. And it didn't mean that something untoward was going on. Otherwise, why write a check in the first place? Why not just give cash like he had done for my payment?

Still, I felt uneasy with the money in my possession. I had no way of knowing the source of the funds. If I delivered the checks without knowing where the money came from, and it ended up being from an unsavory source, was I committing a crime? I could go to the police, but that felt hasty. And anyway, what would the police do with these checks?

I doubted that anyone would ever ask me about the money. But as a precaution, I decided to keep a record of everything. I turned on my computer and the scanner next to it. I retrieved the envelope from my safe, made a copy of the checks and the letter, saved the copies to my desktop, and returned the envelope to the safe.

My doorbell rang. I assumed Betty had come back. What did she want now? I guess I hadn't convinced her to leave things until tomorrow.

I walked to my front door and checked the peephole. Len stood on the other side.

CHAPTER 12

I opened my door and relief washed over me. Len was back safe and sound. "Len, you have no idea how good it is to see you."

His eyes had circles under them, and his shoulders sagged. "Betty said you were looking for me."

I directed him into my apartment. "Yes, please, come in. How are you doing?"

"I'm okay. Sorry I worried you and Betty."

It looked like Betty had dragged me into it and told him I was worried too. I almost laughed out loud. I supposed I was worried, but not in the same way and to the same degree. What did it matter anyway?

"Stay here for a second," I said and walked into my office. I opened the safe and grabbed the envelope. While I was relieved that Len was here, I was uncomfortable telling him I couldn't do this favor for him.

I returned to the living room.

Len pointed to the envelope. "I see you received

the checks."

"Yes, I want to talk to you about that."

"I don't need you to deliver them."

Thank goodness. My luck had changed. I could get this money out of my apartment, and I didn't even have to tell Len no. I was so relieved; I felt like dancing. I handed him the envelope. "The cash is in there too."

"I'm sorry if my request put you in an awkward position. Something came up, which I thought might detain me for longer. I wanted to get these checks out before the end of the year. For taxes and all."

"I understand."

Len had been my landlord for eight months. We had talked a few times but always in the most general of ways. Even though I provided him with a summary of my background today, I knew little about him. "I don't mean to pry, but what came up?"

Len frowned and took a deep breath. "Just a couple of last-minute errands."

"Is everything all right?"

I had a moment of déjà vu; I had asked Len a similar thing earlier today.

"Mostly, yes."

"Is there anything you want to talk about?"

Len adjusted his blazer. "No. Just the usual stress at this time of year. Nothing to worry about."

"All right. If you change your mind, let me know."

"You're very kind. Can we still meet tomorrow?"

"Of course," I said. "I take it you'll be around for a

while?"

He nodded. "I'm not planning to go anywhere if that's what you're asking. After my earful from Betty, I told her I'd give her advance notice the next time I go anywhere. Just to save myself the hassle. Even if all I did was step out for a while."

"Yes, she seemed a bit concerned. The closed blinds and all."

Len shook his head. "I should have known it would be something like that. I'm not allowed to deviate from my routine."

I wasn't sure what to say. I didn't want to get into whatever was happening with Betty. I was just thankful Len was back, even if I wasn't convinced everything was okay. "Let me know if you need anything."

Len walked to the door and opened it. "Thank you for your help."

Before I could say anything more, Betty appeared and was now standing beside Len.

"Hi," she said, a big smile on her face. "As you can see, Len is back, and all is well."

"That's great," I said.

"We got ourselves into a tizzy, didn't we? Did Len tell you that I gave him a talking-to? I informed him he couldn't leave like that without telling anyone."

Len looked at me and smiled. "Yes, Betty, I was just telling Jocelyn all about the error of my ways. Next time, I'll get all my absences approved by you. Maybe even put a notice in the paper."

Betty narrowed her eyes and crossed her arms.

"Well, excuse me for caring about you. I could have just left it alone, and you could've been dead in your apartment for days. How would you like that?"

"If I was dead, what would it matter to me?"

"Anyway," Betty said, long and drawn out. "I'm leaving tomorrow morning. See how that works, Len?"

I was in no mood for Betty's passive-aggressive behavior. In fact, I would've liked it if Betty left. But I was curious where she was going.

"Where are you off to?" I asked.

"To visit my sister. She lives in Indio. I go down there several times a year and stay for a week. We go to the casinos and have a fabulous time."

"Don't blow all your Christmas money, Betty," Len said.

"Don't jinx me," she said and shook her head. "I swear."

Len laughed. "Lighten up, Betty, I'm just joking."

Betty looked at me. "Len has all my contact information if you need to reach me. It's late, so I need to go to bed."

"I should go too, Jocelyn," Len said. "I'll see you tomorrow."

Betty walked away. Len followed her, carrying the letter, checks, and cash.

CHAPTER 13

I arrived at Applewood Deli, my favorite sandwich shop in Brentwood, for a late lunch on Sunday afternoon. The deli was on San Vicente Boulevard, and I used to eat here more often than I do now. Back in the old days when I had a steady paycheck. The real estate company I worked for, ADWR, was located several blocks away, off Wilshire and Federal.

Most of the time, I got my food to go because I was so busy with work. Occasionally, I had time to sit at one of the outdoor tables. Since I worked from home now, I made most of my meals to save money. But I found it good to get outside and do something every once in a while. It was too easy to spend all day and night locked inside my apartment.

I ordered my usual sandwich, which was tuna on walnut bread. The sandwich had green apples, blue cheese, and a tangy coleslaw. It was unique, but I liked it. I added a bag of jalapeno potato chips and iced tea. I ordered dinner to go, another of my favorites: broccoli cheddar soup in a sourdough bread bowl.

I selected a table outside and waited for my order. The weather today was outstanding. A clear blue sky, variable to no winds, and the temperature was seventy-five degrees.

The place was busy, but not as much as on a weekday when working professionals flooded it. Today, being a Sunday, the patrons were in a mix of workout clothes and jeans. Lots of baseball hats and sunglasses, especially on the ones sitting outdoors.

I wore jeans and an old gray sweatshirt with Stauffer University Est. 1878 across the top in red and silver. I had worn it so often that the sleeves frayed at the wrists. I was a little overdressed for the weather, but I felt comfortable in the shade.

A young man wearing a T-shirt and baseball hat with the Applewood Deli logo dropped off my lunch.

He pointed to my sweatshirt. "Do you go to Stauffer?"

"I did. Yeah."

He moved the tray he was carrying to his side. "I applied there. I'm still waiting to hear back."

"That's cool. I hope you get in."

He smiled. "Thanks. Did you like it?"

"I did."

"What was your major?"

"Accounting."

He nodded. "Cool, I'm thinking of doing business."

"They have a great business school."

"That's what I heard. Did you go to high school

around here?"

I shook my head. "No. I'm from the Midwest."

"Oh, cool. How did you end up at Stauffer, then?"

I glanced at my lunch and then back at him. "I had a cousin who went there. She seemed to enjoy it, so I thought I'd go there too."

He flipped the tray behind him. "Cool. I'll let you eat."

"Good luck. I hope it works out."

"Thanks," he said and walked back inside the restaurant.

My cousin, Jennifer Hendricks, attended Stauffer University and moved to Los Angeles after she graduated. Then, in 1995, she was murdered behind a home in the Hollywood Hills. Her killer had been caught shortly after.

I took a bite of my sandwich and tried to shake off thoughts of the past.

CHAPTER 14

After lunch on the patio at Applewood Deli, I grabbed the brown bag holding my soup and bread and walked back to my apartment. San Vicente Boulevard was bustling with people walking to and from restaurants and shops. The large strip of grass splitting the street into two was filled with runners and walkers.

Eating outside lifted my spirits and pushed away any negative thoughts I had been having about starting my business. When I worked at ADWR, I often found myself buried in work or struggling to solve a problem. On those occasions, I made it a priority to eat lunch away from my desk.

Usually, as in this instance, a sunny day would relieve stress. I would then return to my desk, able to plow through the remaining work I had to complete, or solve whatever problem was bothering me.

I walked down Montana Avenue. Cars filled both sides of the street. Today, many people were out and about. It was quieter on weekdays. The neighborhood had a peaceful feel, even though the area was heavily populated.

I entered my apartment complex and went to my mailbox, which was located just outside Len's front door. Then, I remembered today was Sunday. Also, I checked my mail last night.

I glanced at Len's apartment. His blinds were closed. When I left for lunch an hour ago, they were open. I had déjà vu. Then Len's door opened.

A tall, skinny man with a buzz cut walked out. His face was pale, and he looked like he could use a little time in the sun. He wore a red and black flannel and jeans. He had on a beat-up pair of wheat-colored work boots.

Where was Len?

The man nodded in a "what's up" gesture. "Hey there."

I didn't know what to say, because his presence at Len's apartment was setting off warning bells. So I kept it simple. "Hi."

"You live here or what?"

I didn't want to tell him I lived here, but I couldn't deny it. If he was going to be hanging around, he would see me coming and going.

"Yep," I said, trying to sound as casual as possible.

"That's cool. I'm Mikey Zobak."

"Zobak? Are you related to Len?"

"Len's my uncle. And you are?"

"Jocelyn."

"You have a last name, Jocelyn?"

I felt uncomfortable giving Mikey my last name, but what did it matter? I lived up the stairs, and he just came out of Len's apartment. He could find out information about me if he really wanted to. "Bennett."

"Nice to meet you, Jocelyn Bennett. Maybe I'll see you around."

I didn't respond, turned, and headed up to my apartment.

My heart was beating faster than it normally did after climbing two flights of stairs. But why? Because Len's blinds were closed again?

I couldn't help myself, so I entered my office and looked out the window that oversaw the courtyard. Mikey sat in one of the two chairs Len kept on his patio. He looked up in my direction, and I ducked.

Had Mikey caught me looking at him?

CHAPTER 15

I was sitting at my kitchen table with an open can of sparkling water, my laptop, a notepad, and a pen. I was playing Solitaire while killing time waiting for Len, who was an hour late.

I closed out the game and shut my laptop. I was starving and wanted to eat dinner. But I needed to make sure Len wasn't coming. The only way to find out was to go talk to him.

I locked my apartment and went to Len's. I rang the doorbell.

Mikey Zobak opened the door and smiled at me. "Hey, Jocelyn. What's up?"

"I'm looking for Len. Do you know where he is?"

Mikey leaned against the doorframe and narrowed his eyes. "Why's that?"

His friendly demeanor had changed to defensive. I was sure my question was straightforward. "Why's what?"

"Why are you looking for Len?"

"He was supposed to meet with me. Have you seen him?"

"He left for a while."

I raised my eyebrows. "Like on vacation?"

"Yeah. Said he was off to Vegas. Was going to kick back for a few days, that kind of thing."

I almost laughed at the absurdity of what Mikey was telling me. "Are you watching over the place while Len's gone?"

Mikey tapped his foot. "I said I'd help the poor guy out for a while, but that was it. I told him if he didn't come back in a timely fashion, I was out of here, you know? I've got things to do. Anyway, what were you going to meet with him about? A maintenance problem or something?"

None of this made any sense. Len wasn't in Vegas on a gambling spree. "No."

Mikey stepped out of the doorframe. "What then?"

"It's a business meeting."

"That sounds interesting. What kind of business?"

I didn't want to get into this with Mikey, and I knew, thanks to client confidentiality, I didn't have to. "Do you know when he'll be back?"

"No idea. You know how Len is. He could be gone for a while. I can tell him you stopped by."

Sure. This sounded normal. "That's okay. I'll just talk to him later."

Mikey narrowed his eyes. "I'm serious, you know. Tell me. What kind of stuff are you planning to talk about? Or should I say, already talked about. I saw you met with Len yesterday."

Could Mikey have seen my appointment with Len on his calendar? "Huh?"

"What business?"

Mikey wouldn't let it go. I was about to tell him the same thing I told Betty less than twenty-four hours ago. "I can't say."

Something flashed across Mikey's face, but I couldn't tell what it was. "You can't say?"

My stomach filled with butterflies. "That's right."

Mikey walked up to me. "Did Len ask you to do something for him?"

I stepped back. "What do you mean?"

Mikey raised his eyebrows, his forehead creasing. "He asked you for a favor, didn't he?"

"Why don't you ask him?"

"Who, Len?"

"Yeah. Why are you asking me?"

"Because like I told you, Len's in Vegas. And you're right here. And I want to know now."

I had no intention of answering Mikey's questions. "Ask him the next time you talk to him."

Mikey crossed his arms and stared at me. "Fine. Play it like that. You know where to find me."

I nodded but said nothing.

Mikey snapped his fingers. "I guess I know where to find you, too, huh?"

I knew I should leave things alone and not risk escalating the situation, but I felt compelled to respond. "What's that supposed to mean?"

Mikey pointed behind me, and I twisted around to see what he was looking at. It was my front door. He stepped back into Len's apartment and grabbed the doorknob. "Apartment three-oh-two, right?"

More butterflies filled my stomach, and my arms shook. "I need to get going."

"If I don't hear from you, I'll be in touch. Count on it."

CHAPTER 16

I'm on my street, walking to my apartment after dinner with friends. I'm at the building's gate, and he appears. Adam Davis. My boss at ADWR. I'm surprised to see him there; I wonder what he wants.

Then I remember what's happening at work. And how I confronted Adam at the office about the fraud.

Adam Davis slides to stand in front of me. "Who have you talked to?"

My throat is tight. I can barely get any words out, and I wonder if Adam will hear me. "No one."

"I don't believe you. Be honest."

What I'm saying is true; I've told no one what I discovered. "I swear. No one else knows."

Adam steps closer to me. He grabs my arms and pushes me against the gate. "You tell anyone anything, and you'll regret it. No cops, no family, no friends. Are we clear?"

I nod my head.

Adam shakes me more. "You'll be sorry if you tell anyone. Do you understand?"

I shake my head and keep doing it so much that it

feels like it's on a swivel. "I won't tell anyone."

He grips my arms harder. "What's the matter? Why can't you talk?"

I nod again and try to shout. But nothing happens. My mouth opens, but there's only silence.

Adam's face changes. It gets twisted up like he's going to spit fire. He pushes me harder against the metal gate. My head slams into the call box. I should be in pain, but I'm not.

My purse is on my shoulder, and there's pepper spray in it. It's close, but I can't get my arms loose because they are pressed tight to the gate.

I shift my body back and forth, hoping to get loose, but Adam's grip is too tight. I scream. But my voice is still caught in my throat. I give it my all, using everything I can, but nothing, not one sound, will come out.

Then, I thrust my body forward, trying to pull away from the gate, but I'm stuck. I can feel Adam's hands on my arms, but now the rest of my body feels glued to the gate. No part of me moves.

I try yet again to scream. This time, Adam hears me. He releases one of my arms and uses his now free hand to cover my mouth. I think about biting his hand, but I can't. My jaw is locked.

His hand clamps harder on my neck. "Shut up. Remember what I said. You never saw what you think you saw. If you say something, I'll make sure you're implicated. Got it?"

I don't understand. What does Adam mean about implicating me? What will he say that I did?

"Let go of her," a voice says. "I've called the police. They're on their way."

Someone is there, but I can't see him.

Adam continues to hold on to me.

The voice gets louder. "I said let her go."

This time, Adam releases me.

I realize what's happening. I'm in a dream.

Wake up, I say to myself. Wake up now.

CHAPTER 17

My eyes popped open. My pajamas were twisted tight across my body, and my sheets and blankets were pulled up around me. The alarm clock on the nightstand said it was 2:04 a.m.

The nightmare I had just awoken from was a recurring one, which persisted despite nine months having passed since I left ADWR. Even after Adam Davis took a plea and went to prison.

As happened every time I had the nightmare, my mind raced with thoughts about ADWR. I had made a naïve decision: I asked Adam Davis about the discrepancies I found. Initially, I thought they were just that, discrepancies. I didn't want to believe that fraud was happening. That was stuff I read on the news and heard about in accounting training, not something I expected to encounter in real life.

It was late one night in March. I had been at the company for about sixteen months. It was still Busy Season, which started in January and lasted through at least April. This was the period when the bulk of financial reporting was due for most companies.

ADWR's bank obligations required the company to have an annual audit. My old firm, Harman & Haskell, were the auditors. As always, the auditors were working late. Nothing was out of the ordinary.

I stayed until they left each night, in case they needed anything. Adam was also working late but had gone out to pick up dinner. Earlier that day, while I gathered documents for the auditors, I found some things that looked out of place. And because of that, I had questions for Adam. When he returned with his food, I stopped by his office.

I didn't know the chain of events that my questions were about to set into motion. Adam Davis was running a fraud through his real estate company. He had help from Tom Anderson, a real estate appraiser. Greg West, a Harman partner who I had worked for and at one time respected, was also involved.

Adam wasn't at the office the next couple of days after I confronted him. The following Monday everything came apart. I arrived at work to find the ADWR offices closed; my keycard had been deactivated. I ran into a co-worker outside the building, who told me the offices had been emptied. Effective immediately, I was out of a job.

Shortly thereafter, I contacted a realtor and put my condo up for sale. Then, I started the hunt for a new place to live. That was how I found this apartment on Montana Avenue. I missed that fancy condo on Wilshire Boulevard right by Beverly Hills. It was on the tenth floor with a skyline view of

Los Angeles. But my future had become shaky, and owning a home I could no longer afford wasn't a burden I wanted to shoulder.

This apartment had been a blessing in disguise. It was a quiet and secure place. Overall, with a couple of exceptions, the tenants were mellow. Nobody blasted music late at night or trashed the common areas. And Len had been an awesome landlord.

While my nightmare was just that, a nightmare, the events in it had happened. I had dinner with friends at a restaurant near my apartment. I walked home, and Adam confronted me outside of my apartment complex. I didn't believe Adam's threats were idle, and he had scared the crap out of me. Len helped me even though he had no idea who Adam was or what he might do.

I straightened out my pajamas and fixed my blankets. I had calmed down enough to fall back asleep. Then, I heard something.

My apartment door had just closed.

CHAPTER 18

I gripped my blankets. Had I just heard what I thought I did? My breath was shallow, and I felt clammy. My heart was beating so hard in my chest that I thought it might break free from my rib cage and plop onto the floor.

The blinds were closed, and no light came through the sides. I had no nightlights anywhere. It was utterly dark. Pitch black.

While I lay still, unable to move, I strained my ears. I heard nothing, not even the usual sounds like the refrigerator humming. I wanted to jump up and run out of my apartment, yet I felt pinned to my bed.

I took a breath and forced myself to roll onto my side. Just doing this sounded loud. Whoever was in my apartment had to have heard me and was now on his way into my room.

I remained motionless on my side. I glanced out the door but saw nothing. I could still hear nothing. No footsteps stomping down the hall. No creaking floors. Nothing.

I took another breath, placed my feet on the floor,

and sat upright. My slippers were in front of me. I slid them aside so that I wouldn't trip over them.

Now what? I continued to listen, but I heard nothing. Not a single sound.

With a count of three, I stood. My legs were shaking. I grabbed my headboard to steady myself. Then, I kneeled, reached under my bed, and felt around until my hands touched the cool metal of my flashlight.

I pushed up off my knees and sat back on my bed. I gripped the flashlight and yet again felt frozen on my bed. My mind raced, thinking of what to do, how to act, and what steps to take next. But it didn't feel like I could get my body to move. My brain was in panic mode and had locked down the rest of me. I kept picturing someone entering my room at any second. I felt like a sitting duck, just waiting for someone to murder me.

I did my best to take a deep breath. My lungs felt like they had limited capacity. With my next breath, I inhaled more air. In and out, in and out.

I had to get up and do something, not stay here forever. I stood. Slowly. After each movement, I paused, listening for any sounds. There was nothing but silence.

Taking things one step at a time, I moved toward my bedroom door. I was terrified, but I tried to calm myself by remembering that I had a slight advantage if someone was here with me. I knew the layout of my apartment. Now that my eyes had adjusted, I could make out a few shapes of my furniture.

My sense of calm didn't last long. Once the intruder found me, the advantage was with him. I thought I would be safe if I could just reach my front door. Would I make it there?

CHAPTER 19

I inched my way out of my bedroom to the hallway. I had the flashlight in one hand and used my free hand to touch the wall, letting it guide me through the dark space toward my living room.

Even though my eyes had adjusted, everything seemed darker than usual tonight. I could've sworn that at least some light came into my apartment. Either from outdoor security lights or the moon. But no, it was dark, and my pupils strained to make out the familiar shapes of my place.

With each step, my breathing got shallower and shallower. It was like I was holding my breath. I wasn't; I was trying as hard as I could to fill my lungs.

I expected I would run into an intruder any second. Yet nothing happened. Everything appeared calm. If someone was in my apartment, then where was he, and when would he make his presence known? Or had I dreamed the sound? Maybe no one had opened my front door. It had sounded real, but perhaps I was mistaken.

I made it to the living room. Avoiding the sofa and coffee table, I walked through it at a fast clip and reached my front door. I touched the deadbolt and ran my hand along the smooth metal. It was turned to the right, which meant my door was locked. Just like it had been when I went to bed.

I exhaled and felt relieved. I had made it to my escape route. I tapped my hand on the wall until I found the light switch and flipped on the foyer ceiling light. The glare blinded me.

Once my eyes adjusted, I glanced around the kitchen and living room. Both areas looked like they had been earlier in the evening; nothing was out of place.

Gripping my flashlight, I searched each room as I had when I came home from dinner on Saturday night and found the envelope. No one was hiding anywhere in my apartment.

The last room I checked was my office. The safe was still there and appeared undisturbed. I looked at my desk. A couple of manila folders were askew, and the papers were peeking out. Which wasn't how I left them. And one of my desk drawers was open. Someone had been in my apartment while I was sleeping. *Crap.*

I walked back to the living room. I opened the front door and examined both sides of the lock. I saw no noticeable pry marks or scratches anywhere.

The person had to have used a key. This narrowed my list of suspects. In fact, it left me with one prime suspect: the person living in the manager's apartment. The same person who had just shown up today. And who claimed to be Len's nephew.

Mikey Zobak.

PART 2

BACK TO THE DRAWING BOARD

CHAPTER 20

It was early Monday morning and Mikey returned to Len's apartment with breakfast. He'd gone to a nearby fast-food restaurant, one that served regular food before lunch. He set his food on the kitchen table, but the trash he'd left all over the place distracted him.

One day here, and he'd made a mess. Half-filled sodas and empty water bottles littered the counter, along with food wrappers. It had been nice to let things go, but the more clutter, the less he could think.

He opened the pantry, grabbed a garbage bag, and swept the trash off the table and counters. He dropped the bag by the door. The next time he left, he'd throw it in the dumpster.

Mikey looked around the straightened-up apartment. He had restored it to how it was when he arrived yesterday. Tidy, just as that neatnik Len preferred. Then Mikey let out a chuckle. He didn't give a shit what Len liked.

Mikey left the blinds closed, though. Len might

enjoy living like an animal in a zoo exhibit, but not him. He couldn't stand to have people walk by and stare at him as he was going about his day.

Before he ate, he went into Len's second bedroom, where there was a desktop computer. Len didn't have a password, so it had been easy to gain access. He pulled up the page and saw that he'd had a response. Yes. All right. He could kick that off soon. Possibly tomorrow.

He returned to the table and turned on the TV, which he could see from the kitchen. He flipped around. Daytime TV was the worst. A bunch of soap operas and news. He found an old action movie on one of the local channels. It was from the eighties, and he'd seen it a million times, but it would do.

He pulled out his food: two burgers on sourdough bread with bacon and American cheese, mozzarella sticks, jalapeno poppers, curly fries, and a chocolate shake.

He stuffed a popper in his mouth and thought about his current problems. Most were minor and could be considered more of a nuisance than anything. He could nip those in the bud right away.

But he had one major problem. Despite ransacking Len's place, he still hadn't found it. He was close to grabbing a knife and tearing apart the sofas, mattresses, and drywall.

This was his only goal. Finding it. Getting it in his possession. And he knew it had to be somewhere nearby. Like playing that childhood game. He was getting warmer, not cooler. He was sure of it.

Jocelyn, in apartment 302, was the key to this. Len's calendar had two meetings scheduled with her. One on Saturday and one on Sunday.

Mikey heard someone enter the gate. He moved to the large picture window and pushed back the shades in time to see a locksmith climb the stairs to Jocelyn's apartment.

What the hell? Was she changing the locks? Did she know he'd been in her apartment? Obviously, he hadn't been careful enough.

He stared at his lunch, which he had only taken a few bites of. He had other stuff to do. After seeing the locksmith, he no longer felt like hanging around here. He stuffed his food back in the bag to take with him. He grabbed his keys and headed to the parking garage.

Jocelyn could change her locks fifty times if she wanted. It wouldn't stop him.

CHAPTER 21

It was Monday morning, and I felt like a zombie. I spent the rest of the night on the sofa and never fell back asleep. I couldn't stop picturing Mikey creeping into my apartment. So I tossed and turned until the first light illuminated the living room. At that point, I started my day.

The first thing I did this morning, after having a cup of coffee, was to call a locksmith and schedule an appointment. I wasn't looking forward to the unplanned expense, but changing the locks seemed necessary.

I debated going to the police. After all, someone had been in my apartment and had gone through my office.

But what would I say to them? My doors and windows were intact, and nothing had been jimmied or broken into. Also, nothing had been stolen. My only proof was a slight disarray in my office.

For now, I would change the locks, which should prevent Mikey from sneaking in again using Len's key. Of course, I couldn't confirm it was Mikey, but he had access to a key to my place, so he seemed like the most likely person.

The locksmith was in my apartment now. The name Robert was embroidered on a patch on his blue work shirt. He was tall and trim, probably ten years older than me. His brown hair stuck out of the sides of a baseball hat. We had spoken little except for introductions and for me to show him what I wanted him to do.

While Robert worked on the front door, I stayed in the kitchen and made a second cup of coffee. I didn't think the extra caffeine was going to do much to boost my energy, but I had to try.

I had a top-of-the-line coffee maker, something I had bought in my hot-shot corporate days. Back then, I barely spent time at home and never used the thing. I made several cups a day with it now, so I supposed that in the end, the money spent had been worth it.

Robert rattled the doorknob. "Are you afraid a previous tenant has a key to your place or something?"

I preferred not to divulge the details of why I needed new locks. "Sort of."

"You can never be too careful, you know? Did you ever hear the story of the girl who lived around here and went missing?"

I was sure that in Los Angeles, plenty of people went missing. He would have to narrow it down. "No, I hadn't heard. When was that?"

"Oh, it was in the eighties, a long time ago. I just know because the girl's parents were my neighbors. Her name was Tracy."

"I'm sorry to hear that."

Robert continued shaking the lock. "Tracy had just moved out on her own and lived off Barrington Avenue. She just up and disappeared one day."

"She's never been found?"

"Not that I'm aware of. I think it was her landlord, but I guess nothing ever came of it. He was one of those weirdos coming in when the tenants weren't around. Going through underwear drawers and stuff like that."

CHAPTER 22

Robert's face was serious. "You're not having a situation like that with your landlord, are you?"

My landlord was great. Mikey was another story. I wasn't about to get into my woes with Robert, a practical stranger. "No."

He was staring at me like he had analyzed what I said and didn't believe me. "Well, just be careful."

"I will."

Robert shook his head. "A lot of weirdos out there. They look normal, too, you know?"

My skin prickled. Robert was working on my locks while also blocking my only egress. My balcony was three stories up, so escaping out the patio wasn't workable.

His gaze remained fixed on me, so I diverted my eyes to the living room. I didn't like this whole conversation. I knew he was waiting for a response, except I didn't know what he wanted me to say.

"Yeah, I've heard all about Ted Bundy," I said, though I wondered if I was getting us further into the topic by mentioning that.

Robert adjusted his hat. "Yes. He's a perfect example of what I'm talking about."

Thoughts of my cousin Jennifer flashed through my mind. Jennifer had been murdered, but not in her apartment. She had a roommate, I knew she wasn't reckless, and yet it hadn't helped her.

He turned around to the door. "You know what's even stranger? I came by Tracy's place the day before."

It looked like we were back to talking about the woman he knew who went missing. "No kidding?"

"Yeah, I'm from West Covina, and like I said, my family was her neighbor. I was in high school. Her parents asked if I would do them a favor and drop off some food for her. They hadn't heard from her, and they were getting worried."

Robert kneeled and rifled through his toolbox. "I went there to drop off the food, but she didn't answer. I stayed around for a while since I had driven all that way. But she never came to the door."

He stood and inserted a tool into the lock. "And you know what?"

"What?"

"The next day, her parents came and found blood all over the bed. But she wasn't there. Isn't that creepy?"

Did Robert tell this same story to everyone he helped in Brentwood, or was I just the lucky one? I wondered how much longer his work would take. How long would it be before he was finished, and I could be rid of him and his story about the missing woman?

But Robert wasn't done yet.

He adjusted his hat. "Some neighbors later said they heard a scream. Right before I came by. Whoever took Tracy may have been in the apartment when I was outside."

My skin had prickled earlier, but now I had full-blown goosebumps. The more Robert talked, the more I wanted to run over and push him out of my apartment.

"Luckily, someone saw a guy leave her apartment. Who resembled her landlord. And he looked nothing like me. What a relief. For a while there, I thought maybe they would think I did something to her, you know? Being in the wrong place at the wrong time."

Robert jiggled the door knob. "Don't worry. I didn't do it."

CHAPTER 23

I was thinking I had hired the wrong locksmith. Like Robert had feared in the eighties, perhaps I was in the wrong place at the wrong time. I wanted Robert to finish and get out of here.

I again sized up my options for fleeing, considering that Robert blocked my front door. As I had already deduced, my only other door was three stories high and led to a balcony. I supposed I could scream if I had to. I took a deep breath to relax.

Robert continued his work, not saying another word or even looking in my general direction. He'd stopped telling missing women stories. Finally, he put his tools away, and I felt like he was done. I could pay him, and he could move on to his next job.

Robert stuck out his hand, holding shiny new keys. "Here you go. It's all finished."

He produced an invoice. It wasn't as steep as I thought it would be. I grabbed my purse and pulled out the cash to pay.

"Thanks," he said. "You take care."

Robert left. I stayed in my entryway and looked at

my new locks. I still held the keys in my hand. With Robert gone, I felt relief, and my mind wandered back to last night's events. Why did Mikey come into my apartment? What did he want? Was he looking for something? If so, what?

Mikey was interested in my meeting with Len. The only thing to come out of that meeting was Len asking me to deliver the checks. Then he changed his mind and said he would do it himself. Did Mikey want the checks? Did he think I had them? How would he know about them? Did Len tell him? And if he wanted the checks, why? To steal the money?

Mikey could try to cash a check made out to someone else if he forged the endorsement. He may need an ID in the payee's name, unless he could find a place to cash the check where no ID was needed. Then again, he could likely circumvent the required identification by forging the payee's signature. Then, if he signed his own name underneath, it would appear that the payee had transferred the check to Mikey.

Was that what Mikey was after? The checks Len gave me totaled $45,000. It was a lot of money. Plus, Len gave me a thousand in cash.

There might be other explanations for why Mikey had been in my apartment, but none of the ones I could think of made sense. Mikey stole nothing, and he didn't hurt me.

I thought about Len not showing up for our meeting. Where was he? Why hadn't he told me he would be gone? I knew that whatever Mikey told me was bogus. Len hadn't just taken off for Vegas. So why would Mikey make up a story like that? Did he have something to do with Len having gone missing?

I had a million questions and no answers.

Just as I was about to close my door, I looked at the front gate and saw an older man enter the apartment complex, walk up to Len's door, and knock on it.

I stood in my doorframe, hoping to see what happened when Mikey answered.

Mikey never opened the door, despite the man knocking for a while. Then, the man turned to leave. I wanted to talk to him before he got too far. But I wasn't wearing shoes, so I opened my hall closet, slid on flip-flops, and locked the door using my new keys.

The man had left the complex, but I figured he couldn't have gotten far. I ran down the stairs fast enough to catch him, but slow enough to avoid a slip-and-fall.

I ran out of the gate and looked left and right. The man turned right onto Westgate Avenue.

I waved my arms, even though he wasn't facing me. "Hey!"

I ran as fast as I could in my flip-flops. I got to the corner of Montana and Westgate. I looked around, but I didn't see him. I walked down Westgate, my head on a swivel for any sight of him.

He had vanished.

CHAPTER 24

I traipsed up the two flights of stairs to my apartment. I was out of breath like I had run a mile when all I had done was chase a stranger down the street. I kicked off my flip-flops and returned them to the closet.

I sat on my couch and took several breaths, waiting for my heart rate to return to normal. Who was the man who knocked on Len's door? I had never seen him before. Why didn't Mikey answer? Was he gone? Was it for good? I could only hope. And then maybe Len would return.

If I wasn't worried about Len, I would think today was just another Monday in my apartment complex. The building was quiet, as it usually was on a weekday morning.

I was tired from lack of sleep but had the entire day ahead. I couldn't just sit around and do nothing. So I got up from the sofa and went to the kitchen, where my laptop was on the table. I booted it up and then searched the internet for Mikey Zobak. I scrolled through several pages but saw nothing relevant to the person who was downstairs in Len's apartment.

Next, I pulled up the documents I scanned onto my computer on Saturday night, which included Len's letter to me with the addresses and the five checks. I wondered if I could find out anything about these five people if I performed an online search. Maybe something would come up if I used the name and address.

I started with the first one on the list and worked my way down. Not much popped up. The last names, like Baker, were too common, and with just a first initial, there wasn't much to go on, even with the addresses.

I didn't know Len well; our meeting on Saturday was the most I had talked to him since I moved in. Sure, we said hello here and there, just like I did with everyone else who lived in the building, but that was about it. I liked keeping to myself, and most of the other tenants did too.

The situation with Len and Mikey was strange, but did it mean that there was a problem? If Betty was to be believed, and Len stuck to a routine and took time to plan his travel, then something may have happened. Adding credence to the fact that something was wrong was Mikey's bogus story about Len taking off to Vegas on a whim. And of course, someone had been in my apartment last night.

I didn't track the comings and goings of everyone who lived in my building. Still, as long as I had lived here, I didn't remember seeing anyone else in Len's apartment, but that didn't make it true. It just meant I had never noticed it. And since I didn't keep tabs on everyone, I might have missed something.

I sat back. What was I getting myself involved in? Was I worrying about Len because I had no other prospects for work? Was dealing with him easier than dealing with the reality that I had to find clients? Thus, as long as I was concerned about Len, I could avoid facing my fear that my business would fail, forcing me to return to corporate life.

Sure, this might all be my way of avoiding reality, but the fact remained that I hadn't heard from Len despite our scheduled meeting. Besides that, someone was in my apartment last night. And I believed that someone was Mikey. Yes, something strange was going on. And Len and Mikey were involved. And, unfortunately, so was I.

What should I do? Well, Len was missing, so I could try to find him. I wondered if the checks had something to do with his disappearance.

I skimmed the list of addresses. The first person on the list lived in Diamond Bar, which was quite the haul from my West Los Angeles apartment.

But I had to start somewhere. So why not there?

Someone at that house should know Len and might even know where to find him. It was worth a try. I printed the list from my computer.

My gut told me that Len needed help. He helped me when Adam Davis confronted me outside of my building. And now I was going to help him.

CHAPTER 25

I slipped behind the wheel of my black 2003 Mercedes hard-top convertible. My car was a constant reminder of my earlier life. A time when I was moving up and things were going well. It had been one of my first significant purchases, and I felt proud for having been able to buy it.

I owned the car outright and would hang onto it until it fell apart on the freeway. While I was penny-pinching more than ever since college, I didn't cut corners where the car was concerned. I scheduled and kept every service appointment. Whatever the mechanic recommended for repairs, I completed.

I hooked up my iPod and flipped through it until I found my Christmas playlist. I put it on shuffle. I had a vast collection of Christmas songs spanning decades, starting in the 1940s all the way until today. Nothing too slow; I preferred upbeat songs. If it weren't the holiday season, I would likely be playing something from the eighties.

I didn't drive as much anymore since I no longer had a commute and my favorite grocery store,

Gwendolyn's Market, was walking distance from my apartment. Besides saving quite a bit on gas, I hoped that not putting so much wear and tear on my car would prolong its life.

I took a deep breath. Just getting out of my apartment had begun to relieve some stress. Letting my thoughts wander gave me a reprieve from worrying about Len. Perhaps that was because I was out doing something to try to find him. Even if I was unsure whether driving to Diamond Bar was a good idea.

I pulled out Len's list. I was headed to a person named B. Jackson's house. I entered the address into my GPS. Once loaded, I threw on a pair of sunglasses and exited my parking garage. I made a right onto Montana Avenue. The sun was out. The day was warm, even though it was only late morning. My car's thermostat read seventy degrees, though it felt hotter than that. My vehicle was probably still cold from being parked in the covered garage.

At the stoplight on San Vicente Boulevard, I put the top down on my convertible. The sun hit the top of my head and flooded my car with light. I was overdressed for the weather in my sweater, jeans, and white Converse sneakers. I pushed up my sweater's sleeves and inhaled the fresh air.

As I waited at the red light, I looked around the neighborhood. A gas station on the corner was filled with cars. Everywhere I looked, people were going about their day. Then, the light turned green.

I continued on San Vicente to Wilshire Boulevard,

where I made a left. Then, I got onto the 405 south freeway. I closed the top to avoid blowing away and started the long trek across town.

An hour later, with light traffic, I was outside B. Jackson's house. Diamond Bar was still part of Los Angeles County, though it bordered Orange County. As an auditor for Harman & Haskell, I had been all over the county. I had been everywhere in Los Angeles at least once.

Having arrived at the house in Diamond Bar, I wondered if maybe I was off-base with this. Perhaps.

What was the worst that could come of knocking on a stranger's door?

CHAPTER 26

I exited my car and surveyed the residential neighborhood. B. Jackson's house was two stories, but the neighboring homes were one-level ranches.

The street was deserted. I didn't see any gardeners, which seemed weird considering I rarely passed a street in Brentwood that didn't have at least one lawn mower whirring.

It was hard to tell by looking whether anyone was home. No cars were in the driveway, and the two-car attached garage was closed. The blinds were open except for one room on the top floor.

I walked up the neatly manicured pathway and rang the doorbell. I waited, my hands clasped behind my back. I felt like a door-to-door salesman. All I needed was a vacuum cleaner or a set of knives. At a minimum, a clipboard.

The house had no signs prohibiting soliciting, not anywhere I could see. Not the nice ones attached to the home's siding. Nor were there any homemade ones printed from a computer with "Beware of Dog" and a clip art canine baring its teeth.

No one answered, and I debated what to do next. If it was me and a random person came to my door, I most likely wouldn't answer.

I rang the bell one last time since I drove an hour to get here. Still, no one answered. And I doubted anyone would. Either the residents weren't home, or they were avoiding me. My persistent ringing wouldn't change that much.

I walked back toward my car, feeling at a loss. I had driven forty-five miles without being able to talk to the home's occupant, thus not getting any more information on Len.

The next-door neighbor was now outside. He was an older man, thin, with gray hair. He wore jeans, a button-down shirt, straw hat, sunglasses, and gardening gloves. He was pruning rose bushes that ran along his house.

I walked down the driveway; the neighbor saw me.

He waved. "Are you looking for Belinda?"

Belinda? Did that mean B. Jackson was Belinda Jackson? I figured it did. "Yes."

"She's not home. Works at the golf course down the way. I don't know when she'll be back. Want me to give her a message?"

The man's willingness to reveal his neighbor's schedule to a stranger surprised me. But I'd take it. I put my hand over my eyes to block the sun. "The course off the sixty?"

He nodded. "That's the one."

"Thanks. I'll stop by there. No need to leave a

message."

He waved again. "You haven't seen a turtle, have you?"

I didn't know what to say. "A turtle?"

"Yes. Well, it's a tortoise. Very big. Walks slow."

"No, I haven't seen it."

"It's a pet. It got loose the other day. I'm devastated. If you see it, well, you know where I live."

I couldn't tell if he was serious, but I figured he wasn't joking. "I'll let you know."

CHAPTER 27

I left Belinda's neighborhood and headed to the golf course off the 60 freeway. Thanks to the helpful next-door neighbor, I knew Belinda was probably B. Jackson.

I saw the golf course when I drove into Belinda's neighborhood earlier. Luckily, the course was public, meaning I didn't have to figure out how to talk my way into a private club.

I pulled into the course a few minutes later. Ample parking was available, and it wasn't too busy on a Monday around lunch. I walked into the clubhouse, a large A-frame building. The entire place smelled like a deep-fat fryer.

I wandered around. A man appeared from out of nowhere. He was tall and wide and wore dress slacks, a dress shirt, and a tie. The pin on his shirt told me his name was Matt.

Matt spotted me and put his hands behind his back. "Can I help you?"

"I'm looking for Belinda. Does she work here?"

Matt tilted his head. "She does, but she's busy

right now. We just had a large group come in. She won't have a break for a couple of hours."

I had surmised that Matt managed the clubhouse and Belinda was a waitress in the club's restaurant. "Okay."

"I can give her a message for you."

Just like Belinda's neighbor had offered. I didn't want to leave a message and would rather talk to Belinda in person. Especially since I drove all the way across Los Angeles. I put together a quick Plan B. "Can I eat in the restaurant?"

Matt narrowed his eyes like he was trying to determine whether I had circumvented his authority. "Of course. But Belinda has to work, so keep that in mind."

I nodded, showing I understood. "I'm just hungry, is all."

Matt stared at me, and neither of us moved. Before it could get too awkward, he started walking. "I'll take you to the restaurant."

I followed Matt around the clubhouse. A golf shop was on my right. An older man was inside, flipping through the racks of golf shirts.

When we got to the back of the clubhouse, a restaurant appeared. It was big with lots of tables. The dining room was decorated like it was Christmas in the sixties, with an explosion of tinsel and Christmas lights with large bulbs. It went well with the clubhouse's A-frame architecture though.

Overall, it wasn't busy, at least not as much as Matt had tried to make it out to be. A large group of twelve, a mix of men and women all sporting the same green golf shirt, were seated in the middle. It looked like a company outing.

Matt grabbed a maroon menu from a stack at the restaurant's entrance, and I followed him until he stopped at a table by the floor-to-ceiling windows.

I sat down. My view was of the entire golf course, which included tightly mowed grass with a backdrop of a cloudless blue sky. Several golfers were out, and two wobbly golf carts zoomed past my window.

Matt handed me the menu, which was heavy and opened like a book. "Here you go." He looked like he wanted to say something else. Instead, he walked off.

I held the menu, and my eyes caught Matt speaking to someone. A woman in black pants and a white button-down dress shirt. She wore a black waist apron with pockets. She was short and had a dark brown bob. I figured it was Belinda.

I'd bet Matt was warning her not to spend too much time talking to me. I didn't want to get Belinda in trouble and hoped that just being here wouldn't cause a problem.

While I waited for Belinda to stop by, I perused the menu. The restaurant offered a variety of salads, sandwiches, and soups. Even a couple of steaks.

Eventually, the woman I had guessed was Belinda approached my table. She looked nervous. "I'm Belinda. Matt said you're looking for me."

CHAPTER 28

I set down the menu and cut to the chase, not wanting to waste Belinda's time and risk her getting in trouble with Matt. "Do you know Len Zobak?"

Belinda stared at me, still looking nervous. Like she didn't trust me.

I wondered if she needed reassurance that I understood she was at work. "I'm not trying to get you in trouble."

She smiled, but it looked forced. "It's okay. Matt's harmless, but he's always stressed out."

"If it helps, I'm planning to order food. But my main reason for being here is to ask you if you've seen Len Zobak."

Belinda pointed to the large table. "Their food is almost out, so I have to take care of that first. Then I can talk."

"Do you care if I order?" I asked.

"Of course not. Go ahead."

I didn't need another look at the menu. "I'll have the Hole in One." It was a bacon cheeseburger with curly fries.

Belinda scribbled down my order. "I'll be back when I can."

I stared out the window. More people were on the course now. Several golf carts zipped by. One looked like a beverage cart, and two others carried golfers.

Sometime later, Belinda and Matt each carried a tray of food and brought it to the large group.

After they distributed the plates to the table, they both disappeared. Then Belinda emerged carrying my burger and fries.

She set a plate down in front of me. "Here you go."

My food looked good. And smelled even better. "Thanks."

She placed her hands on her hips. "What was it you said earlier? That you want to know if I've seen Len? Why's that?"

I felt some relief. It sounded like Belinda knew Len. "I'm looking for him."

She glanced around the room, but Matt wasn't anywhere that I could see. The table of twelve was busy eating and laughing, and it didn't look like they needed anything.

"Why are you looking for him?" she asked.

I gave Belinda a summary. About how Len was my client. About how he was missing. For confidentiality, I left out the part about the checks.

Belinda stuck her hands in the pockets of her apron. "Huh. That's concerning. Len is great. He used to be my landlord."

"Really?"

She nodded. "Yes, I used to live in Brentwood."

"On Montana?"

She smiled. "Yes."

"I live there now."

"No kidding. I miss that part of town. But I started dating someone who lived here, and you know how it goes. His job was here; it made sense. We bought a house. Well, I did; it's in my name. Then he dumped me and stuck me with a mortgage."

"I'm sorry. That stinks."

She shrugged. "What can you do?"

"Have you seen Len?"

Belinda tucked her hair behind her ears. "It's funny that you ask. I saw him yesterday."

"Sunday?"

"Yep. Early in the morning. Len wanted to give me something. He called first, said he had a surprise for me and asked if it would be all right to swing by."

Since Belinda had brought it up, I felt comfortable asking. "Did he give you a check?"

She blushed. "I felt bad taking it, but Len insisted. He knew about my situation. The mortgage. It was the best surprise. I still can't stop thinking about it."

It seemed like, in this case, Len had given money to Belinda to help her out. "How did he seem?"

"Tired. Len said he had a lot on his mind, things he needed to take care of. An old problem, or something like that, had returned. Something about a tenant. He said as soon as he got that under control, he'd be great."

I wondered who the tenant could be. Was there any chance it was Mikey? "Did he say who this tenant was?"

"No, and I didn't ask. Len's a private person. Oh, sure, he'll listen to you all day and night. But he prefers to keep his own stuff to himself. I was surprised he said as much as he did."

I ran my hands along my plate. "Did Len say anything about giving money to anyone else?"

"No, we didn't talk for long."

"Did he say what he was doing after?"

"After he gave me the check?"

I nodded.

"No. I was on my way to run errands. I didn't think to ask. He just left."

Matt came up to our table. "Belinda, I'm about to seat a party of eight."

Belinda adjusted her apron. "I'm sorry. I have to go. I hope you find Len."

CHAPTER 29

Mikey approached a two-story traditional house with white siding and red brick accents. He was in Playa del Rey, which was close to the large harbor in Marina del Rey. From Len's apartment, the home was a quick jaunt down the 405 south freeway.

This place had to have cost a fortune. First, it was huge. Second, it was basically at the beach. He checked his paper to confirm he was at the correct address. Yep. He was.

Dang. Life had been good to Barry Corcoran. Very good.

He lost contact with Barry, and a lot of time had passed. Things had been crazy back then, what with getting wasted all the time and wreaking havoc.

Mikey needed to talk to him. Make sure they were still on the same page, even after all these years. That included confirming that Barry intended to keep his mouth shut.

The thing was, Barry wasn't returning his calls. Mikey wasn't even sure he had the correct phone number. Which was why he came by the house. To see for himself just what was going on. Before he did anything hasty.

A man was trimming the bushes in the tiny front yard of the house, which included a pathetic patch of grass. The rest seemed to be shrubs that could survive with very little water.

Despite all the time that had transpired, Mikey recognized Barry. He had the same curly blonde hair, which stuck out of the top and the sides of the visor on his head. He also wore basketball shorts, a T-shirt, sunglasses, and flip-flops. Really, dude, flip-flops to trim the hedges? Mikey didn't do jack shit for manual labor, but if he did, he wouldn't use a power trimmer basically barefoot.

A cord dangled from Barry's ears to one of his pockets. He was no doubt listening to music, though Mikey didn't know how he heard anything over the whir of the trimmer. It was a Monday around lunchtime. What was Barry doing at home in the middle of the day? Mikey realized he should worry less about why Barry was home and be thankful he'd had some luck finding the guy.

Mikey had done an internet search; that was how he found Barry's phone number and address. He saw that his old buddy was working as a financial planner. Barry even had some fancy certificate proving he was trustworthy and shit. Yeah, right. The stories Mikey could tell about Barry.

One thing Mikey was sure about. Barry had started a new life. And he'd done a decent job of it. It was like Barry had wiped away the past. No doubt he didn't want any reminders of said past either. Like an old friend who came calling.

Well, tough toenails, this wasn't Barry's lucky day. Mikey got out of his car and walked up Barry's driveway. He stood behind Barry a few feet. Waiting. Patiently, at first, then creeping closer. Finally, Barry turned off the trimmer.

Mikey tapped Barry on the shoulder. Barry's whole body flinched. He whipped around and pulled off his sunglasses. It took a second, but Barry recognized Mikey. And Barry looked like he'd seen a ghost. In a way, he had.

Mikey slapped Barry on the back. "What up, dude? Are you glad to see me or what?"

Barry's eyes flickered. "Yeah. Of course. How're you doing?"

"I'm doing all right. How about we go inside?"

Barry scanned the street as though he were looking for help. Except none of the neighbors were outside. Some eyeballs might be on them, catching a glance from a nearby house. But no one was around. No deliverymen, no gardeners, no exercisers. Just Mikey and Barry, two old friends, having a friendly conversation.

Barry glanced toward his house and then looked at Mikey. "It's a nice day. Let's talk out here."

Barry's voice was nervous, though he tried to act cool. Barry always had a terrible poker face.

Mikey pointed to Barry's house. "Let's talk inside."

Barry stared at the trimmer. "Oh, sure, no problem, sounds good. Just let me put this away."

Barry walked toward the detached garage at the top of the driveway. Mikey followed.

The garage was filled with all the usual crap people stored in them. Among the boxes and tools sat a beautiful, pristine Porsche. Yep, Barry had done very well for himself, all right. Very, very well.

Mikey rapped his knuckles on the car's hood. "Sweet ride."

Barry set the trimmer on a bench against a wall. "Oh, that? It was my dad's."

Barry grew up in Palos Verdes Estates. He surfed and had a pretty pampered life compared to Mikey. He was sure that had been the allure for Barry in being Mikey's friend. Barry had been in his rebellious phase. Mikey, well, Mikey was just living life.

Mikey pushed the garage button. Barry froze, looking startled as the garage door rumbled shut. Darkness descended around them.

Mikey could make out Barry's head darting around, likely having figured out that something was wrong. That he had become trapped in the enclosed space with Mikey.

Mikey smiled. He had waited ten years to make Barry pay. Who did he think he was, starting a new life? Wheeling around town in a fucking Porsche?

Barry swung his fist and tried to punch Mikey. Mikey ducked, grabbed Barry's wrist, and twisted Barry's arm behind his back.

Barry yelled, but Mikey was too quick. He threw an arm around Barry's neck and put him in a chokehold. Then, he squeezed. Hard. Barry flopped around like a trout on a fishing line. Barry had some strength, but Mikey was stronger.

A few minutes later, Mikey left Barry's crumpled body on the concrete floor. He could cross this one off his list; things were going his way. Now it was on to his other problems, which included Jocelyn.

He slipped out the garage's side door and paused. Should he take the Porsche while he was still feeling lucky?

CHAPTER 30

I left the golf course with my bacon cheeseburger and fries in a to-go box. Eating lunch there by myself, while Belinda served the other patrons, felt awkward.

Belinda knew Len. She needed money. Len knew this, which was why he gave her a check. The others on Len's list might be this way too. I learned nothing about where to find Len, and if I were to visit the remaining four addresses, I might not find out much either. Maybe I should rethink all of this.

But since I was already so far from my apartment, I would make another stop on my way home. Despite my doubts that I would have luck with any other names on the list, I could try one more person: M.R. Watts in Pasadena.

I entered the Pasadena address into my GPS and drove out of the parking lot. I took the 57 north to the 210 west. Thirty minutes later, I exited the freeway onto Fair Oaks Avenue. A short time after that, I pulled onto a tree-lined street with well-maintained homes. The address provided for

M.R. Watts was two stories tall and looked like it was from the 1950s. In fact, it reminded me of the Cleaver home from *Leave it to Beaver,* with its second-floor windows poking out of the shake-shingle roof.

The house was decorated for Christmas. Garland was wrapped around the mailbox and front door. Despite being daytime, I could see icicle lights strung along the house.

I parked on the street, finding an open spot several houses down. I felt similar to how I felt at Belinda's home. Like a solicitor. Still, I walked to the front door.

The home had two driveways. One was large and circular. The second jutted off the circle driveway and led to a detached garage behind a gate.

I rang the doorbell. I heard dogs yipping. Then, the door opened. An older woman with gray hair tied into a bun, wearing jeans and a zip-up sweatshirt, answered the door.

"Hi, I'm Jocelyn Bennett. Are you M.R. Watts?"

I felt like I had marbles in my mouth. Len had written the names using initials, but I doubted M.R. Watts went by M.R. Watts. Just like Belinda Jackson did not go by B. Jackson.

The woman looked me up and down. "I'm Marsha, Mrs. Watts's housekeeper."

"May I speak with her?"

"She's not home. What's this regarding?"

"I have a question for her."

Marsha eyed me warily. "What do you want to ask

her?"

I wondered how much I should reveal about why I was here. I would keep it vague. "I want to ask her if she knows someone."

"You'll have to be more specific."

"Len Zobak."

Marsha tilted her head. "That doesn't sound familiar. You'll have to ask her."

"Okay, no problem. Do you know when you expect her back?"

"I can't say for sure. She's at her salon. Sometimes, she runs other errands."

I pulled a business card from my purse and handed it to Marsha. "Could you tell her I stopped by?"

Marsha stared at it. "You're a CPA?"

"Yes."

She looked down at the card again. "You're not a salesperson?"

"No. As I said before, I'd like to ask Mrs. Watts about someone."

She tucked the card into her back pocket. "That's right. Who was it again?"

"Len Zobak."

"Of course." The woman began to close the door. "I'll give her the message."

CHAPTER 31

My stomach growled once I was back in the driver's seat of my car. I had worked up an appetite spending nervous energy this morning.

Of course, I had a burger and fries on the passenger seat. I supposed I could just eat that, but it didn't sound good. That type of food didn't keep well. I wasn't even sure why I had taken it with me.

I was about forty-five minutes from my apartment at my current location in Pasadena. If any of the multiple freeways I had to take to get home were jammed, that would set me back even longer. My fridge at home had little, and I was hungry now. So I could eat the lukewarm, soggy burger and fries, or I could grab something around here.

I remembered a café nearby that I had been to several times when I worked at Harman and had a client in Pasadena. It was off Colorado Boulevard, called Magnolia Street Café. The restaurant was known for sandwiches, salads, and a house-made banana walnut bread that people went crazy over.

A few minutes later, I parked my car in a structure

off bustling Colorado Boulevard and started walking toward the restaurant. I kept my phone in vibration mode this morning but turned on the sound in case I got any calls while eating. Mary Watts could be gone all day, but I didn't want to miss her call if she wasn't. Then again, she might never call.

The restaurant was busy but not too bad for a Monday. Lots of business people coming in and picking up to-go orders.

Even though I was in a mess with my client, seeing the harried looks on the faces of the people wearing business casual made me realize I did not want to return to office life. I would resume networking as soon as I could get this Len situation straightened out. I was determined to figure out how to make it on my own.

When it was my turn in line, I ordered a steak salad and Diet Coke. Then, I found a window table with a view of Colorado Boulevard. I sat and sipped my Diet Coke while I waited for my food to arrive.

I wasn't sure what to do after lunch. Should I continue visiting all the people on the list or move on? Visiting Belinda Jackson and M.R. Watts hadn't done me much good. So far.

In what seemed like record time, my salad was delivered. It was a large platter filled with romaine, grilled sirloin, caramelized onions, blue cheese, and walnuts. On a separate plate was the famous banana bread. And a massive slab of butter.

I had eaten a few bites of my salad when my phone rang. It was a number with a 626 area code, which I knew included Pasadena. And so, it could be M.R. Watts.

I answered. "Hello?"

The voice was smooth, calm, and that of an older woman. "May I speak with Jocelyn Bennett?"

"This is Jocelyn."

"This is Mary Rosemore Watts. My housekeeper said you came by and that you want to speak with me. Stop by now if you can."

CHAPTER 32

Thirty minutes later, I returned to Mary Watts's home in Pasadena and parked in the same spot on her street. I had packed up my remaining salad and banana bread, and it sat on the passenger seat next to my meal from the golf course. I was collecting quite an assortment of takeout.

I exited my car and walked up the driveway. Before I reached the front door, a petite woman with wavy brown hair cut above her shoulders, and who looked to be around sixty years old, appeared on the porch. She wore a striped silk blouse, black slacks, and high heels.

I waited for her to approach me. When she did, I smiled and extended my hand. "I'm Jocelyn Bennett."

Her face looked serious. "I'm Mary."

We shook hands.

"It's nice to meet you," I said.

She nodded but looked guarded. "Yes, same to you. How about we sit outside?"

Mary clicked a button on a remote she had in

her hand, and the gate to the backyard swung open. I followed Mary, and we walked to the backyard. The yard was expansive, with green grass and large, mature trees. A small patio table and chairs was under an overhang.

Mary motioned toward a chair. "Have a seat if you like."

Mary and I sat across from each other. A curtain moved behind the nearby back door. I figured Marsha was watching things.

"Marsha said you wanted to ask me about someone I might know."

"Yes. Len Zobak."

I watched for Mary's reaction, but she had none, so I couldn't tell whether she recognized the name.

She shook her head. "I don't know him."

"Are you sure?"

She nodded. "I'm sure."

What did I do now? If she didn't know Len, then why was he going to give her money?

Mary crossed her legs. "What's this about?"

I wondered where I would even start. "It's a long story."

"You came all the way to my house. Twice. Why not tell me?"

I clasped my hands together. "Sure, no problem. To start, I'm a CPA."

"Yes, I gathered as much from your business card. What of it?"

"Len Zobak is my client, so there's only so much I can get into."

Mary smoothed her hair. "But I just told you. I don't know him. I don't understand why you've come here. Talking to me about someone I don't know."

"All I feel comfortable saying is that Len may have wanted to give you something."

Mary blinked several times. "What do you mean? Like a gift?"

"Something like that, yes."

Mary narrowed her eyes. "Why would he give me a gift? What gift?"

I didn't want to say too much, since Len had a right to privacy. "I'm not sure I should say."

"Well, this must be a mistake."

I doubted it was a mistake. Mary may not know Len, but he knew her. "I'm not so sure."

She fidgeted in the chair. "I don't understand. Why do you care? Why are you interested in this?"

I had hoped Mary would know Len. But it didn't look like she did. I debated how much detail to go into with her. "Len's missing, and I'm trying to find him. I'm tracking down people who might know him. To see if anyone saw him."

"Well, I'm very sorry to hear he's missing, but you can cross me off the list. I don't know the man; I've never seen him."

I sat forward in my chair. "All right."

"You're sure it was me, Mary Watts, that he was looking for?"

"Well, he wrote your name down as M.R. Watts."

She tilted her head. "That's strange. Technically, I

am M.R. Watts, but no one calls me that. You have the wrong person. I'm sure of it."

Mary stared off, and I remained silent. So far, this visit hadn't proven helpful at all.

Her body stiffened. "Wait a second. How did you find me?"

"Len has your address."

"My address? And that's how you found me?"

"Yes."

"I don't understand. Why does this Len person have my name? And my address? And why would he want to give me a present? I'm a complete stranger."

It wasn't a present; it was cash. I guess that could be considered a present. Either way, I didn't want to reveal the specifics. "I don't know. That's what I was hoping you could help me with."

Mary rubbed her hands on her arms like she had the sudden onset of a chill despite the warm weather. She stood. "You should leave. And please don't come back."

CHAPTER 33

It was Tuesday morning. Despite not wanting to have another run-in with Mikey, I sucked it up and went down to Len's apartment to see if he was back.

The blinds were still closed. I rang the doorbell. No one answered. Not even Mikey. I heard nothing and didn't see any movement behind the curtain.

I returned to my apartment and debated what to do. I felt like I was prying into Len's life, a life he liked to keep private, according to Belinda. But Len hadn't returned, and I still felt the checks were relevant, but I didn't know how.

I thought about what had happened yesterday when I visited two of the five addresses. First, I saw Belinda in Diamond Bar. She knew Len; he had been her landlord. He knew she was struggling to pay her mortgage. Len had given her a check on Sunday morning.

Then, I met Mary Watts in Pasadena. Mary didn't know Len, didn't know why he would want to give her a gift, and didn't like the idea of a stranger knowing where she lived. I didn't blame her, but she had a connection to Len, even if I hadn't figured out what it was.

I wished I could've asked Mary more questions, but Mary had requested that I leave. Since I'm not keen on being seen as a stalker or interested in being arrested, I obliged.

The remaining three addresses were in Torrance, Sherman Oaks, and Thousand Oaks. Torrance wasn't too far away, and neither was Sherman Oaks. Except the two were in opposite directions. Thousand Oaks was a hike; it was past Sherman Oaks. I could knock off Sherman Oaks and Thousand Oaks in the morning. I could go to Torrance in the afternoon. The question was, did I want to?

The main issue I had was navigating the traffic and how long these visits would take. I thought of an alternative to driving to each one. I could do a reverse lookup and see whether any addresses had a phone number listed. Landlines were becoming rarer in this age of cell phones, so I wasn't sure whether I would have any luck.

I searched for the address for A. Baker, which was the name provided with the Sherman Oaks address. There was a number listed. I called it. No one answered, and no answering machine picked up either. The phone rang and rang until I hung up.

I next searched for J. Cecil in Thousand Oaks. I couldn't find a landline listed.

The last address was for P. Hernandez in Torrance. I found a potential number. I called, but no one picked up. I did, however, get an answering machine. A woman's voice told me I had reached the Hernandez residence and to please leave a message. I hung up without doing so, unsure what I would say.

Even though no one had answered at two of the addresses and I found no landline for a third, I could still go to these houses. Sure, it would take a considerable amount of time. But by showing up in person, I might run into someone at home. It might be a massive waste of time, or maybe I would find Len.

I heard voices arguing outside. I went into my office and looked down to the courtyard. One of the longtime residents, Chris, stood outside Len's door with Mikey. I had just been to Len's apartment, but no one answered. Had Mikey been home the whole time?

Chris was in his forties and had a full head of dark brown curly hair. He was trim but wasn't big in the muscular sense. He looked tiny compared to Mikey.

Chris was flailing his arms. I couldn't hear what the two were saying. So I dashed out of my office, went to my front door, cracked it, and listened. Their voices echoed, distorting some of the speech, but I could make out bits and pieces of what was being said.

"Your car is in my spot. You need to move it," Chris said.

We had assigned parking. Chris and Betty had two of the best spots. Seeing how they were the two longest residents, it made sense. Both spots were close to the door going into the building.

"I'll give you a different one," Mikey said, stepping closer to Chris.

"Who are you to come here and take my spot? I've been parking there for ten years."

"Well, too bad. Until Len gets back, find another spot."

Chris threw up his hands. "There are no other spots. They're all taken."

Mikey made a shooing gesture. "Go away. Park in the street or something."

Chris raised his hands like he might do something. Mikey stepped closer to him, an unsaid "what are you gonna do about it?" in his body language.

Chris froze.

Mikey smirked. "That's what I thought."

Chris returned to his first-floor apartment. Mikey waited until Chris closed his door, then he stomped into Len's apartment. He slammed the door as a finishing flourish.

I shook my head and closed my door.

I had seen Mikey's car downstairs. It was a big old hunk of a thing. The vehicle was too long for the spot, so it stuck out, making it even harder for the other cars to navigate.

Poor Chris. Hopefully, for all our sakes, Len would return and tell Mikey to pound sand. And then peace could be restored. If not, I might need to move. I didn't want to, but I couldn't live in this chaos.

Mikey was a menace. And this whole thing was turning into a nightmare. Any doubts I had about visiting the last three houses had gone away. I was going to find Len.

Except I would see about bringing someone with me on my next stops. I knew just the person to call.

CHAPTER 34

At ten o'clock, I was driving north on the 101 freeway. The day was sunny, and the light traffic made the long trek pleasant. I was wearing sunglasses, jeans, Converse sneakers, and a short-sleeved T-shirt. I had pulled my hair into a ponytail.

Jeff Monroe sat in the passenger seat. He was tall and thin, with dark brown hair and eyes that matched. We met at Harman & Haskell. Jeff had also been an auditor. He left Harman long ago and now ran his own true crime blog.

He lived in a guest house at his parents' home in Brentwood. What Jeff sometimes called a pool house. He had a flexible schedule and often invited me over for lunch and an afternoon swim. We had dated for a while, but now we were just friends.

The address for J. Cecil in Thousand Oaks was entered in my GPS. A thermos of fresh coffee sat in my console. My iPod was plugged in and playing a techno remix of an eighties song.

We cruised through the San Fernando Valley. As we drove farther into the Valley, the landscape became less congested and massive green hills appeared.

Jeff grabbed my iPod and flipped through it. "You're taking me all the way up to Ventura, huh?"

"Is Thousand Oaks in Ventura County? I wasn't sure."

"Yeah, I'm almost certain it is. If it isn't, it's pretty close."

I had called Jeff earlier this morning and asked if he wanted to tag along. I'd like to think he would help for nothing, but the sushi lunch I promised him was what likely sealed the deal.

I gave Jeff a rundown of my situation, including how I had gone to Diamond Bar to talk to Belinda Jackson and Pasadena to talk with Mary Watts.

Jeff adjusted his seatbelt. "Well, that stinks about Len."

"I know."

"And you think these checks have something to do with it?"

I shrugged. "It's the only thing I have to go on."

"I'll admit, it's interesting."

"Don't get any ideas."

Jeff laughed. "What do you mean? For the blog?"

"Yeah."

"No promises. If this turns out to be something big, how can I not cover it?"

"That's not why I'm bringing you along."

"Then why? Moral support?"

I smiled. "Something like that. Thanks for coming with me if I didn't say it already."

"No problem."

When we exited the freeway, Jeff helped me navigate the neighborhood. It was all blue skies, green grass, and newer homes with immaculate yards. We arrived at a sprawling two-story Mediterranean-style house perched on a hill.

I parked my car down the street from the house.

Jeff unbuckled his seatbelt. "What now?"

I reached across and locked my purse in the glove box. "Knock on the door?"

Jeff smiled. "That's why you're a genius. What do you need me for, anyway?"

I returned the smile. "I don't like to eat at restaurants by myself."

"I knew you were just using me."

We got out of the car and walked toward the house. A bright red Jeep Wrangler was in the massive circular driveway. Just then, a woman opened the front door and came outside.

She looked young at first glance, but upon closer look, she was probably five years older than me. She wore low-slung jeans, big white sneakers, and a sparkly pink tube top. Her dark blonde hair was piled high on her head in a messy bun. She was wearing large silver hoop earrings that almost grazed her shoulders.

She looked like she was about to get into the Jeep.

I nudged Jeff. "I'm going to talk to her."

I increased my pace to reach her before she got in the car. "Excuse me."

She looked at me suspiciously. "No solicitors."

"I'm not selling anything," I said.

She rolled her eyes. "The only people that walk around here are selling something. Or cops." She thrust her hands on her hips. "Is that what you guys are? Cops?"

CHAPTER 35

Jeff and I were neither solicitors nor cops. For the life of me, I couldn't figure out how she got that impression from us.

"I asked you a question," she said. "Are you guys cops?"

I responded as simply as possible. "No."

"Then you're salespeople?"

"No, we're not."

"Well, those are the only people who come around here."

I stared at her and wondered how much of a debate to get into. "I'm sure other people have been in this neighborhood before."

She crossed her arms. "Oh, really? Do you live here? Are you an expert at what goes on?"

Maybe she thought I was being sarcastic or something. I had tried my best to sound normal, but I could see how my statement could be interpreted other ways. Oh well.

"No. You got me there," I said. This time, I didn't care if she detected sarcasm.

She rolled her eyes. "Yeah, I don't think you guys are salespeople. You guys are cops."

I could tell Jeff was about to laugh. I had never in my life been mistaken for a person of authority. Like they said, there was a first time for everything. "We're not cops."

"Yeah, right. I've seen this before. You wear jeans and act friendly. You just want to ask a few questions. That's how people get themselves into trouble."

I wasn't sure what more I could do to convince her we weren't the police. "I promise you we're not. Search my purse. You won't find a badge. I'm just looking for someone named J. Cecil."

"Jay? There's no one here by that name."

I shook my head. "Not Jay, the name. J, the initial."

"Either way, I can't help you."

I wasn't about to give up, so I gave it another try. "What's your name?"

She put her hands on her hips. "Yep, definitely cops. Am I under arrest? If not, I don't have to talk to you."

Jeff laughed, apparently unable to hold it in any longer. "Jeez. We're not cops. And besides, what are you worried about?"

"Uh-huh, yeah, that's exactly what a cop would say."

I looked toward the house. A woman was standing by the door, watching everything that was going on in the driveway.

She opened the door and peered out. "Jessica? Is

everything okay?"

Jessica. Jessica Cecil? As in J. Cecil? Could Jessica be the person I was looking for?

Jessica waved at the woman. "It's okay, Mom."

The woman didn't seem satisfied, so she stepped out of the house and walked toward us. She had the same dark blonde hair. Also piled into a messy bun like Jessica. She wore yoga pants and a sparkly off-the-shoulder top. She eyed Jeff and me. "Who are you?"

Jessica pointed at us. "They say they're not cops, but they act like it."

I answered the woman's question. "I'm Jocelyn Bennett. This is Jeff Monroe."

"I'm Candy," the woman said but didn't extend her hand. "What's going on here?"

Maybe I could get something out of Candy since Jessica wasn't helpful. "Is this the Cecil residence?"

"Why are you asking?"

"We're looking for someone," I said, even though I figured I had already found her.

"Who is it?" Candy asked.

"Someone with the first initial J and the last name Cecil."

Jessica leaned against the Jeep and adjusted her hair. "I'm the only one with a J initial."

I looked at Jessica. "Do you know Len Zobak?"

Jessica flinched as though she recognized the name. But she recovered, straightening up and crossing her arms. "No. Why would I know him?"

"It was just a question."

Candy stared at Jessica. "What's this about, Jessica. Why are they asking if you know this person?"

Jessica looked at her mom. "Beats me. I don't know these people, and I don't know anyone named Lynn."

"Len," I said.

Jessica frowned. "I'm going to be late."

Candy looked at Jessica then turned to me. "Why would my daughter know him?"

I didn't want to mention the check, so I did my best to avoid it, though I realized how bizarre what I was about to say would sound. "We're not sure. We were hoping she could tell us."

Jessica nodded but looked about to cry. "They're cops, Mom! Haven't you figured that out yet?"

I realized how stilted I sounded, but that was the best way to ask without revealing too much. I wondered why Jessica was so paranoid about whether I was a cop.

Suddenly, Jessica jumped into the Jeep. She turned it on and slammed it into gear. The Jeep bounced as she peeled around the circular driveway and sped into the street.

CHAPTER 36

I watched Jessica's Jeep speed away. The car didn't kick up dust, but I expected it to.

Jeff walked to the driveway's edge and glanced up and down the street. He turned back to me. "Whoa. What's with the Dukes of Hazard exit?"

Candy stood close by, so I resisted making comments about her daughter that she could overhear. She tapped me on the shoulder, and I turned around.

"Will you please tell me what this is about?"

I repeated what I had said earlier. "We're looking for J. Cecil. J is an initial. I'm guessing that's Jessica."

Candy nodded. "Jessica is the only one who lives here whose name starts with a J. And you want to see if she knows someone, is that right?"

"Yes."

"And what was the name again? I didn't catch it."

"Len Zobak."

Candy rubbed her forehead. "That doesn't sound familiar. Why would Jessica know him?"

She had asked this question earlier. And I had told

her we hoped Jessica could tell us. I still wasn't sure what to say. I gave her the same response as earlier. "I'm not sure."

Candy crossed her arms. "Oh, come on. You must know. If not, why are you asking?"

I gave Candy an abbreviated version of the story. "Len's my landlord. He's missing. I got her name from him."

"What do you mean? Are you saying he's looking for Jessica? This makes me extremely uncomfortable. She's just now getting back on track. I don't want anything to derail her."

"Getting back on track from what?"

Candy shook her head. "Just an awful experience with an old job."

"What job?"

"A good one. Jessica enjoyed it, and then something happened there."

I wanted to ask Candy more questions. I had no problem asking business-related questions. But with personal questions, I always felt like I was prying. But I had driven from Brentwood and wanted to find Len. I would have to push through my discomfort. "What did she do at this job?"

Candy frowned. "Look, I don't know what this is all about. You're obviously not telling me everything. You must know why your landlord is looking for her. She's always lived at home, never in an apartment. If he's collecting unpaid rent or something, he has her mixed up with someone else."

"He's not looking for money."

"Then what? Where does this guy live?"

"In Brentwood."

"That's a good hour's drive from here. Is that where you live too? You came all this way to find Jessica?"

Driving to Thousand Oaks from Brentwood wasn't like traveling to the Arctic Circle. People did it all the time in Los Angeles. I knew people who had worse commutes than that. "Yes, that's where I live."

"Do you have a card or something?"

I pulled a card from my purse and handed it to her.

Candy read it aloud. "Jocelyn Bennett. CPA." She stared at me. "Why don't you just admit Len is trying to get money from her? Whatever you think she's done, you've confused her with someone else."

"That's not the case at all."

"Then what?"

I wondered how much it would hurt to tell Candy why Len was looking for Jessica. As with Belinda and Mary, I was worried about privacy issues. I could probably skirt around the check issue, without revealing too much, similar to what I had done with Belinda and Mary.

Candy sighed. "You know what. I'm done with this." She held up my business card. "I'll call you if Jessica knows anything about the guy."

"Len Zobak."

"Yeah, whatever."

Candy walked up the driveway. She waved to get our attention when she got to the front porch.

"Please leave my daughter alone in the meantime, okay?"

Her tone was polite and not aggressive. Then Candy went inside and closed the door.

CHAPTER 37

The large house looked empty. I didn't see anyone staring at us, but I was fairly sure Candy was keeping a lookout.

I turned to Jeff. "Well, that was a total bust."

"I thought it was fun."

"Is that sarcasm?"

Jeff laughed. "I don't know."

"Let's at least get off this property," I said.

Jeff stepped into the street, looking in both directions like he expected Jessica and her Jeep to squeal back into the driveway any second. "You think Candy'll call the police if we don't leave?"

"I don't know. It depends on if she thinks we're the police."

Jeff snorted. "She knows we're not. Plus, you gave her your business card. What cop poses as a CPA?"

I walked to my car and got in. I turned on the vehicle.

Jeff slipped into the passenger seat. "How weird was that whole thing?"

"You mean Jessica fleeing the scene like she's got

warrants?"

Jeff stared straight ahead. "Yes."

"Can I ask you something? I didn't mention the check because I'm not sure how much I should say about my meeting with Len. You know, privacy issues and all that. Do you think I should've told Jessica or Candy about the check?"

"What do you mean?"

"Well, maybe if I had said that Len had a check for Jessica that might've helped. Maybe they would've said more."

Jeff shook his head. "I don't think so. You got as far as you were going to get."

"Yeah," I said, though I didn't feel convinced.

"Len's your client. I agree you can keep your meeting private. I don't think you need to mention the check. And even if you did, like I said, I don't think it would've helped any."

"Belinda Jackson knew Len and brought up the money, so I had no concern there. Then when I talked to Mary Watts, I told her that Len wanted to give her a gift. I guess I could have said the same thing to Jessica. You know, just vaguely mention a gift."

Jeff smiled. "It's okay. Neither of those two was going to tell you much more."

I felt better having broached the subject of privacy with Jeff. I felt I was doing the right thing, but it was easy to second guess.

I reached into my console and grabbed my coffee. "Jessica's long gone. Don't you think?"

"She has to come home sometime."

I sensed Jeff had put on his true crime blogger hat. "What are you suggesting? A stakeout?"

"If you want."

I laughed. "I doubt that'll help. You said yourself that we wouldn't get any more info from Jessica."

"Well, not by talking to her. Who knows what we might find out if we follow her. What's next? You said there was a place in Sherman Oaks."

I pulled out the scanned letter from Len which contained the list of addresses. "Yeah. A. Baker."

Jeff looked at the list. "You know, it would've been helpful if Len had included full names. Then you wouldn't be going around asking for people by initials."

I put the paper in the console, next to my coffee. "What would've been helpful is if Len hadn't disappeared."

"Why are you so interested in finding him? You know you don't owe him anything, right?"

"I kind of do," I said.

Jeff tilted his head. "How so?"

I had told no one how Adam Davis confronted me outside my building. I only told the police, because Len had called them. I don't know why I said nothing about it. Maybe because I was still scared. Even when I reminded myself that Adam was in jail, some fear persisted. "It's a long story."

"You should tell me sometime."

"Maybe," I said. "Would you still be willing to stop in Sherman Oaks?"

"I'm down if you are. You owe me lunch either way."

I sipped my coffee. "My first visit went okay. At the second one, I got kicked out. At this one, Jessica peeled out like she's on the FBI's Most Wanted List. It's getting worse each place."

"Well, expect that you're gonna get some weird responses when you show up places uninvited," Jeff said.

"Good point. All right. Let's go to Sherman Oaks. We have to go there for lunch anyway."

Jeff laughed. "Dare I say it?"

I put the car in drive and drove down Jessica's street, on my way back to the 101 freeway. "Say what?"

"What's the worst that could happen?"

CHAPTER 38

Christine sat in a booth next to a window in a diner in Claremont. She looked out to a tree-lined street. She had a packed schedule tomorrow but had no classes today and was free to work.

Her short light brown hair was still damp from the shower. She had been running late this morning and didn't take the time to dry it. It would likely be a frizzy mess later.

Coming to this diner before heading to her job as a bank teller had become part of her routine. She didn't want to miss it; she could deal with a little frizz.

Claremont was in the easternmost part of Los Angeles County and was home to many universities, including the one Christine attended, Stauffer University.

She had ordered the breakfast platter, which included eggs, bacon, pancakes, hash browns, and a biscuit. All that she had left was the biscuit. She smeared it with butter and strawberry jam.

It was a lovely day in Claremont, but most days

were like that here. Sure, occasionally there were some clouds and even rain, but the weather was mostly perfect. Being from Indiana, she knew how rare that was. The problem was that she always liked to be outside on a nice day. Except she had school and work to attend to.

She had ordered her coffee in a to-go cup, and when the waitress came by to drop the check, she refilled Christine's drink.

Christine added half-and-half to her coffee and finished the biscuit. She placed cash on the table, enough to cover the breakfast and a generous tip. She grabbed her coffee and exited the diner.

Her shift started in ten minutes, but she wasn't looking forward to it because she was extra-tired this morning. She had been up late the night before, cramming for her upcoming finals. The last thing she felt like doing was a shift at work.

She entered the bank, and the familiar ding of the bell went off as she did. She greeted everyone and set up at her spot.

One customer was already inside. He was an older gentleman, and he stood at the center table, filling out a form. She recognized him. Tom was his name. He came in every week to withdraw cash, and it was always for the same amount. He once told her it was to cover his weekly expenses; this was how he kept to his budget.

A young woman walked in. She looked like a high school student. Too young to be in college, though Christine thought she looked a lot like someone in her history class.

She wore a tight striped T-shirt, which showed off her belly button ring. She also had on low-slung jeans with gemstones glued to the pockets. Her curly, dark brown hair was cut short and loaded with so much gel that it looked crunchy. She wore oversized dark sunglasses, which she had so far not removed. And that was strange.

Christine tried not to get too many unsettling feelings from customers. If she did, she would become paranoid that every customer was about to do a stick-up.

The woman walked up to Christine's counter.

Christine smiled. "How can I help you?"

The woman's head swiveled around, like she was checking things out. "I'm withdrawing money for someone. He's old and can't come in."

Withdrawing money on behalf of someone else wasn't unusual. Christine saw it all the time. Many people did banking for elderly relatives.

Christine grabbed the correct form and slid it across the counter. "Please fill this out."

The woman scrunched her hair. "I don't have the info for the forms. He's on the phone. Can you talk to him? Get the information from him?"

Christine felt a twinge in her stomach. Was it the diner's food or her intuition? She glanced around but didn't see the security guard. He was useful most of the time, but he took an awful lot of cigarette breaks. And he always seemed to take these breaks around the side of the bank rather than the front. So maybe he wasn't that helpful after all.

Christine's manager was down at the other end of the bank. It was too far to ask for help subtly; maybe Christine could give her a signal.

The customer placed a small black cell phone on the counter. "Here. He'll give you everything you need."

Christine stared at the phone, sighed, and grabbed it. "Hello?"

The man on the other line responded.

That was when Christine knew this wouldn't be a good day.

CHAPTER 39

Jeff and I arrived in Sherman Oaks about thirty minutes after leaving Thousand Oaks. We were now back in L.A. County and not too far from home. Brentwood was just over the hill.

We drove down Ventura Boulevard, the major thoroughfare not just for Sherman Oaks but the entire San Fernando Valley. Finally, we turned onto A. Baker's street, which was lined with cars on both sides. I lucked out and found a spot directly across from the house. We exited my car, and I surveyed the area. The neighborhood was quiet, with not much activity this Tuesday morning.

The beige one-story house had a protruding attached garage, which was open and lined with shelves filled with boxes. Tall shrubs blocked the windows and front door. A white conversion van was parked in the driveway.

The house looked dated. But it was clean. And the paint appeared new. The grass needed mowing, and a man out front was fiddling with a lawn mower and gas can.

He had shaggy blonde hair and wore baggy jeans, a black sleeveless undershirt, and Adidas sneakers, giving him an air of youth. But the closer I got, the more I realized he was probably in his thirties.

He saw us coming and eyed us cautiously.

"Hi," I said, trying my best to sound friendly and unassuming. "Anyone here named A. Baker?"

He set down the gas can. "My pops is Andy, but he's not here."

"And you are?" I asked.

"I'm Tony."

Tony was often short for Anthony, which obviously started with an A. So was I looking for him or his dad?

Tony rubbed his hands on his jeans, and his eyes moved between Jeff and me. "My pops do something? Are you guys undercover cops? Private detectives?"

First it was Jessica and now Tony. I didn't see how Jeff and I were giving off this vibe. Maybe it was the questions I was asking. "No, I just want to see if he knows someone."

Tony pushed his hair out of his eyes. "Yeah, who's that?"

"Len Zobak," I said.

"No, my pops doesn't know anyone by that name. Sorry."

Considering I still didn't know if I was looking for Tony or Andy, I had a couple of follow-up questions. "Do you ever go by Anthony?"

"Well, yeah, that's my official name. But only my

parents ever call me that." He smiled. "And cops."

"I know you said your dad doesn't know Len, but do you know him?" I asked.

Tony tapped his chest. "Me? No, ma'am, I don't."

He didn't know Len and didn't believe his dad, Andy, did either. But Andy might know him. The only way to be sure was to talk to him. "When will your dad be back?"

"Depends. He works late, especially right now."

"What does he do?" I asked.

"He's a contractor. Works on houses. Everyone wants things done before the holidays. You get all those relatives in your house. You wanna know your plumbing's gonna hold up, you know what I mean?"

I gave Tony my business card. "Will you ask your dad to call me?"

Tony slid the card into one of the huge pockets on his jeans. "Sure." He smiled at Jeff. "Anybody ever tell you that you look like a pimp?"

I tried to see Jeff's reaction, but he didn't look at me.

Jeff bit his lower lip. "No, man, that's a first."

"Total pimp, dude. The car, the girl. You know you're straight pimpin'. Don't lie to me."

Jeff hooked a thumb toward me. "The car belongs to her."

Tony's eyes got big, and he looked at me. "No kidding. How did you afford a car like that?"

"Accounting pays big money," I said. I wanted to use some slang, but I couldn't think of any.

"No kidding, my pops always says I should get

into accounting. He tells me it's a real stable career and shit. But there's no way I could sit in some dank office all day. Can you see me wearing a suit?"

"Things are a bit more casual these days," I said. "You could get away with slacks and a dress shirt."

"What's the difference? That sounds uncomfortable as hell," Tony said. He waved his arms up and down, showcasing his current attire. "This is what I like to wear."

I agreed with Tony. Business clothes were uncomfortable as hell. It was also expensive to maintain. Dry cleaning alone could cost a fortune.

I wanted to circle back to Tony's dad. Then Jeff and I could leave. "You said you'll give your dad my card, right?"

"Yeah, of course. I'll have my pops call you."

I nodded. "Thanks. Like I said, I want to ask him if he knows Len Zobak."

"He doesn't, but I'll have him call you."

Just then, a beat-up black conversion van, similar to the white one in the driveway, rolled up to the curb and shuddered to a stop, blocking the driveway.

CHAPTER 40

I glanced at the vehicle at the end of the driveway. The window was down, giving me a clear view of the driver. He had a long brown ponytail and beard and looked like he was wearing a white sleeveless undershirt.

The man kept the car parked where it was, blocking the entire width of the driveway. My stomach flipped. Who was this person, and what did he want? And why on earth had he parked like that?

The man jumped out and slammed the door. It squealed as it shut. Despite the slight belly hanging over his jeans, the man was tall, and I could tell muscle was hiding underneath the fat.

The man pulled up his jeans, leaned against the van, and looked up and down the street.

I turned to Tony. His eyes looked like they had bugged out of his head. He hadn't spoken a word until now. "Fuck, it's Doug."

Tony said it like we knew who the hell Doug was.

I frowned. "Who's Doug?"

"This asshole who keeps bugging me."

Doug waved. "What's up, Tony?"

Tony's eyes darted around, scanning the street. Hoping for a savior. "Hey."

Doug gestured toward the lawn mower. "You thinking about cutting the grass? Because you should. Your yard looks like shit. Be a better neighbor."

Tony laughed, a nervous, high-pitched laugh. "What do you want?"

"You know."

I didn't know what to do. I looked at Jeff. His eyes were glued to the situation unfolding in front of us.

Doug smiled. It was a big smile that took over his entire face. "Didn't think I'd find your house, huh, you punk ass."

Tony laughed again but didn't say anything. His eyes continued their rapid motion, scanning the scene like he expected someone to pop out of the bushes and rescue him.

Doug opened the van's sliding door and retrieved a bat. "You got my money or what?"

I stepped off the driveway into the small patch of grass on the house's side. My car was parked behind the van, which meant I had to pass Doug to get to it. My other choice was to sprint away and return for my vehicle later.

Jeff stayed in the driveway, not budging since Doug arrived, and I wondered what he was thinking. If only I could silently communicate to him that we needed to cut and run. *Now.*

Doug rolled the bat in his hand. "You hear me? I'm

talking to you."

Tony's eyes darted from Jeff to me and then back to Doug. "I don't have it!"

Doug continued rolling the bat. "Bullshit!"

Tony pulled on his shirt, and it looked like the wheels in his head were turning. Like he was trying to put together an escape plan. "It's true! I don't!"

Doug took a couple of steps up the driveway. Tony jumped and sprinted into the house, his baggy jeans not slowing him down at all. The front door slammed a few seconds later.

Doug ran up to the door and started pounding. "Open up! Or I'll bust this fucker down!"

CHAPTER 41

With Doug and Tony occupied, Jeff and I had a limited window of time to escape. Jeff must have thought the same thing.

He ran over to me and grabbed my arm. "Let's go."

We darted to my car. I could still hear Doug pounding on the front door. Then, he moved to the garage, just in time for it to close. He started hitting his bat on the closed garage door.

At first, no damage occurred, but after repeated blows, dents dimpled the lightweight metal door.

Jeff ran around to the passenger seat. "What does he think he's doing?"

I unlocked my car and jumped in. "I don't know."

Jeff was now seated next to me. I locked the doors and started the car. Doug was still slamming his bat into the garage.

Jeff placed his hand over mine, which was on the gear shift. "Let's wait a second. I want to see how this plays out."

"Isn't that stupid?"

"We'll go if there's a problem."

I put the car in drive and kept my foot on the brake, ready to hit the gas if I needed to. I wasn't so sure that Jeff had the right idea. "Looks like a problem to me."

Jeff rolled down his window.

I flinched. "What are you doing?"

"I want to hear."

Doug was screaming so loud, we could hear him even with the windows closed.

Doug stomped back to the front door. "Open up, Tony! Open this door now!"

My eyes caught a movement. Tony was at the side of the house, carrying a backpack.

Tony peered around the garage, bobbing his head. He bent forward, paused for a few seconds, and sprinted to the white van. His baggy pants swished, and the backpack bounced.

Tony opened the driver's side door, flung the backpack in, hopped in, and pulled the door shut.

Doug turned from the porch and rushed to the van, baseball bat in hand. He slammed the bat into a headlight. It shattered. He started on the other headlight. *Crack!* Finally, taking the bat in both hands, he started smashing the hood. His muscles were taut, and he was sweating.

Tony rolled down the window an inch. "Knock it off, man! I don't have your money!"

"Yeah, right, what's in that backpack? Hand it over. You can't hide. I know where you live, you little shit."

Tony turned on the van. It rumbled and

shuddered, like it was thinking about whether it wanted to work.

Doug blasted the door closest to Tony and a big dent appeared.

Tony rolled down the window another inch. "Stop, Doug! Seriously, stop!"

Doug ignored Tony and continued slamming the bat into the van.

Suddenly, Tony reversed at a diagonal onto the grass. He sped backward across the front yard, running over the tall blades of grass. The back tires dropped off the curb and the vehicle bounced into the street, headed straight for my car.

I braced for impact, waiting for the inevitable crunch as it smashed into mine. But just as the vehicle was inches from my door, it lurched to a stop, the front tires landing with a thud on the pavement.

Tony threw the van in drive, hit the gas, and raced off, tires squealing.

Doug sprinted to his own van. He jumped in. His van also hesitated to start. When it did, he peeled off in the same direction as Tony.

Both vans were gone, and things were calm again on the street. Tire streaks were all that remained.

CHAPTER 42

Jeff and I sat at a small table along the wall at one of the larger sushi restaurants on Ventura Boulevard in Sherman Oaks. We looked calm, like nothing exciting had happened to us today. We were just a couple of people in on a Tuesday for a relaxing lunch.

The restaurant was pretty packed. People in suits, slacks, and tailored dresses filled the sizable sushi bar. Most of the tables in the dining section were also full.

Our server had dropped off my glass of iced green tea and Jeff's pot of hot tea. Jeff filled his tiny mug. We were both looking at the piece of paper to mark down our rolls.

I scanned the page. Everything sounded good, but I stuck with the basics today: California, rainbow, and spicy tuna rolls. I borrowed the little pencil and put a checkmark next to my choices.

I slid the paper to Jeff. "I've figured out mine."

Jeff grabbed the pencil. "I'm starving." He began filling in what he wanted. He was more adventurous than me, marking down many selections of sashimi, which was plain fish, along with a variety of rolls.

My mind was reeling from what had happened on the visits to Thousand Oaks and Sherman Oaks. I believed J. Cecil was Jessica Cecil. Tony or his dad, Andy, was A. Baker.

Then there was Doug, who was after Tony, looking for money. What was Tony into? If Len intended to give the money to Tony, why was that?

This led me to believe Len was looking for Andy, Tony's dad, and not Tony. If that was the case, I still needed to get a hold of Andy.

Jeff finished with his selections and set the paper down. "Well, that was interesting. And by interesting, I mean, what is going on?"

The server picked up our order and dropped off a bowl of edamame.

I waited until she was out of earshot. "Really? I thought what happened was totally normal." I had a tough time saying it with a straight face.

"I never expected to see so many cars tearing down residential streets," Jeff said.

"I like to keep you entertained."

He laughed. "No kidding."

I grabbed an edamame. "Do you think we need to go to the police?"

"About what?"

"Tony."

"And what about him?"

"What if something happens to him? You know, Doug does something to Tony?"

Jeff looked confused. "You mean like murders him?"

"Not murder. But hurts Tony or something. Would we be responsible for not reporting it?"

Jeff snorted. "We didn't see anyone get hurt."

"You know what I mean. Not reporting the threat."

Jeff picked up an edamame. "Well, Doug never threatened to kill him or anything. Just wanted his money."

"Doug was beating on that garage door pretty hard. And Tony's van. Should we report that, or do you think we're okay?"

"I don't want to be involved."

"But we're already involved. Don't you think?"

Jeff shook his head. "No. We're not. All we did was observe two people having a private dispute. We don't know what's going on."

CHAPTER 43

Our server placed one large platter of sushi between Jeff and me. Jeff cracked open his chopsticks, rubbed them together to smooth any splinters, and grabbed a piece of fish.

He held it and looked at me. "Is there anyone else on your list?"

I stared at the platter, wondering where I wanted to start. "One last name. In Torrance."

"Are you thinking of going?"

This morning, I called my friend Bethany Scott in Hermosa Beach to see if she wanted to meet me for dinner. Hermosa Beach was close to Torrance; both were in the South Bay. My plan was to visit the last address and meet Bethany for dinner afterward. "Yes, later today. Do you think I should reconsider?"

Jeff shrugged. "It's your choice. But I mean, you were right earlier. This is getting worse."

I smiled, slid my napkin onto my lap, and picked up a piece of the California roll with my chopsticks. "Well, you said you'll get strange responses when you drop by unannounced."

"Did I say that? You should definitely not listen to me. What just happened was more than weird."

"I know," I said.

Jeff placed two pieces of sushi on his plate. "I want to make sure I understand what's going on. Your landlord wants tax advice. You give it to him. He asks you to deliver five checks. Then he changes his mind. He's supposed to meet with you. But he doesn't show up. And you haven't seen him since. Is that right?"

"That's the gist of it, yes. And someone named Mikey, who claims to be Len's nephew, showed up at his apartment."

"Mikey, you said? Have you looked him up or anything like that?"

I grabbed another piece of the California roll. "Yes, but I didn't find anything."

"I can look."

"If it's not too much trouble."

Jeff smiled. "Not at all. I'm interested now."

I laughed. "Okay."

"Do you have a last name for Mikey?"

"Zobak. Same as Len."

"How old is this guy?"

"Mikey looks young, but I think he's older. It's hard to tell."

Jeff picked up another piece of sushi. "I'll see what I can find. Do you want to come by and swim later?"

"Sounds nice, but I better take a rain check since I'm going to Torrance later today."

"Oh, right, you said that. Just to confirm, are you

okay going by yourself?"

Was I acting stupid for going alone? Especially after how things went in Thousand Oaks and Sherman Oaks? "I think so, yeah. I'm meeting Bethany afterward, so I can always ask her to come with me if I get concerned."

"Okay. I have plans tonight, but if you change your mind and want to go tomorrow, I could do it then."

"Should I go to the police?"

Jeff laughed. "Are you still worried about those two guys from earlier?"

"No. I mean to report Len missing."

"When did it happen?"

"Len going missing? Sunday was when we were supposed to meet."

Jeff looked like he was thinking. "And today's Tuesday. I would give it some time. I don't think it hurts to poke around. But maybe I should reconsider saying that after what happened earlier."

Even though I felt something was wrong, I agreed with Jeff that it was premature to file a missing person's report. I had little information for them to go on. They would probably just brush it off.

We worked our way through the platter, finishing everything we ordered. Then, the waitress dropped off the check.

Jeff put his hand over the bill. "I got it."

I tried to grab it from him. "I'm supposed to pay. You're helping me."

Jeff slid the check out of my reach. "How much did

you say you made the other day?"

I smiled. "Forty bucks."

"Yeah, that's what I thought. I'll pay."

"Thanks, I appreciate it."

Jeff shook his head. "Don't worry about it."

We exited the restaurant and were back out in the bright sun. I saw a red Jeep Wrangler parked across the street from the restaurant.

I nudged Jeff. "Look."

"What am I looking at?"

"Red Jeep Wrangler. Right by the curb."

Jeff turned to me. "You think it's the same one?"

"It looks like it."

"I see those all the time. I doubt it's the same."

I stared at the Jeep, and it looked like someone was in the driver's seat. A woman? Around Jessica's age? I doubted it. Still, it made me wonder, even if it was just my imagination.

CHAPTER 44

I returned to my apartment after dropping Jeff off at his house. I had some time before I needed to leave for Torrance.

The air was becoming stuffy on this warm afternoon, so I opened my sliding glass doors. I walked around my place, straightening things up.

Today was only half over, but I was exhausted. I was still full from my sushi lunch, and I felt like taking a nap. I had time before I had to leave. I rested my head on the couch and took a few deep breaths. The breeze from my open sliding doors felt nice.

Someone knocked on my door. Could it be Len? Had he returned safe and sound?

I looked out the peephole. It was Tara, a tenant whose apartment was on the first floor. She had lived in my building for about six months. Tara and I met the day she moved in. She had been hauling in boxes when I was checking my mail.

I opened the door. Tara was petite with long golden brown hair and dark blue eyes. She wore a similar outfit every time I saw her: ripped jeans, a vintage T-shirt, and flip-flops. She once told me she was thirty-five. Tara was enrolled in a graduate extension program involving art at UCLA.

I had just seen Tara on Saturday night while looking for Len. Betty had given her the business about doing laundry past eight.

Tara smiled. "Hi, Jocelyn. Sorry to bother you. Have you seen Len?"

"No. I haven't. I'm looking for him actually."

Tara raised her eyebrows, and fine lines creased her forehead. "You're looking for him too?"

I would leave out anything confidential, but I wanted to find Len. The more people who knew he was missing, the better. "I was helping Len with something. We were supposed to meet on Sunday, but he never showed up. I haven't seen him since."

"But there's someone in Len's apartment."

"Mikey."

Tara tilted her head. "Who's that?"

"I'm not sure. He said his last name is Zobak and Len is his uncle. But I have no idea if that's true."

"Hmm. That's interesting."

"Yeah, and Mikey showed up right around the time Len went missing."

Tara's eyes grew wide. "That's sketchy."

I wanted to add that Tara should stay away from Mikey, but she was with it. She didn't need someone telling her what to do. So I just gave a simple response. "I know."

"And you're trying to find him all by yourself?"

I thought about the older gentleman I had

seen knocking on Len's door yesterday after my locksmith left. I didn't know who he was or whether he was trying to find Len. "Right now, it looks that way."

"Len's awesome. I love living here. I hope he's all right."

"Me too. What did you need to see him about?"

"Oh, it's not important. The dryer in the laundry room isn't working right. It doesn't seem to get hot."

"I'm guessing you don't have a dryer in your apartment?"

She shook her head. "I have a studio. There's no hook-up; I don't know where they'd put it even if I wanted one."

"You're welcome to use mine."

"Thanks, that's nice of you. I'll just go to a laundromat."

Tara walked away, stopped, and turned around. "You know, you're the first person I've asked who noticed Len is gone. I hope he comes back soon."

CHAPTER 45

I parked across the street from a modest house in Torrance belonging to P. Hernandez. Torrance was in the South Bay region of Los Angeles and about twenty miles south of my apartment in Brentwood.

The home had a pinkish beige stucco exterior with a tan roof. The driveway was long and narrow, leading to a detached garage. There were a lot of plants, all potted in brick-lined planters that ran along the house's perimeter.

This was my last visit. I was at the fifth and final address on Len's list. Despite what happened in Thousand Oaks and Sherman Oaks, I came alone. Jeff had plans tonight, and Bethany was still at work. Maybe I was being stupid, but I wanted to get this over with. Hopefully, I wouldn't regret my impatience later.

Before I drove down here, I called the landline I had found for the house. Just like when I called this morning, no one answered.

But it looked like someone was home, because an older man with dark brown hair wearing a navy windbreaker and jeans was outside. He had a watering can in one hand and steadied himself with a cane using his other. The man ambled around to various potted plants in the yard, putting a little water into each one.

I locked my purse in the glove box and exited my car. The sun was setting, and the street was quiet. Many homes had cars parked in the driveway, but I saw little action.

The day was cooling off. I was still wearing my jeans and Converse from earlier, but I had changed from a short-sleeved T-shirt to a sweater.

The man watering his plants wasn't facing me, so I approached carefully, not wanting to startle him.

"Hi there," I said.

He turned around and lowered the pitcher. "No, thank you."

I shook my head. "I'm not selling anything. I'm looking for someone."

The man balanced himself on his cane. Then he bent down and set the pitcher on a small bench on the patio. He stared at me like he didn't believe me.

"I promise. Is this the Hernandez residence?"

He narrowed his eyes. "Yes. What do you want?"

I felt more at ease now that I was at my last address. I started my well-rehearsed spiel. "My landlord is missing, and I'm looking for him. His name is Len Zobak. He might know someone who lives here."

The man tilted his head. "Len's missing?"

"Do you know him?"

"I know Len, yes."

Relief washed over me, and I felt like I might get somewhere. "Do you mind if I ask your name?"

"I'm Pete Hernandez. And you are?"

It looked like Pete Hernandez was P. Hernandez. Perhaps he could direct me to where I could find Len, and I could put an end to this once and for all. Would I be so lucky? I walked closer and put out my hand. "I'm Jocelyn Bennett."

We shook hands, and I stepped back to give Pete space. "Do you know where Len is?"

"Right now? No, I don't."

"But you know Len?"

He nodded. "Yes."

"How do you know him?"

Pete ignored my question. "Len's your landlord, and you're looking for him. Do I have that right?"

I put my hands in the pockets of my jeans. "That's correct. We had a meeting scheduled on Sunday. He didn't show. I haven't seen him since."

He nodded like he was processing what I was saying. "And your search led you to me?"

"Yes, it did."

"How so?"

I wasn't sure what to say. I didn't want to give up confidential information but needed to provide Pete with more details. "Len was planning to give you something."

Pete used his cane to help lower himself onto the patio bench. Then, he rested his cane next to it. "You must be talking about the money."

I felt more relief. "Yes. Did Len give you a check?"

Pete rested a hand on the bench's arm. "Len mentioned one of his tenants was helping him with that. Is that you?"

"Yes. I'm an accountant. He asked me about gift taxes."

Pete nodded. "Ah, that makes sense. Do you know who I am?"

I figured Pete was asking about more than what we had already established. Which was that he was Pete Hernandez. Outside of that, I didn't know what he was getting at. "Just that Len wanted to give you a check, that's all."

"I've known Len for a very long time."

"You're friends?"

He stretched his legs out. "The word friends isn't entirely accurate."

Pete wasn't being forthcoming. For every question I asked, I got a miniscule bit of information. I had, however, found someone besides Belinda who knew Len. I was already doing better than I had earlier today.

I wondered if Pete was just another acquaintance that Len was helping. Pete used a cane and had a limp. Perhaps there were some medical bills Len wanted to assist with.

I asked Pete the same question I had earlier, the one he didn't answer. "How do you know Len?"

"I was a bank manager. At the Bank of Santa Monica. The one in Century City."

I shifted from one foot to the other. "Does Len do

162

his banking there or something?"

Pete shook his head. "Not exactly."

It was the same drip, drip, drip of information. I was progressing but at a snail's pace. "I'm sorry. Could you explain?"

Pete frowned. "You don't know?"

I felt myself blush. Obviously, I was missing something, but I didn't know what it could be. "No."

"Len never told you why he wanted to give me the money?"

Len didn't provide the reasons for his gift-giving. It wasn't in the scope of our meeting. And it honestly wasn't my business at the time. "No. He didn't get into that."

"Do you know who Mikey is?"

I nodded. "Mikey and Len are related, is that right?"

"Len's nephew, I think."

"What about Mikey?"

"My bank was robbed. Len believes Mikey did it."

CHAPTER 46

My arms tingled, and my vision blurred, as I processed what Pete told me. That Mikey might have robbed a bank in Century City.

The sun continued to set, casting long shadows across the driveway and the front of the house.

I stared at Pete. "You're saying that Mikey Zobak robbed your bank?"

Pete raised his right index finger. "To start, I don't know that it was Mikey. What I said was that Len believes it was Mikey. And second, Zobak isn't his last name. I can't remember it off the top of my head, but I'm sure that it starts with an M."

Did the fact that Mikey's last name wasn't Zobak explain why nothing came up in my online search for him? Or was it possible that Pete meant a different Mikey? But Pete said that Mikey was Len's nephew, which tracked with the Mikey who moved into Len's apartment. I was sure we were talking about the same person, but I would try to confirm that somehow. "Do you know what Mikey looks like?"

"I've only ever seen him in a blurry picture in the newspaper. I wouldn't know who he was if I passed him on the street."

"Mikey was in the paper?"

Pete nodded. "He's been in trouble before."

I wondered what else Mikey had been up to, but my more pressing questions related to what Pete just told me about the robbery in Century City. "When was your bank robbed?"

"January twelfth, nineteen ninety-five."

"The robbery happened over ten years ago? And Mikey hasn't been charged?"

"No one has."

A robbery that took place over a decade ago remained unsolved? If the police had enough evidence, someone would've been charged by now. "Do you think anyone will be?"

Pete leaned forward. "Arrested? No. The statute of limitations ran out. And anyway, I've made peace with what happened, and I've moved on."

I wanted to explain more about what was happening on my end. To see if that would spark something in Pete that might help me. "Someone using the name Mikey Zobak is staying in Len's apartment. And he showed up right around the time that Len missed a scheduled meeting with me."

"That's interesting."

I wasn't sure which aspect Pete was talking about. "What is?"

"That Mikey is now going by Mikey Zobak."

"Do you think he's the same person?"

"Well, I've never met Mikey, so it's hard to say."

"He says that Len is his uncle."

"It sure sounds like him." Pete frowned. "You said he was at Len's apartment? And that Len is gone?"

I nodded. "That's right."

"Well, you should be careful."

I assumed Pete was referring to the fact that Mikey was a suspect in a bank robbery. But I wanted to ask anyway, just to be sure. "Why's that?"

"If it's the same Mikey, he was convicted of two other robberies and went to prison."

CHAPTER 47

Mikey eased his car into a parking lot outside a bar in Van Nuys in the San Fernando Valley. It was still early but almost dark outside since it was December.

Doug McCall had parked his black van on a side street. Mikey knew he'd find Doug here, since this was the guy's hangout back in the day.

Doug was hunting for the money. Not surprising. Doug wasn't a guy who just gave up, especially not when he was after something he wanted. Or, in this case, felt he was owed. But all of Doug's asking around was just looking for trouble.

To add to Mikey's problems, his keys were missing. A set that he needed. They must have fallen out when he was at Barry's. Those keys could be connected to him, so as stupid as it was to go back, he had no choice.

He'd seen nothing in the news about Barry. Maybe nobody had found him. That figured. Probably lived alone. Being that Mikey left the body in the garage, it might take a while. Regardless, he had to go back to Barry's house. Tonight.

His thoughts switched to Jocelyn. He had to figure out where she was keeping it and that meant going into her place again. He could try for a time when she wasn't home. If that wasn't possible, Mikey would have to force his way in. He was running out of time.

Mikey eyed the bar's door. So far, no one was coming or going. He wondered how long he would have to wait for Doug. He didn't want to miss him, so he would hang out in Doug's van until he arrived.

Mikey exited the parking lot and pulled his car onto a neighborhood street behind the bar. His car was enormous, and most cars nowadays were more compact. He found an open area on the residential street, locked up, and walked up to Doug's van.

He tried the passenger door. It was unlocked. *Bingo*. He was in business.

Mikey sat back and closed his eyes. Just as he was about to doze off, the driver's door opened. Doug hoisted himself in, and Mikey smelled the alcohol before he even saw Doug's face. Doug turned and noticed Mikey waiting for him.

Unlike Barry, Doug didn't appear panicked or scared. Of course, Doug still looked the same. The same long brown hair in a ratty ponytail with a dirty beard. And, of course, he still drove the same shit van.

Doug grinned, big and wide. "Look who it is. You got my money or what?"

"I don't have shit for you."

Doug exhaled, blowing out stale beer breath.

"I'm done with this. Pay up or deal with the consequences."

Mikey pulled out a knife he kept in his right pocket. "Consequences? I'd like to see you try that, man. That would be fuckin' hilarious, all right?"

Mikey raised the knife and brought the blade down. Just as he reached Doug's stomach, Doug grabbed Mikey's wrist and twisted it. Mikey heard a sickening snap; pain spread up his forearm. Mikey screamed. The knife tumbled from his hand and landed somewhere in the van.

Doug jumped across the console and was on top of him. He punched Mikey in the face once, landing his blow right on Mikey's jaw. Mikey punched back with his one usable hand, but he missed and slammed his knuckles into the dashboard. He pushed Doug's face and tried to force him away so Doug couldn't hit him again. But Doug was heavy and applied all his body weight on Mikey.

Then, Doug jumped out, ran to the passenger side, and flung the door open. He yanked on Mikey's flannel shirt until it choked him, one button jamming into his Adam's apple.

Doug dragged Mikey from the van and dropped him onto the sidewalk. Mikey landed with his messed up wrist underneath him. The pain was unbearable.

Doug slammed the door. "The fuck is wrong with you? Ambushing me?"

Mikey couldn't speak; all he could do was grab his wrist.

Doug punched Mikey three more times. Once in the jaw and twice in the stomach. Mikey dry-heaved from the blows to his abdomen.

Doug leaned close, his sour breath in Mikey's face. "I want my money. Get it to me by tomorrow, or there'll be a problem."

Doug walked around the van, jumped back into the driver's seat, and rumbled away, leaving Mikey slumped over on the sidewalk.

CHAPTER 48

I stared at Pete as panic washed over me. Mikey had been in prison? Had he just gotten out? I felt like I was frowning, but I was trying not to. "He was convicted of two robberies? You mean, besides the one at your bank?"

"Yes."

"Is there anything you know about them?"

"Both were branches of the same bank."

"The Bank of Santa Monica?"

"Yes, the same bank I worked for."

Mikey had struck two branches of the Bank of Santa Monica. It seemed plausible that he robbed the Century City location of the same bank. "Do you know which locations the other two were?"

"Well, I'm pretty sure they were also on the Westside. That's one reason Len was so convinced Mikey did Century City."

I had checking and savings accounts with the Bank of Santa Monica. They had branches everywhere on the Westside. "But you don't know which ones specifically?"

"Don't quote me on this, but one was in Santa Monica, and the other was, I want to say, in Playa Vista? Again, it's been a long time."

I stepped back, absorbing what Pete told me. "I understand. Any idea when these robberies took place?"

"Before Century City. But I don't have specific dates."

"Okay," I said. "Did you read about these other two in the paper?"

Pete shook his head. "Len told me most of these things."

"You mentioned you saw Mikey's photo in the paper."

"I read something about Mikey. I know that. Because I remember seeing a tiny black-and-white photo of him. Blurry. How headshots look in a newspaper."

"And you're still not sure that Mikey robbed your bank?"

"No, I'm not. But Len is. Believe me, I've thought about it over the years. I tried to remember anything I could that might prove it was Mikey. But nothing ever came to me. It didn't help that the robber covered his entire face."

I considered what Pete just said. "If it was Mikey who did Century City, and he covered his face there, I assume he would've covered up at the other two. So how did he get caught for those?"

Pete threw up his hands. "I'm sorry, I don't know. I only know what happened at my bank. I'd tell you to ask Len, but since you said he's missing, well..."

I thought of something that I wanted to ask Pete. It would be pure speculation, but it didn't hurt to get Pete's take on things. "Do you think Mikey could have hurt Len?"

Pete shrugged. "That's hard to say. But if Mikey is the one who robbed my bank, then I'd say there's a good chance that he could."

"Why's that?"

Pete sat back on the bench and grabbed his cane. "Well, he shot me in the leg."

CHAPTER 49

Pete's cane and limp now made sense, and thinking of Mikey shooting Pete made me shiver. I wanted to get more information on what had happened that day. I hoped I wasn't asking about things that weren't my business.

But the fact was that Len was missing, and now I was finding out what kind of person Mikey was. The situation didn't look good for Len.

Prying or not, I had to find out more. "He just shot you?"

Pete nodded. "He perceived me as intervening, even though I hadn't even had a chance to process what was happening."

I felt like we needed to back up a few steps. "Can you tell me how things started?"

Pete leaned back, gripped his cane, and stared at the sky. "There were so many customers that morning, more than usual. And people seemed to be in a hurry, too, so there was this growing impatience. You could feel it. Plus, we were short-staffed as one of our tellers had called in sick. And another teller was new, and she worked slower."

"How did it happen?"

"Kind of out of nowhere. I remember that there was an older woman in a wheelchair. She was struggling to get into the bank. We had a door that was supposed to open if you pushed a button, but she couldn't reach it. She didn't seem to have a caretaker, so I went outside to help her. I was gone for thirty seconds, tops, and the robber showed up."

"What do you remember about him?"

"He was dressed like a farmer. Or at least a city person's idea of a farmer. Overalls, straw hat. And he completely covered his face. He had sunglasses and a bandana. It was a bizarre getup. Like a Halloween costume."

"Was there anything else?"

Pete gripped his cane. "The last thing I remember is that I came back inside and before I could process what was going on, the robber yelled "stop" and then immediately shot me." Pete sighed. "I have to ask. How do you think this will help you find Len?"

"That's a good question. I don't know."

"Because going through these details, well, it's not something I like to do, do you understand what I'm saying? It was a long time ago."

I nodded; I was running out of time with Pete. I needed to circle back to the check. I had gotten little information out of Pete on that. "Did you think it was weird that Len wanted to give you money? Regarding something that happened so long ago?"

"That's his business."

A woman, who looked about Pete's age, opened the front door and came outside. "Pete, we have to leave soon."

Pete pushed himself up and walked toward the house.

"Wait," I said. "I just have a couple more questions. I'll make it quick, I promise."

Pete sighed but stayed put.

"You said you've known Len for a long time, is that right?"

"Yes, Len came to see me after it happened. To see how I was doing."

"You met him in ninety-five?"

"Yes, sometime that year."

"Did you ever see Len again after that?"

Pete shook his head. "No. But he called me Sunday morning and told me he wanted to come by with a check. He said it was for pain and suffering and that what happened to me was wrong. I told him I couldn't accept the money. And that was that."

Len had delivered the check to Belinda on Sunday morning and had also called Pete that same day. Before he disappeared.

Pete walked to the front door. "I have to go. I have dinner at my daughter's. You take care and good luck finding Len."

CHAPTER 50

Bethany Scott and Erica Cruz were my two closest friends from Stauffer. I was now sitting in a restaurant in Hermosa Beach with Bethany. Erica couldn't meet us because she had a yoga class.

I had just had dinner with Bethany and Erica at The Grove on Saturday night, back when I was feeling happy about my first client. How things had changed in just a few days.

According to Bethany, this restaurant had just opened and was the new hotspot. I wasn't even sure what the actual name of the place was, as there was no sign on the door or on the menu. That was supposed to make the place seem exclusive. It was close to the beach, like many other restaurants and bars in Hermosa Beach. This was one of the major attractions for living here.

Bethany was taller than me and had long blonde hair. She hadn't changed out of her work clothes, which included a lavender button-down dress shirt and black pinstripe pants.

I gave Bethany an update on what happened

to me today. I started with Thousand Oaks, then Sherman Oaks, and finished with Torrance. My mind was still racing, processing everything that Pete had told me, and I felt like I was talking a mile a minute.

I covered how Mikey was a bank robber who had been in prison. Mikey shooting Pete in the leg. Len wanting to give Pete money to atone for what he believed Mikey had done. That I had started to wonder whether others on Len's list were also Mikey's alleged victims. People like Jessica Cecil, Mary Watts, and either Tony or Andy Baker. How maybe they were there that day in Century City.

I finally stopped rambling.

Bethany frowned. "What in the world is going on?"

I knew her question was rhetorical, but I answered it anyway. "I just told you."

She shook her head. "No, I know, believe me, you told me. I don't understand why you're looking for this guy."

I couldn't tell if Bethany was joking, or if she didn't understand my situation. "I already told you. Len was supposed to meet with me on Sunday. And he never showed."

"So what?"

Was she not getting it? "Mikey showed up just as Len went missing."

"And?"

No, Bethany definitely wasn't getting it, and I was done trying to explain. "Never mind."

I was sorry I had even brought it up. And I regretted I had scheduled this dinner. I wanted nothing more than to go home and research what Pete Hernandez told me. Based on my visits to Thousand Oaks and Sherman Oaks, I figured I wouldn't find out anything useful. But Pete had given me a lot to work with. I wanted to see what I could find.

The only positive thing about this dinner was that it helped me ride out the evening traffic. I supposed I could deal with a little inane conversation.

Bethany grabbed a menu. "Are you still going to do this?" She waved her hand around.

"Do what?"

Bethany rolled her eyes. "You know. Your own little business or whatever."

I slid my napkin onto my lap. "Yeah, I mean, that's the plan."

"But you worked for Harman. That's a top accounting firm. Can't you just go back there?"

I struggled to explain why I wanted to do what I was doing. Bethany had a nine-to-five corporate job and didn't seem to have much stress. I wondered if that was why she thought I should go back to sitting in a cubicle. "I could. But I don't want to."

"I just don't get it, that's all."

Bethany wasn't the only one who didn't understand. My parents were the same way. And Bethany was sounding like them, making me further regret that I had committed to this dinner.

Bethany set down her menu. "You know, I know people. I have a lot of connections if you want to go back to accounting."

I didn't want to get into a thing with Bethany, but I had to at least correct the record. "I'm still doing accounting."

"You said you're doing forensics."

"Yes, forensic accounting."

Bethany frowned and pursed her lips. "But this isn't forensic accounting."

She was right. What I had helped Len with wasn't forensic accounting. However, I knew there would be times I would need to do other types of accounting to make ends meet. "I'm aware of that."

"Okay, whatever. But I have some contacts. So just let me know."

I grabbed my menu and hoped to move on to another topic. I noticed Bethany was now staring off. Her gaze was distant. I turned to see what she was looking at. "What is it?"

Bethany's eyes darted around the restaurant. Then she looked at me. "It's nothing."

"Come on. It has to be something."

"Just some guy staring at me. It gave me the Willies."

CHAPTER 51

I turned around again to see if I could identify who she had been talking about. All I saw were people eating dinner, all engaged in private conversations. No one was staring at Bethany. "Who?"

Bethany sighed. "He's gone now."

"Just like that?"

"Yeah, he's gone, I don't know."

Could Bethany have been mistaken about someone looking at her? Either way, something about the way she said it gave me a strange feeling, but I wasn't sure why. "What did he look like?"

"Thin. Wearing a baseball hat of all things. And a sweatshirt. Can you imagine? I couldn't see much else. It was like he was hiding in the shadows."

I glanced around the dimly lit restaurant. Most tables were full, but there wasn't a wait. And this was a dressier place. It didn't seem like a restaurant where I would expect people to wear baseball hats. But what did I know? It was L.A., so things were more casual. I had been in expensive steakhouses in Beverly Hills and seen people wearing two-hundred-dollar sweatpants.

I wondered if the man had just been looking around the restaurant. As dark as the place was, it could be hard to tell if someone was looking at you or just in your general direction. "Maybe he was meeting someone."

"What? No. Definitely not. The guy was a full-on creep. And he left once you turned around. Tell me that's a coincidence."

I got goosebumps. Was it possible this person was looking for me? Had I stirred up something with my visits yesterday and today? I should be careful, just in case. "Was he sitting at a table?"

Bethany shuddered. "No, he was just standing by the wall. Staring. Like. A. Creep. Did I mention that already?"

I might have laughed at Bethany's repeated insistence that the guy was a weirdo. But I was too worried about whether this mysterious person was looking for me. "Let me know if he comes back."

Bethany nodded. "Oh, I will."

We had dinner. Bethany ordered salmon, and I got the roast chicken. We didn't discuss Len or my career, and I was thankful for that. We even laughed, which helped shake me out of the mood I was in when I arrived. The creep never returned. At least not that Bethany saw.

We split the bill, left the table, and walked outside the restaurant. The wind had picked up, and a definite chill was in the air. I was glad I had changed into my sweater earlier.

Bethany had a concerned look on her face. "Do you want me to walk you to your car?"

"It's pretty far away and opposite from your apartment."

Bethany smacked her lips. "Still. I'm creeped out by the guy."

I had calmed down and was no longer as concerned about the person who may or may not have been staring at Bethany. "I'm sure it was nothing."

She clutched at her purse. "It doesn't help that I've been hearing rumors that some guy has been snatching women off the pier."

I got goosebumps again, but I wasn't sure if it was the cool air or Bethany's story. "What? When did you hear this?"

"A while ago."

Was this something real or just a rumor? "I haven't seen anything in the news."

Bethany's hair swirled around. "How often do you check the news?"

"Periodically."

"Well, I don't know if it was reported on or not. That doesn't mean it's not happening."

The wind was whipping through my sweater, and my hair blew across my eyes. I was eager to get safely into my car and stop hearing about a potential serial killer. "I guess not."

Bethany held down her hair. "I'm freezing to death. I don't think you should walk to your car alone."

"Like I said, my parking spot is past your apartment. You'll then have to walk by yourself back home."

"That guy skeeves me out."

"You haven't seen him again, have you?"

"No."

An idea came to me. "How about you walk me to my car, and I'll drop you at your apartment?"

Bethany's eyes lit up. "Yes!"

Bethany and I walked up Hermosa Avenue to find my car, and I saw a red Jeep Wrangler.

I knew that this was what sometimes happened. You got a new car, and all you saw was that car. When I first got my Mercedes, I saw black Mercedes coupes everywhere.

Plus, a Wrangler wasn't some vintage car no one drove anymore; plenty of people owned them. We got in my vehicle. I locked the doors and put on my seatbelt. I dropped Bethany at her apartment.

Afterward, I started my drive home. It didn't take long before I noticed a silver car following me.

CHAPTER 52

I kept checking my rearview mirror. To see if the silver car stayed behind me. It did. I was still on Hermosa Avenue and decided to do a maneuver I had read about years ago.

I made the first right I could, which was Pier Avenue. Then, I made a right onto Manhattan Avenue. I turned right once more onto Tenth Street. Three turns in quick succession, yet the silver car remained behind me.

I hadn't been mistaken; I was being followed.

I had no clue where to find a police station in Hermosa Beach. But I knew of one close to my apartment in Brentwood. It was off the Santa Monica Boulevard exit of the 405 freeway. I would head there.

I got back onto Pier Avenue and drove away from the beach. When I got to Pacific Coast Highway, I turned right. Then, a left onto Aviation Boulevard. Finally, a right onto Rosecrans. I merged onto the 405 north.

The silver car stayed behind me the entire time,

though I could tell it hung back so as not to get too close. Every once in a while, I switched lanes. Not right away, but within thirty seconds, the car would drift into my lane.

The car was an expensive one. I could tell by the smooth lines and aggressive styling. But I hadn't been close enough to see the make.

The night was dark. Despite being past eight, the traffic was heavy. My mind raced, and I wondered who was in the car behind me. What did the person want? Did this have something to do with Len and the addresses I had been visiting? Or was this something random? Like the man snatching women off the Hermosa Beach Pier?

The closer I got to my exit, the more anxious I got. It was strange. I felt an odd sense of calm out here on the open road. It was even easy to pretend that I wasn't being followed at all. Even though the silver car made the same three consecutive turns that I made in Hermosa Beach. Even though the car got onto the 405 north. Even though the car had stayed behind me, all these miles later.

The police station was on Butler Avenue; the nearest exit was Santa Monica Boulevard, and I was getting closer by the second. The sense of calm I felt earlier vanished as traffic slowed down.

The fast clip I had been driving for most of the way was done. All I saw now were brake lights. Things always seemed to get congested around this area, and tonight was no exception.

I glanced in my rearview mirror. I could no longer

see the silver car and wondered if by some miracle it was gone. The traffic was now at a standstill. I inched along until I got to the exit. It too, was jammed up. I crawled along the off-ramp, and it took three lights before I could turn left onto Santa Monica Boulevard.

I drove toward the police station. I passed Corinth Avenue, so I knew I was getting closer. I checked the rearview mirror again. And there it was. The silver car. Still behind me and now there were no other vehicles between us.

Then, I saw Butler. As I approached, the light turned red. I applied the brakes, but I didn't want to stop. I had visions of the driver getting out, dragging me from my vehicle, and executing me in the street.

The car was so close that I couldn't see the front license plate. Despite its proximity, I also couldn't see the driver's face. I thought I saw a baseball hat, but maybe I was hallucinating. Or maybe this was the same man staring at Bethany at the restaurant.

The light turned green, and I inched forward, waiting for the lanes to clear. When they did, I turned left. I drove for a bit, and then I saw them. Police cars. It was dark, but I knew I had reached the station.

I stopped behind a police car. I left space between the car and mine in case I needed to drive around it. I kept my car in drive with my foot on the brake.

The silver car had also turned left. It sat behind me. Then, in one quick motion, it zoomed around me and sped down Butler, too fast to allow me to read the license plate.

I parked my car, turned it off, and went inside. I would file a police report, or at least try to. I had no information though. Just a silver sports car. I was sure there were just a few of those in all of Los Angeles, right?

CHAPTER 53

This had turned out to be one of the most bizarre days of my life. I was sitting across from Mary Watts.

We were at Café Coffee, my go-to coffee place less than a block from my apartment. Tonight, I drove here and parked in the tiny lot behind the building.

Mary called me while I was driving home after filing my police report. She told me she was in my neighborhood and asked if we could meet. Despite being exhausted, I didn't want to miss the opportunity to meet with her. Especially since she was in Brentwood.

Mary's wavy brown hair was again styled perfectly, with not a hair out of place. She wore another silk blouse, slacks, and heels, similar to the outfit she had on when I was at her house yesterday.

I had a slight chill earlier, but I had ordered a hot chocolate, and that had taken care of it. "What did you want to talk about?"

Mary sipped her tea, and the tag dangling from the mug showed it was a caffeine-free herbal blend. "Yes, you're probably wondering why I called you."

I had a general idea, but I wanted to ask, anyway.

Mary clasped her hands together. "You won't believe this, but I have a friend who owns a condo up the street from here. She's a retired judge. I was having dinner with her tonight. Afterward, I thought I'd see if you were available to meet. To continue our earlier conversation."

"About Len Zobak?"

She nodded. "Yes."

I wondered what had changed from yesterday. "Do you know Len?"

"No, I don't know him."

Pete told me that Len visited him after the robbery in 1995. I had a hunch that Mary was at the Century City robbery and that, like Pete, she was also a victim. If that was the case, I wondered why Len had never reached out to her back then. But was that important?

I scooted my chair closer to the table. "If you don't know Len, then what did you want to talk to me about?"

"Well, the name Zobak sounded familiar when you first mentioned it. I couldn't figure out why. Then it came to me. I've never met Len, who you say is missing. But I know who his nephew is."

"Are you talking about Mikey Zobak?"

Mary gripped the handle of her mug. "Sometimes, he uses the alias Mikey Zobak. But his legal name is Mikey Miles." She leaned closer. "Please keep that between us. I'm not supposed to tell anyone."

I flashed back to my conversation with Pete.

How he thought Mikey's last name started with an M. It looked like he was right. This new piece of information energized me.

"How do you know Mikey?" I asked, wanting to find out if my hunch about Mary being at the bank was correct.

"He robbed a bank I was at."

And it looked like I was right. "Was this bank in Century City?"

"Yes!"

"What makes you think Mikey robbed the bank?"

Mary tilted her head. "What?"

"My understanding is that Mikey's never been charged for that robbery. How do you know it's him?"

A bell rang in the coffee shop as another customer entered. Mary glanced at the person and then turned back to me. "Well, it's because he robbed those other two."

Despite most likely knowing the answer, I was prepared with my next question. "You mean in Santa Monica and Playa Vista?"

Mary nodded. "Yes, those are the ones."

"Because of that, you believe he robbed Century City?"

Mary smiled. "I have some sources that I won't reveal."

I wondered what sources Mary was cryptically alluding to. Most likely it was her friend, the retired judge. "And these sources believe it's Mikey?"

"Well, sort of."

"Then why wasn't he arrested for Century City? I assume there was video evidence. Didn't he look like the same person from the other robberies?"

Mary shook her head. "From what I understand, he wore a different disguise."

"Even so. The body shape, the way he walks. A different outfit would not disguise him that much."

"You have a good point. But even if the authorities could show a similarity with how the robbers looked and moved, it's difficult to convict someone on just that. And there are a couple of other reasons too."

"Like what?"

"The footage at the Century City location wasn't very good. And of course there's this other thing."

"What other thing?"

"Well, Mikey supposedly has an alibi."

I sat back. "What?"

"He said he was at work. I guess he did maintenance. No one was living in the house he was working on. But a neighbor saw his car and was pretty certain on the time it was there. And his employer swears he was there too."

"Is there anything else?" I asked.

"I guess if one wants to nitpick, then there is."

"What's that?"

"There was a lag between the first two robberies and the third. The first two were in July 1994. The third one was in January 1995."

I crossed my arms, trying to process what Mary just told me. It was looking less and less like Mikey had committed the Century City robbery. But that didn't change the fact that he served time for the other two robberies.

Mary frowned. "I know how this must sound. But Mikey did it. Of that, I have no doubt."

CHAPTER 54

I wasn't sure what to make of all of this, but I might as well press ahead and see what else I could find out. "Is there anything else you can tell me about the Century City robbery?"

Mary sat forward and leaned her head closer like we were in a clandestine meeting. "Oh yes. How much time do you have?"

I was exhausted, but I would make time for whatever she might have to say since she seemed willing to talk. I was hoping Mary could add details I didn't already have. "However long it takes."

Mary straightened in her chair. "This all happened in ninety-five. Keep that in mind, okay?"

"I will."

A self-satisfied look spread across Mary's face. "But you're in luck. Despite how much time has passed, I remember everything."

I sat back and sipped my hot chocolate, letting Mary talk.

"I shop in Beverly Hills a few times a year. You know, I make a day of it. I do a lot of preparation.

I figure out what I need, what stores I plan to visit, and where to go for lunch. This time, though, I ran out of time to get cash."

Mary cupped her drink. "I like cash for tips and valet. Rather than delay my drive to Beverly Hills by stopping at my usual bank in Pasadena, I went to a branch in Century City."

"And this was in the morning, right?"

"Yes. And when I arrived, there was a line of people. The bank manager was outside helping someone. There were a few employees working, but it still didn't seem like enough, not with how busy it was."

Pete also mentioned the place being short-staffed. "Then what happened?"

"A man stormed in, dressed like he was coming from plowing the fields. He was waving this gun around and yelled for everyone to lay on the floor face down. He went right up to a teller, threw her a bag, and told her to give him all the money. Just like in the movies!"

"What else happened?"

"Well, he shot the manager."

"Pete Hernandez?"

Her eyes grew wide. "Do you know Pete?"

"I met him today."

Mary sipped her tea, then set it down. "He also grabbed me, put a gun to my head, and told everyone in the bank not to try anything or he'd kill me.

Pete had already given me the rundown of what had happened at the bank that day. But he never mentioned the robber putting a gun to anyone's head. "That sounds awful."

"It was horrible. The teller gave him the money and just like that, he was gone. The police showed up not too long after that."

"Is there anything else?"

Mary perked up. "One thing, but it's more like a rumor. I heard it years ago."

"What's that?"

"Now, keep in mind, this is only a rumor."

"Okay."

"There was an eyewitness. Someone who saw the robber's face. Nothing ever came of it, but it always gave me hope Mikey would be charged."

"I thought the robber wore a mask."

"He did. But the eyewitness was outside the bank. And Mikey took off his mask then."

Mary took another sip of tea. "Like I said, it's a rumor. Silly for me to believe it. I mean, wouldn't the person have come forward by now?"

I didn't want to burst Mary's bubble, so I didn't say the first thing that came to mind. Which was that even if there was a witness, it was probably too late. Over ten years had passed. Pete said that the statute of limitations had already elapsed. "How did you hear this rumor?"

"From a friend of mine."

"The judge?"

Mary smiled. "No. The bank is in a business district. Lots of offices all around there. My friend is a partner in a law firm about a block away. Naturally, we discussed the robbery. My friend talked to one of her associates. That person heard that someone was hanging around outside the bank."

It looked like Mary's rumor had been through a game of telephone. "Did your friend tell anyone besides you?"

"Of course. My friend reported the information to the police. I wish the witness would do the same."

"Maybe there was no witness, and that's why."

Here I was, feeling like I was bursting her bubble, which was what I didn't want to do. I would let it go. What did it matter whether Mary believed this, especially since it was too late? Besides, we were talking about a hypothetical person who possibly saw something.

Mary frowned. "There was a witness. I'm sure of it."

CHAPTER 55

Mary cupped her tea. "Oh, I thought of something else. If you need to go, let me know. Once I get talking, it's hard for me to stop."

"It's okay. What is it?"

"Well, it's something that's always nagged at me. I've told the police. After the robbery, I think I told anyone and everyone who would listen. But it never panned out."

"What's that?"

"The bank teller. The one Mikey demanded the money from. I think she knew more than she was letting on."

I wondered about the likelihood that this was true. "Do you remember her name?"

"Yes, I remember her name because I'm very observant. She wore a pin. It said Jessica."

"Jessica? Do you know her last name?"

"I found out later. It's Cecil. Jessica Cecil. She was a rail thin little thing, very young."

I met Jessica Cecil this morning in Thousand Oaks. According to Mary, Jessica was a teller at the

Century City bank. Was Jessica another victim, like Pete and Mary? Or was she, as Mary was implying, somehow involved?

Jessica seemed paranoid that Jeff and I were cops. But that alone didn't mean anything. Plenty of people were wary of police. And if she was doing something illegal, it wasn't necessarily connected to a robbery from over ten years ago.

I leaned forward. "Why do you think she knows more than she's said?"

"Because I did some research after all this happened."

"What research?"

Mary sipped her tea. "I talked to some people familiar with the bank. And I may have gotten some inside information."

"Like what?"

"Well, I'm not bragging, Jocelyn, but I'm well-connected in Los Angeles. So I knew who to ask. I won't say who that is. It's been ages, but I'm not interested in anyone getting into trouble for what was told to me all those years ago."

I knew little about Mary Watts. She might be blowing smoke. Or she might have connections. I had no way to confirm. "Of course. Is there anything you can share with me? Without breaking confidences?"

Mary closed her eyes for a second and sighed. "A few days before the robbery, Jessica started asking the other tellers all sorts of questions."

"Like what?"

"Questions about security cameras, the alarms, how much money there was."

I remembered Pete saying one of the tellers was new. Was that Jessica? "Couldn't those just be questions of an employee who's trying to learn how the bank works?"

"She already had her training. They weren't that type of question."

"You're saying that the questions were red flags?"

"Yes, when she asked them, the other employees found it odd. Also, it was the way she was asking, like someone else had given her a list of questions."

"Do you believe she was checking things out for someone?"

Mary nodded. "Yes, that's exactly what I believe."

"Was there anything else?"

Mary touched an earring. "Well, of course there's the fact that she quit right after." She raised a hand. "I know what you're going to say. The situation was traumatic and that's why. Who could blame her?"

"That seems reasonable."

"Yes, on its own, it does. But I found out that she didn't live anywhere near the bank."

"You find that strange?"

"Yes, I do. There are banks everywhere. Why not find one closer to where you live?"

"Maybe nothing was available."

"She was from somewhere in the San Fernando Valley. That's a long drive to Century City."

Everything Mary said was circumstantial. Likely the police thought so too, which was why Jessica had never been arrested. "And this is why you think she knew more than she ever said?"

Mary nodded. "Yes, that's part of it. It's hard to explain, but I also got a feeling about her."

"Could you try to explain?"

"When the robber first came in, she was just a little too, you know, calm about the whole thing. She seemed to follow his instructions robotically."

"Like she knew him?"

Mary nodded. "And there was the fact that Mikey made all the tellers, except for Jessica, lie on the floor in front of him. He chose her. Why her? Because they knew each other, that's why. I'm sure of it."

"Maybe he just happened to pick her. He had to choose someone."

"It's not just that. I felt like they were speaking in code. If he would have said, 'stick to the plan we came up with,' I wouldn't have been surprised."

Mary made a somewhat persuasive case for Jessica's involvement. But there was just one problem: she didn't have any proof. Jessica asking strange questions was hearsay.

If Jessica really asked these red flag questions, wouldn't they have been brought to the manager's attention? Pete didn't mention them, and I would think that he would, considering he got shot over the whole thing.

And the rest was just Mary's interpretation of Jessica's actions during the robbery.

Plus, I was sure that Len was giving checks to those people he viewed as victims of the robbery. If

Jessica wasn't a victim, then why would Len give her money?

I glanced around the coffee shop and then looked at Mary. "You said you talked to a lot of people about this, right?"

She nodded. "Just about everyone I thought could help."

"And nothing happened?"

"Nope. Eventually, I dropped it. What else could I do?"

CHAPTER 56

Mikey emerged from a hospital near Santa Monica. Finally. Jeez Louise. What a nightmare. He had to wait forever to get help.

Granted, his situation wasn't as dire as some others at the overcrowded emergency room. Just because he wasn't riddled with bullets or spraying blood all over the walls didn't mean he didn't have a legitimate problem.

They x-rayed his wrist, and a doctor informed him of the obvious: it was broken. He continued waiting until they fixed him up. Finally, he walked out, wearing a brand-new cast and carrying a prescription for pain meds. The wrist hurt like a mother, and he needed something.

He walked two blocks down the street, made a right, and then walked several more blocks until he arrived at Santa Monica Boulevard. He stopped into a twenty-four-hour pharmacy and waited again for what felt like forever. But he left with his meds and a Coke. He popped two pills into his mouth, washed them down with soda, and used his cell phone to call a cab.

Ten minutes later, he had jumped into a clean taxi that smelled like pine and was heading to Playa del Rey. He directed the driver to a grocery store a few blocks from Barry Corcoran's house. This way, the cabbie couldn't blab to the police he had dropped off a man at Barry's house. Going back for his keys was already taking a colossal risk. He had to stay on high alert and be extra-vigilant. No more silly ass mistakes like dropping keys in a dead man's garage.

Fucking Doug. Breaking his wrist. And demanding money. By tomorrow too. Well, no dice. He'd deal with Doug, but he had other things that took precedent. Like getting his keys.

Of course, he also had to check Jocelyn's apartment.

The cab stopped, and the driver looked over his shoulder. "Here you are."

Mikey slid out his wallet with his good hand, peeled off some cash, and was on his way. He walked toward the grocery store, pretending to go in. Once he could no longer see the cab, he changed course and headed to Barry's house.

Arriving in Barry's neighborhood, he looked around. He didn't see anyone; it was as deserted as it was on Monday. Which he expected given the time of night.

Barry's house was dark. A good sign. No police officers. No black-and-whites. No yellow tape. No one had found Barry. If someone had, the place would be lit up like New Year's Eve in Times Square and crawling with people, mainly the neighbors. They'd all be rubbernecking. Trying to get a look. Asking questions.

Why did this happen to Barry? How could this happen here? Who do you think did it?

But there was nothing.

Mikey jiggled the garage's side door. He couldn't remember if he had left it unlocked. It seemed stuck, but he twisted it, hard, and it opened. Either it was already unlocked, or it was just a shitty old door. He closed it behind him. The garage was pitch black. He had left Barry's body on the other side.

He shuffled his feet, feeling for the keys, but found nothing. He didn't want to turn on the light, so he tapped his foot around but started feeling dizzy. He wondered if the meds were making him trip out.

A dark thought came to him: the police had already found Barry. Perhaps they just didn't put up any tape because they were waiting to see if he, the killer, would return. And he had, like an idiot. Was he about to be surrounded by a thousand cops yelling at him?

Put your hands up! Get on the ground! Don't move!

But he heard nothing.

He walked out of the garage and went to the side of the house. He took a deep breath to get a handle on himself. Then, he listened. It was silent. Much too quiet for an ambush, he was sure of that. No, nobody was there. Barry hadn't been found.

He returned to the garage, dropped to his knees,

and ran his good hand around the smooth, dusty concrete. Finally, his hands touched metal. He had found his keys. What a relief.

He could move on to his other problems. Like Doug. And Jocelyn.

CHAPTER 57

I had figured out Belinda Jackson, Mary Watts, Jessica Cecil, and Pete Hernandez's connections to Len Zobak. If I could find out how Tony or Andy Baker knew Len, I would have all five connections nailed down.

While Mary sipped her tea, I asked her a question. "Does the last name Baker sound familiar to you?"

Mary frowned. "No. Should it?"

"I was just wondering if anyone at the bank that day had the last name Baker. An employee or a customer, maybe."

Mary gazed off like she was thinking. "As for employees, I only remember Jessica. I met a few customers afterward, but I don't remember Baker."

When I met Tony, I guessed he was around thirty, which would have made him about twenty back then. I didn't know how old Tony's father was. "How many other males were there that day?"

Mary frowned, and I felt like I had confused her. "Let me think."

I was almost done with my hot chocolate, so I

finished it.

Mary sighed. "There were so many customers that day. I don't remember who was who."

"That's okay," I said. "It was a long shot."

"Who is this Baker person? Maybe if you tell me more, I'll remember something."

"It's another person connected to Len. Except, I don't know if it's the father or the son."

"What can you tell me about them?"

"Well, the son was probably in his twenties back then. Shaggy, blonde hair, dresses in baggy clothes. I've never met his father."

Mary tilted her head. "I'm sorry, I don't remember anyone like that."

"It was worth a try."

Mary shuddered. "You know, talking about all of this brings it back. And now that you say that Len is missing, it's distressing, you know? I'm just glad Mikey's in prison and won't be getting out for several more years."

Mary didn't know Mikey was no longer behind bars? I wondered whether a victim of a crime could keep tabs on the perpetrator. If so, what did that mean for Mary? She wasn't a victim of the robberies that Mikey had served time for. I didn't know how any of that worked.

But now I wondered about Mary's alleged contacts. Even if Mary couldn't have kept track of Mikey, couldn't one of them, like the judge, have done it for her? Given her a heads-up that he was out?

I had to tell her. I clasped my hands together. "Mikey's out of prison."

Her face went slack. Her skin turned pale, her eyes were wide, and she was blinking rapidly. "What?"

"Mikey's out."

Her hand, which was still holding her tea, started shaking, and she looked on the verge of tears. "He got out early? This is horrible. Really horrible. When?"

She tried to stand but wobbled and plopped back into her seat.

I jumped up and moved to her side of the table. I hoped she wouldn't pass out. "Please, stay where you are. I'm going to get you some help."

Mary took a deep breath. "No. I'm fine."

"Let me call your friend who lives around here."

She pushed herself up and away from the chair. "No. I'll be okay. I just need to catch my breath. I wasn't expecting that news. I knew Mikey could get out early, but I didn't think it would be so soon."

I felt uncomfortable letting Mary walk out of the coffee shop by herself. "Are you sure there's nothing I can do for you?"

"I'm sure. I'll be okay."

Mary straightened her blouse and seemed to have composed herself somewhat. "I considered tracking him over the years, but I thought it would make me obsessed. You know, keep him too much on my mind. I decided it was better to wait until it was closer to the time he got out. I guess I thought I had more time. I really didn't expect this."

I didn't know how to respond. But it didn't matter. Before I could say anything, Mary walked out of Café Coffee.

CHAPTER 58

It was early Wednesday morning, and my head was a muddled mess. I felt like I was running on low batteries. Burned out and stressed out. I needed a break, but it would have to wait until I found Len.

I sat at my kitchen table with a fresh coffee and my open laptop. I thought about the crucial details Pete Hernandez and Mary Watts had given me. I now knew that Mikey had been in prison for two bank robberies and that he was suspected, but never charged, in a third. I also had Mikey's legal name: Mikey Miles. Armed with this new information, I had enough to start my research.

I searched using the keywords "Mikey Miles" and "bank robbery." I added the three locations: Santa Monica, Playa Vista, and Century City.

An archived article for a magazine called *Westside Happenings* was the top result. My cousin, Jennifer Hendricks, used to write for the magazine.

I took a deep breath and clicked on the link. I couldn't believe what I was seeing. Jennifer wrote the article, which was published on May 15, 1995.

This was less than two months before she was murdered.

I was staring at one of the last articles Jennifer ever wrote. My skin tingled, and I felt lightheaded.

Jennifer's murder wasn't something that I thought much about these days. The man who killed her was serving his life sentence somewhere in a California prison. My parents didn't talk about Jennifer, shut down questions about her, and clammed up if the conversation even got close. Over the years, I learned to let it go.

But here I was, in 2006, staring at an article that Jennifer had written. *Westside Happenings* was a glossy lifestyle magazine I still saw on the shelves at grocery stores.

The banner across the top of the website stated that the publication covered the people, the lifestyles, the culture, the entertainment, the fashion, the art, the architecture, and the news defining West Los Angeles.

I read the article's title and lead sentence.

*String of Robberies Leaves Westside
Residents on Edge*

*Mikey Miles accepted a plea for holdups
in Santa Monica and Playa Vista, but
Century City remains unsolved.*

I skimmed the article. It reiterated much of what I learned from Pete and Mary. That Mikey had been sentenced to prison for two robberies. But not for a third, similar robbery. It included many details about Mikey's prison term.

Jennifer interviewed several people. One person was Mikey's relative, who asked to remain anonymous. Could the relative be Len? If so, how strange that my cousin had interviewed Len all those years ago.

The article quoted Mikey's relative as unhappy with the length of Mikey's sentence but hoping that Mikey would eventually be charged in the Century City robbery.

Had Mikey read this article? Did he figure out who the anonymous relative was? Did he know or suspect it was Len? If so, did this explain Len's disappearance? Was Mikey getting revenge against the man who spoke out against him?

The article contained some details about Mikey's first robbery in Santa Monica. Tina Tompson worked as a teller there. She was the employee Mikey had demanded money from. Tina was quoted throughout. Since she had put herself out there by speaking with the media, I wondered if she would talk to me. It was worth a try.

I searched online for Tina Tompson. According to the search results, I found a landline and address for a Tina Tompson in Santa Monica. There were other Tina Tompson's scattered throughout Los Angeles and the country, so I hoped this one was the correct Tina Tompson.

I pulled out my phone and called the number.

"Jody's Hair Design and Spa, Santa Monica," a woman's voice answered.

I figured I had the wrong number, but I asked anyway. "May I speak with Tina Tompson?"

"I'm sorry, no one here goes by that name."

The phone clicked in my ear.

I drummed my fingers on the kitchen table. The landline was for a business. Did that mean the Santa Monica address was inaccurate too? Since Santa Monica was close, I could always drive over there and see.

I realized I hadn't finished Jennifer's article. I read the last paragraphs and froze. At the robbery in Santa Monica, Mikey had taken a hostage when he left the bank. Her name was Corinne Reynolds.

I shuddered. My doorbell rang.

CHAPTER 59

I checked the peephole. It was an older gentleman. I recognized him; he had stopped by Len's apartment on Monday after my locksmith left.

I opened the door. The man looked like Len. He had the same dark blonde hair and light blue eyes, and he even wore a collared shirt and sweater.

The man pointed to his chest. "I'm Jan Ryba. Len Zobak's friend. I understand Len met with you. He said the woman on the third floor, apartment three-oh-two. Is that you?"

"Yes, that's me."

"Have you seen him?"

"No, I haven't."

Jan put his hands behind his back. "But you are the one Len talked to about taxes, right? The accountant?"

"Yes, I'm the accountant."

Jan looked past me into my apartment. "I'm returning home to Poland for a visit. Len's taking me to the airport tonight. I came by to confirm our plans."

"I haven't seen him," I said, reiterating what I told him moments ago.

"Has Len ever told you about Poland?"

Len had never told me much of anything. He never talked about Poland. In fact, I didn't even know he was from there. "No, he hasn't mentioned it."

"Len and I came to the United States in the eighties. Len doesn't like to talk much about it. Me? Well, I'm an open book. We didn't know each other there. We met in Los Angeles."

Jan had piqued my curiosity with his references to Len's past life. I was tempted to ask more, but my time was better spent seeing if Jan could tell me anything to help me find Len. "When was the last time you saw him?"

Jan shuffled his feet. "Saturday. In the morning. I came by Monday, but he wasn't home. But you and Len, you talked about taxes, right?"

"Yes."

"When was that?"

"I met with him on Saturday. We were supposed to meet again on Sunday, but he didn't show up. And he hasn't been around since. I've been looking for him."

Jan furrowed his eyebrows. "That's not like Len. You know, I can't find Betty either."

"Betty's at her sister's. Do you know anyone Len would contact if he went somewhere?"

Jan nodded and pointed at his chest. "Me! Do you think he went somewhere?"

"I don't know. What do you know about Mikey?"

Jan looked like he had just sucked on a lemon. "Ahh. He's no good."

"Do you know about Mikey's past?"

Jan blinked several times. "Oh, yes, I do. I told Len that he better make a plan. I told him, 'Len, Mikey is going to come here, and he will expect a place to live once he gets out.' If I told him once, I told him a thousand times."

"Did Len agree with you?"

"He told me not to worry. He said Mikey wouldn't be staying at any of his properties."

I wondered if I had heard Jan correctly. "His properties?"

"Yes. Len owns this building and many others."

Len had always presented himself as the manager, never the owner. But now that I thought about it, Len seemed to take care of most things around here.

"Where are these properties located?" I asked.

Jan waved his hands toward the courtyard. "Around this area. Brentwood. I own the building around the corner."

He said it like we weren't surrounded by apartment buildings. In this part of Brentwood, it was pretty much condos and apartments everywhere you looked.

I had to get more information from him. "But where?"

"Len can tell you sometime. I just know they're around here. He lives at this one, so I visit him here."

"You don't know where the others are?"

He waved his hand again and smiled. "Around. Not far. Blocks away."

I wanted to ask Jan more about the properties, but I felt I had reached the end with this line of questioning. "Okay."

Jan took several steps back and seemed eager to leave. "When you see Len, can you tell him to call me?"

"What will you do for your ride if Len doesn't show up?"

He looked at me like this wasn't even a possibility. That of course Len would take him to the airport. "I suppose I'll arrange for a taxi."

Jan's body stiffened. "Wait a second. What you said earlier. Why did you ask about Mikey?"

"Mikey's been here."

Jan clenched his hands into fists. "Here. As in, at this apartment?"

"Yes."

"You know this for a fact?"

I nodded. "He came out of Len's apartment, and he introduced himself as Mikey Zobak, Len's nephew."

Jan tossed his head and laughed. "He wishes his name was Zobak. Mikey's not Len's nephew."

"Are they even related?"

"He's a very distant cousin. Mikey is from New Jersey, and his family visited Len when he was growing up. Then, Mikey moved to Los Angeles after high school. But all he did was get into trouble. It's been nothing but headaches for Len. Len tried to help Mikey, but it did no good."

Jan shook his head. "This is not good. This is what I warned Len about. You said you were to meet with Len on Sunday? And today is Wednesday. You haven't seen him since?"

"No."

Jan gritted his teeth. "I have to go.

"Will you still be going to Poland?"

Jan appeared to be assessing how much to divulge. "I will still go to Poland, yes."

"And you still want me to have Len call you when he returns?"

Jan walked away and then turned to look over his shoulder. "Yes, please do. And stay away from Mikey. He's bad news. This is all bad news."

"Wait," I said.

Jan turned around.

"Where can I reach you?"

"I live around the corner. The big white building. Looks like this one."

Not helpful. "But which one? In case I need to find you."

"I'll find you."

Still unhelpful. "What does that mean?"

Jan headed down the stairs. "If I need your help, I'll let you know."

In under a minute, he had left the building.

CHAPTER 60

It had been about thirty minutes since Jan left. I had my breakfast of champions in front of me: scrambled eggs, hash brown patties, and a fresh coffee.

I was feeling lost and overwhelmed and didn't know what to do or where to look. And my concern for Len had grown even more after Jan stopped by.

Until talking to Jan, I had taken little time to consider what could have actually happened to Len if Mikey was involved. I had hoped it would be easy to find Len. But several days had passed, and I had come up empty. I needed to be realistic.

I was now sure that Mikey was involved, but what did that mean? Did he kidnap Len? Or worse?

I wasn't ready to accept the worst-case scenario, which was that Mikey had killed Len. I had to hope that Len was still alive. Maybe since I was having such dark thoughts, it was a sign I should file a missing person's report. I would consider it.

If Mikey had kidnapped Len, where was he keeping him? Thanks to Jan, I now knew that Len owned various properties in Brentwood. Could Len be at one of his other properties? It was a long shot, but since Mikey had been in prison until recently, I didn't see how he would have had the time to secure a place to stash Len. But a property that Len already owned and which Mikey knew about? Well, that seemed like a strong possibility.

I had to find out the addresses of Len's Brentwood properties. Jeff looked up stuff like this all the time for his true crime website. I never asked how he got the information, and I wasn't sure I wanted to know. But considering my current situation, I wasn't afraid to take advantage.

I called Jeff, and he answered right away. "Hey there. I'm heading to the airport in a couple of hours."

Jeff's family owned a home on Maui and went there every year for Christmas.

"I didn't realize you were leaving already," I said.

"We're going earlier this year. Oh man, I spaced out. I was supposed to look up that guy for you. What was his name? Mikey something?"

"Yeah, Mikey. It's okay. I've already looked into him."

"Sorry about that. I got busy packing and doing some stuff for the blog."

"It's okay. I was calling you for another favor. But I guess I'm too late."

"You're in luck. I'm packed and just killing time until the car service arrives. This is about your landlord, isn't it?"

"Yep," I said.

"He still hasn't turned up?"

"Not yet, no."

"Fire away," Jeff said. "What do you need?"

"Len owns some properties in Brentwood. Is it possible to find the addresses?"

"Yep. I'll get right on it. Are you by your computer? It'd be easier if you just emailed the info. That way I get the correct spelling of his name and all that."

"Sure, I'll send the request over," I said. "Can you expand the search? Beyond Brentwood?"

"Of course, just include everything you want in the email. By the way, I forgot to ask what you're doing for Christmas."

"I'm supposed to go to Omaha."

"Supposed to?"

I shifted in my chair. "I don't know if I want to go. My parents separated."

"No kidding? When did this happen?"

I suddenly felt hot, like the thermostat had been jacked a thousand degrees. "I found out around Thanksgiving. I just haven't felt like talking about it."

"That sucks. Well, if you want to talk, let me know."

"Thanks."

I had thought little about my parents' separation. I told my parents I would be back for Christmas, but now I wasn't sure. Going forward, everything was going to be different. I wasn't sure if I was ready for all that change.

I pushed aside those thoughts and emailed Jeff with my request.

CHAPTER 61

While I waited for Jeff's email, I figured I could visit Tina Tompson in Santa Monica. After talking about my parents' separation with Jeff, I felt antsy, like I needed to get out.

I jotted down Tina's address, grabbed my purse and keys, and headed out. I passed the laundry room.

Chris came out of it carrying a basket of folded, dry clothes. His curly brown hair flopped around his head. The last time I saw him, he was arguing with Mikey about his parking spot.

I pointed to his laundry. "Is the dryer working?"

"What do you mean?"

"I heard it wasn't getting hot."

Chris adjusted the basket. "It worked for me. Hey, let me ask you something. Have you seen that guy in Len's apartment? Do you know who he is?"

"He said he's Len's nephew."

Chris shook his head. "Strange, don't you think? I've lived here ten years and have never seen him before. And now Len's gone, and he's here?"

It didn't hurt to mention to Chris what was going on. Maybe he knew something. Or maybe he could help. "It is weird. I was supposed to meet with Len on Sunday, but he never showed up. I haven't seen him since."

Chris shrugged. "Well, I'm sure he'll be back. Look, I gotta run. I've got something in the oven."

So much for that. At least I tried.

I continued down to the parking garage, got into my car, and put the top down. I exited the garage onto Montana Avenue and started toward Santa Monica.

The day was excellent; it was a perfect beach day. My hair was down and blowing all over, a few strands sticking to my lip gloss. But the air on my face felt refreshing, so I'd leave the top down.

I was wearing a short-sleeved T-shirt, jeans, and Converse sneakers, which was turning into my uniform when I left my apartment lately. The day had warmed up, and the sun on my arms felt nice. My head slowly cleared.

Tina Tompson's address was on Ocean Avenue. Back when I was living the high life, I had considered living in a building on the same street. All the units had an ocean view.

That life was long gone. In my current life, I was hunting for my missing client. My first client. My *only* client. I had made forty bucks. It wasn't the best start to my new business. I smiled to myself. But it was a start.

I arrived at Ocean Avenue. The street and area

were busy, and I figured parking would be tricky. Of course, I thought this every time I came to the beach but always found a space. Today, I located one a block away. Not too bad. I exited the car and saw countless exercisers, all out and about on this lovely Wednesday morning.

Tina's building stood four stories tall and looked like it was built in the seventies. It had a white stucco exterior and glass patios, giving the units a Pacific Ocean view.

The lobby was locked, but there was a call box outside. I pushed the button for unit 404, which hopefully belonged to Tina Tompson. A few seconds later, a woman's voice answered. "Yes?"

"Hi, I'm looking for Tina Tompson."

"What's the reason?"

The most straightforward response seemed best. "I want to talk to Tina about Mikey Miles."

I received no answer. But I heard a click, and the lobby door unlocked. Someone had let me in.

CHAPTER 62

I walked into the spacious, bright white lobby and up the stairs to the fourth floor, where Tina Tompson's unit was. I knocked on the door.

A woman answered within seconds. "I'm Tina."

Tina had red hair styled like a groupie from an eighties rock band: long, fluffed up, and sprayed until crisp. She wore a loose, bright white T-shirt, a thousand bracelets, tight boot-cut jeans, and cork-soled wedge sandals.

Tina's minimal makeup brought out her features despite the obviously fake hair color. Her brown eyes seemed to sparkle against the hair. She had a handful of fine lines on her forehead and around her mouth.

We shook hands. "I'm Jocelyn Bennett."

"Come on in."

Tina let me into her condo without so much as a question. I was still surprised all it took for her to let me into the building was a mention of Mikey Miles. I thought Tina might be more open to talk, considering she had been interviewed by Jennifer at

Westside Happenings. But for someone who had been held up at a bank, I expected a little more precaution.

The condo looked like it hadn't been updated since the building was erected. The place had wood paneling, an avocado-green shag carpet, and was done up in orange and gold tones. The flocked Christmas tree standing in the corner was almost too perfect. It wasn't my style, but somehow it worked here.

A man walked down the hallway. He had a buzzed head and was all muscles under a T-shirt with a burger joint logo. I supposed I now had my explanation for why Tina wasn't afraid to let me in.

"This is my boyfriend, Dan," Tina said.

Dan smiled and gave me a light, friendly handshake, which felt disproportionate to the frame the hand was attached to.

"I'm Jocelyn Bennett."

"Nice to meet you," he said.

Dan folded a piece of paper into a square and put it in his back pocket. "Anything else you want me to pick up?"

"No, just whatever's on the list," Tina said.

Dan eyed me but didn't seem afraid of me. Not that he would be. But he also didn't seem concerned about leaving me with Tina.

"Jocelyn wants to ask me about Mikey and the robbery."

I had never mentioned the robbery, just Mikey. But since Mikey had held up Tina's bank, she correctly assumed that was my reason for being there.

Dan turned to me. "Are you another reporter?"

"No. My landlord's missing. He's related to Mikey. I wanted to talk to Tina to see if she could help me."

Tina gasped. "Len's missing? It has to be Mikey."

CHAPTER 63

I had a million questions for Tina but didn't know where to start. She knew Len? And what made her think Mikey would be responsible for whatever happened to Len?

Dan stared at Tina, lines cutting across his forehead. "Are you sure you're good?"

Tina nodded and stuck her hands in her front pockets. "I'm fine."

He grabbed a set of keys from the counter. "All right, then I'm going to head out."

Dan left, and the condo fell silent. The sliding glass doors that faced the ocean were open. A light breeze flowed through the room, and the condo was surprisingly quiet for being next to such a busy street in Santa Monica.

Tina smiled. "Dan's the best. He worries about me though. He thinks I need to move on and stop talking about what happened. I know it's been forever, but I can't forget it. Believe me, I've tried."

I clasped my hands and picked up where we had left off. Tina knew who Len was when I said he was

Mikey's relative. "You know Len?"

"I've known him for a long time. Since the robbery. I'm assuming you know about that?"

"Yes, I've just learned about it."

Tina shook her head. "Just terrible. It happened not too far away from here. I don't work there anymore, but I always pass by."

Tina continued, "You know, Mikey's out of prison. And Len is missing? Like I said, Mikey must have something to do with it."

"How did you know that Mikey's out?"

"I kept very close tabs on him over the years."

"What makes you think he had something to do with Len?"

"Just that I know what kind of person Mikey is."

"Have you seen Len?"

"Sort of. I hadn't seen him in ages, but he came by the other day."

"When was that?"

"Saturday evening."

This must have been an errand Len was running when Betty thought he was missing. "Do you mind if I ask why he stopped by?"

"Oh, well, I wasn't home. But he left me a note and dropped something off. I tried to call him, but I couldn't reach him."

Had Len given Tina a check too? Was it possible that the five checks Len asked me to deliver weren't all the checks he planned to distribute? "Stop me if I'm prying, but what did he give you?"

"A check. Len said it was for my troubles. I haven't

decided whether to cash it."

"You never reached him?"

"No, unfortunately not." Tina gestured for me to sit. "Do you want to talk about what happened? At the bank?"

I figured any information I could get would be helpful. "That would be great."

"How about some coffee first?"

I sat on a gold sofa. "Sure, that sounds good."

Tina disappeared into the kitchen. She returned, carrying a small tray that had two glasses filled with ice, a small carafe of coffee, a little pot of creamer, and a dish filled with sugar cubes.

Tina filled a glass and then motioned for me to help myself. "It's cold brew. I make it myself. I hope that's okay."

I filled my cup and sat back on the sofa. "That's great, thank you."

Tina held onto her glass but didn't drink. "That day was just so crazy. Working at a bank, I always feared that something like that could happen. But I had worked there for over five years, and nothing ever did. At a certain point, you start to believe that it never will."

"But then it did."

Tina sipped her drink. "Yep. And nothing was ever the same again. Mikey came up to my counter. We were in a large office building with security in the main lobby, so I always felt safe, like they would stop something. But they weren't in the bank and had no way to know what was going on."

I set down my glass. "You worked at the Bank of Santa Monica, in Santa Monica?"

Tina fluffed her hair. "It's a mouthful, huh? But yes, there are several locations in Santa Monica. I worked at the one on Main Street."

"Okay."

She leaned forward and rested her elbows on her knees. "Mikey got his money. Then he took a hostage. It was crazy. We all begged him not to leave with her, but he did."

Jennifer's article mentioned the hostage. "Was she okay? Did he let her go?"

"He released her a short time later. She claimed Mikey had two accomplices. But they've never been caught."

CHAPTER 64

I sipped my coffee. The Westside Happenings article gave the name of Mikey's hostage, but I couldn't remember it off the top of my head. The article didn't provide many details about the situation. I hoped Tina could fill in the blanks. "Is there more you can tell me about the hostage?"

"Her name was Corinne Reynolds."

Yes, now I remembered; that was the name reported in Jennifer's article.

"She had a camera on her shoulder with her purse. Mikey got pissed and accused her of taking photos of him. She started to cry and said she brought it into the bank because she didn't want it stolen from her car. She had just come from an overnight photoshoot and was depositing the money she made. He grabbed her. Once he had the money, he left with her. Said he liked blondes."

"Wow, that's pretty scary, I have to say."

"Yeah, no kidding."

"Did Corinne say anything about Mikey's accomplices?"

"You'd have to ask her, but she said Mikey was his own getaway driver. He was parked down the street. Then, he took Corinne to a house somewhere. Two other people were waiting there for Mikey."

"Did she see the other two? Their faces?"

"No, she was blindfolded, but she was sure there were two. They didn't use names, and since she never saw them, there wasn't much for the police to work with."

"I understand."

"Corinne couldn't even tell where the house was. She knew they drove for a while after leaving the bank, but that's it. The next day, Mikey put her in his car, drove her around for a while, and then dropped her off by the Santa Monica Pier."

"And Corinne never saw his face?"

Tina bit her lip. "Nope. Not his or the others. Then Mikey got arrested and that was it. No one seemed interested in anyone else."

"But you think Mikey had accomplices?"

"Corinne says he did, and I believe her. She said they had walkie-talkies and were communicating. They were acting as lookouts."

"How do you know so much about Corinne?"

"Oh, that's easy. I found her after the robbery. I wanted to check that she was okay. We've become friends. Well, sort of. We see each other occasionally. She's a nice person, but our only connection is the robbery."

I thought of something to ask, but I wasn't sure if Tina would know the answer. "Do you think Len was going to give Corinne a check too?"

Tina shook her head. "I don't know. Besides, even if he wanted to, he would have to find her first."

"What do you mean?"

"Corinne doesn't want anyone to know where she lives. Even I don't know where she lives. She's like that; she's worried Mikey's accomplices will find her. I've assured her that she likely doesn't need to worry about that."

Tina drank some coffee. "You can call Corinne if you like. She would be okay with me giving you her number."

I wasn't so sure about that. Corinne didn't want Tina, her friend, to know where she lived. Would she be okay with Tina giving her number to a stranger? "I'll think about it."

"I'm serious. Corinne might have some helpful information."

I wondered about that. I had learned a lot about various robberies but little to nothing about where to find Len. Plus, I didn't want to cause Corinne more problems.

I clasped my hands together. "Like I said, I'll think about it. I don't want to dredge things up just to dredge them up."

"I see your point. You know, I've talked about the robbery a lot; that was my way of dealing with it. Others do things differently. Corinne became a hermit; that was how she got through it. But what happened to her was pretty scary. She was convinced she was going to die. That's a lot to deal with."

Tina was reinforcing my belief that Corinne wouldn't want me calling her out of the blue.

"I agree," I said.

"Here, give me a second."

Tina disappeared into the kitchen. She returned a few minutes later and handed me a piece of paper. "This is Corinne's contact information. It's her cell phone. I also included my number. Call either of us any time, and if there's anything I can do to help Len, I would like to do it. I can't speak for Corinne, but I can't imagine she'll be happy when I tell her Len's missing."

I decided I had taken up enough of Tina's time. I put the phone numbers in my purse, we said goodbye, and I headed back out into the bright sun.

CHAPTER 65

Mikey didn't want anyone at the Montana Avenue apartments to get suspicious about Len's absence. So he stopped by to make sure nothing needed attention. Things like a burst water pipe or a tenant burning the place down.

So far, nothing had happened, and no one had asked questions, except for Jocelyn. Oh, and that one asshole making a fuss about his parking spot.

The good thing was that it was still mid-December. Rent wouldn't be due for another couple of weeks. He had to be gone by then; otherwise, he'd have to figure out how to handle that.

Mikey was still sure that Jocelyn had what he was looking for. And he was more confident than ever that it was in her apartment. Tonight, he was going in and ending all of this.

Just then, there was a knock on the door. Mikey froze but realized it was just a light tapping. Not the banging the police make before they bust in.

He opened the door. He recognized the woman on the other side; he'd seen her around the building.

She was good-looking with long golden brown hair and dark blue eyes. She reminded him of someone, but he wasn't sure who. A movie star? An actress from one of those TV shows in the nineties? He couldn't remember which.

He smiled. "What's up?"

She put her hands in her pockets. "I'm looking for Len. Is he here?"

Mikey leaned on the doorframe with his good arm. His wrist didn't hurt as much thanks to the pills, but the cast was annoying. It got in the way and slowed him down. "Len's out of town. What can I help you with?"

She diverted her eyes from him. "It's a maintenance issue."

Of course. Mikey had just been thinking about how smooth everything was going, and now he'd jinxed himself. "I'm looking out for the place. What's the problem?"

She touched the ends of her hair. "The dryer in the laundry room. It doesn't seem to get hot, so it's not drying my clothes."

Like he gave a wet fart about any of this. Len's apartment had a washer and dryer. Didn't all the units?

He crossed his arms. "Don't you have one in your apartment?"

"No. I have a studio. It's not very big. There's no hook-up."

Wonderful, just wonderful. Mikey didn't need this headache today. He thought of a solution. "You can use mine." He stood back and motioned for her to enter.

She backed away. "No, that's okay. I'll figure it out. I just thought Len might want to know."

"What's your name?"

She took another couple of steps back. "It's okay. I'll go to a laundromat."

He shook his head. "Suit yourself. But you're welcome to use it. I won't bite." Then, he smiled one of his best smiles. He knew he was intimidating and hoped the smile would diminish that effect.

She stepped forward. "Are you sure?"

"Come on, it's no big deal. I'm not using it. You can get your stuff dried and be on your way." He wanted to add, "unless you want to have a drink," but he didn't.

Len had a bottle of whiskey in a cabinet, and Mikey had been buying Coke. He could throw together a quick happy hour.

She tucked her hair behind her ears. "Okay. I'll go get my stuff."

Mikey smiled another of his most pleasant smiles. She smiled back. His charms were working.

She left, and he saw her walk to her unit on the first floor. Her door was visible from Len's apartment.

She came back with a small laundry basket filled with damp clothes.

He waved. "Come on in."

She entered Len's apartment. "Thanks for the help. When will Len be back?"

"I don't know. He went to Vegas for a few days. I'm watching over the place. Is that okay?"

She shrugged. "Sure. Doesn't matter to me. Where's the dryer?"

"Here, I'll show you."

He led her down the hallway. "Do you want a drink while you wait? I don't have much, but Len has some whisky."

Mikey tried to say it casually, so he didn't alarm her. He was already shocked he had persuaded her to come into the apartment. Why was he so surprised? He could be smooth. He was just out of practice.

She laughed. "Isn't it early?"

He tapped his head. "You're right. Silly me. Forget it."

She pushed her hair out of her face. "No, that's okay. I could have one drink."

He was sure he knew her from more than just TV. "You never told me your name."

"Tara. What's yours?"

"Mikey. Don't I know you?"

"I don't think so," she said.

At that moment, Mikey had forgotten all about his problems, namely Jocelyn. Then, a thought flashed through his mind. Tara would look so much better as a blonde.

CHAPTER 66

I walked the block from Tina's condo back to my car. When I arrived at my vehicle, I noticed a silver sports car parked a few spots behind it. I tensed up. Was this the same car from last night? Had the driver followed me to Tina's condo?

I glanced around Ocean Avenue. The sun was high in the sky, and everyone outside appeared to have a carefree attitude. Like we were all in a bubblegum commercial. No one knew I was looking for my missing landlord and that an unknown silver car was following me.

I didn't see anyone in the car, so I walked up to it. Upon closer examination, it was a Porsche. I didn't know if this was the car that was following me, but it looked like it. It was very similar. I took Tina's paper and found a pen in my purse. I jotted down the license plate number.

Then, I returned to my car, and my stomach growled. It was still a little early for lunch, but I wanted something to eat.

A nearby burger place made awesome smash

burgers. I didn't go as often as I liked because you needed divine intervention to find parking, but I was hungry, so I'd try my luck.

I pulled from my parking spot and drove down Ocean Avenue, eventually making a left on Pico Boulevard before turning right onto Main Street. I checked the rearview mirror several times, but no silver cars were following me.

I arrived at the restaurant and after circling the block twice, I found a parking spot. Main Street Burgers was a little walk-up stand with no indoor seating. Just outdoor stools and tables in bright colors, which were drilled into the concrete. Christmas tinsel was draped across the order window, and a large string of vintage Christmas bulbs was wrapped around the red roof.

I ordered at the window. Two smash burgers, a whole pickle, and a Diet Coke. I also asked for a couple of extra sides of what they called fry sauce. It was like Thousand Island dressing, only better.

I stood around until my order was called. Once I had my food, I sat at a small orange table.

The burgers were as good as I remembered. I ordered mine with the works, which included American cheese, pickles, onion, tomato, shredded lettuce, and fry sauce. The sauce dripped down my hands and threatened to continue up my arms.

I grabbed a few more napkins and continued eating.

I thought about the silver Porsche by Tina's condo. I hadn't been hallucinating; someone had followed me from Hermosa Beach last night. If I had to guess the reason, I would deduce that it was because of someone I had visited in the past couple of days. But which person? And why?

I shivered. Was I safe? So far, the person had only been tailing me. Would he or she escalate things? Regardless, I had a license plate number for a silver car. I could return to the police station with that additional information. I would also file a missing person's report on Len; I felt like I no longer had a choice. After all that I had discovered, I was still no closer to finding him.

Everything was a big cluster of a mess from which I couldn't untangle myself. Here I was, searching for Len, when I had no other clients. Not even another prospect. If I didn't figure things out, I was looking at a swift return to an office job.

I also had to figure out my Christmas plans. Spending the holidays alone sounded depressing. But so did going to Omaha. I didn't feel like dealing with the drama, fighting, and negativity that came with my parents' separation.

I took another bite of my burger and looked up at the cloudless sky. It was a nice day; my lunch was great. I had to at least try to give myself a short break from my worries.

CHAPTER 67

I had finished my first burger and was halfway through my second. Main Street Burgers was getting busier. Most customers were ordering food to go.

One man stayed. He sat at a red table furthest from mine, flipping through a newspaper in between bites of burger.

Our eyes met for a brief second, before he returned to reading. The man looked older than me, maybe in his forties. He was pretty good-looking and wore a Stauffer Law sweatshirt, a navy Polo baseball hat, and a giant gold watch.

I finished lunch and made one last attempt to wipe my hands. No matter how many napkins I used, they still felt covered in the burger sauce. I remained at the table, staring at my empty wrappers. It was back to reality. What were my next steps? I reviewed what I knew so far.

Mikey Miles was Len's cousin, who posed as his nephew. He had been in prison for two robberies, one in Santa Monica, the other in Playa Vista. He showed up at Len's apartment sometime on Sunday.

Around this time, Len disappeared.

Len had planned to give money to at least five different individuals. Belinda Jackson had a personal connection to Len. Mary Watts and Pete Hernandez had been at the Bank of Santa Monica in Century City when it was robbed. Len and Mary believed Mikey had robbed the bank; Pete wasn't as sure.

Jessica Cecil was also at the Century City bank the day it was robbed, but I didn't know if she was a victim. Or, as Mary believed, if she was involved. If it was Mikey who robbed that bank, was it possible she was helping him? Did that explain why Jessica peeled out of her driveway after I asked her about Len? If she was an accomplice, why would Len want to give her money?

I hadn't figured out whether it was Andy or Tony Baker that Len was looking for. Getting back in touch with Tony seemed like a bad idea; I didn't know what he was mixed up in. Tony said he'd pass my business card to his dad, but I doubted that had happened. If I wanted to talk to Andy, I would have to make the effort myself. The question was, would Andy be any help?

Then, there was Tina Tompson, who was the teller at the Santa Monica robbery that Mikey was convicted of. Len dropped off a check to her on Saturday night. Corinne Reynolds was Mikey's hostage from the same robbery.

I knew a lot about the robberies in Santa Monica and Century City but nothing about the second robbery in Playa Vista. But was that important?

I had traversed across L.A. County, and I hadn't found Len. He was still missing. I had to face the fact that I had reached the end. I needed help. I should go to the police and file a missing person's report.

My phone rang. It was Jeff. I answered.

"I'm heading to the airport, but I wanted to let you know that I emailed you a list of Len's properties."

CHAPTER 68

I pulled into my parking garage and headed up the stairs. Before I went to the police, I wanted to look at Jeff's email with the list of Len's properties. Yes, this was my last sliver of hope.

I was grasping at any straws I could at this point. I wanted to find Len. But I knew this was bordering on wishful thinking, and it was also turning into a bit of foot-dragging on my part.

I walked by the front gate on my way up to my apartment, and as I did, I saw Betty at the entrance. She was balancing two bags of groceries while trying to open the gate. The bags wobbled, close to tipping over. I thought Betty said she was going to be gone for a week. It was only Wednesday. I wondered what had changed.

I ran up to her. "Here, let me get that for you."

I pushed open the gate, and Betty walked through with her two bags from Gwendolyn's Market, the grocery store I often went to just up the street on San Vicente.

She smiled. She rarely smiled, and it often seemed

fake or forced when she did. Today, her smile seemed genuine. "Thank you so much."

I stepped aside to let her in. As I did, I thought I saw Mikey's car speed away from our building, heading toward San Vicente. I looked back to Betty. "You're welcome. I see you're home."

Betty's smile disappeared. "Yes, I'm back. And I may never speak to that sister of mine ever again. I swear, she makes me so mad."

I didn't want to get involved, but my curiosity got the better of me. "What happened?"

"What happened? She won everything! And all I did was lose! I was just one big loser. The more she won, the more obnoxious she got. I mean, she's unbearable. I couldn't stand it. So I came back early."

"No luck, huh?"

Betty sneered. "None! We play slots. I couldn't get anything going. Not once. Not one hot one. My sister, though, everything she touched, bam, she won."

"That's how it goes sometimes."

Betty narrowed her eyes. "Not for me. I'm always *very* lucky."

Except for now, I wanted to say but didn't.

Betty set her grocery bags on her porch and turned back to me. "Have you seen that hunk of junk down in the garage?"

I assumed Betty was referring to Mikey's car. "The black one?"

"Yes, the Bonneville. I drove in and wondered if I had slipped back to the seventies. It has to have been twenty years since I've seen a car like that." Betty put her key in the lock. "It's in Chris's spot. I can't imagine him trading in his BMW for that."

I was unsure what to say. Should I tell Betty about Mikey? Maybe, but I wanted to think about it before I did.

Betty opened her door and picked up her bags. "That thing was blocking the door, so I couldn't get through with these groceries and had to come all the way around to the front. I'm just glad you were there. Thank you very much for the help."

"No problem," I said and returned to my apartment.

CHAPTER 69

I opened my email and found the one from Jeff. I was relieved and thankful that Jeff had come through for me. I owed him dinner, at least. Of course, I previously offered him lunch, and he wouldn't let me pay. I doubted he'd let me treat him to dinner.

Jeff had provided a list of six properties that Len owned. I recognized the first address because it was my building. Three others had Los Angeles as the city and 90049 as the zip code, which meant they were in Brentwood. The buildings were on Gorham, Darlington, and Mayfield Avenues.

I recognized the street names and knew they were close by. But I pulled up a map anyway, just to be sure. I was right; they were all within walking distance of my apartment.

The last two properties weren't in Brentwood. One was in Long Beach. I had been there once to see the Queen Mary ship when my parents visited me. Long Beach was at least thirty miles from my apartment. The other was in San Pedro, which wasn't too far from Long Beach.

I printed Jeff's email and retrieved it from my printer.

I heard someone screaming for help. It sounded like Betty. A few seconds later, someone pounded on my door. "Open up, Jocelyn!"

It was Betty. I ran to my door, but not quick enough for her. She continued pounding. "Jocelyn! Jocelyn!"

"Just a second!" I yelled, but I didn't know if she could hear me. I opened my door.

Betty was wringing her hands, and her face was pale. "It's terrible. You have to help."

What had happened since I had just seen her downstairs a few minutes ago? "What's wrong?"

"Oh, it's just awful. Please. I need help."

"Tell me what's wrong first."

"Blood is everywhere. I don't know what to do. Can you help me?"

My mind went to Len. I felt like I might throw up. "What?"

Betty couldn't stop wringing her hands. "He's dead! In the apartment. He's just dead."

My body felt like it was floating, and I had detached from reality. Had Len been there the whole time? Was Mikey coming and going, stepping over a dead body?

Maybe I should've figured out a way to check inside Len's apartment. Maybe I should've tried to find Betty in the desert. Maybe I should've gone to the police earlier.

Maybe, maybe, maybe. It was too late now.

"Jocelyn, are you listening to me?"

Betty had been talking, but I hadn't heard what she said.

"I said that he's dead in Len's apartment. I need your help."

I looked at Betty. She wasn't crying. Not one tear had trickled down her face. She was amped up but not hysterical like I would expect if her close friend was murdered. "Is it Len?"

Betty stared at me like I'd just lit a cigarette and blew smoke in her face. "Of course not! I don't know who the hell he is."

CHAPTER 70

I felt a massive sense of relief. So much so, that I grabbed the door handle to steady myself. It wasn't Len. But if it wasn't him, then who was it? Mikey?

Betty's skin was still pale, but she had relaxed her hands. "You need to come with me. Please. I need your help."

Then, she turned and tore down the stairs; I'd never seen her move so fast. My Converse were sitting by the door. I put them on as quick as possible and ran after Betty.

I arrived at Len's patio. All the tenants who were at home seemed to have gathered around and were murmuring loudly. I assumed they had been prompted that something was wrong because of Betty's earlier shrieking. The group was blocking the view of Len's doorway, so I couldn't see inside.

Betty pushed her way through them, barking orders. "Out of my way! Now! Move it!"

"I called the police!" someone yelled.

Some tenants I knew by name, while others I had only seen once or twice. I didn't realize how many people were around on a random Wednesday.

Betty stood guard in front of Len's door. "Stay back, all of you. Someone said they called the police?"

I saw Chris. He raised his hand. "I called nine-one-one."

"What did they say?"

"That they're on their way. What else would they say?"

Betty moved away from the door and walked up to Chris, her eyes narrowed into little slits. "I'm just asking, is all."

Chris backed away. He saw me and came over to where I was standing. "Do you think it's that guy that's been staying in Len's apartment?"

"I don't know. I can't see anything."

"I couldn't see anything either. But I bet it's that guy." He smiled. "Looks like I can get my parking spot back."

Chris turned and walked toward his apartment on the first floor. He opened his door and once he was inside, slammed it shut.

Betty walked back to Len's door, resuming her position as guard.

"Where's Len?" someone yelled.

"I don't know," Betty said. "Has anyone seen him?"

No one responded to Betty, but the crowd started moving closer, the murmuring getting louder, working its way up to a dull roar.

Most of the conversation was about Len. *Where is*

*he? Have you seen him? Is that him? Is he dead? If it's
not him, did he have anything to do with this?*

I wanted to figure out who was dead in Len's
apartment. Could it be Mikey?

The tenants moved in one large mass closer to the
door, and I shuffled with them.

Betty sensed the crowd getting closer and waved
her hands like a crossing guard. "Stand back. We
can't contaminate things. This entire area is a crime
scene."

"Why don't you back away then?" someone
yelled.

Betty continued waving her hands. "The police
will be here. They will want to talk to all of you."

She was portraying herself like she was an expert
in criminology when at most she was an expert in
Law & Order.

Betty bobbed her head like she was taking a
mental inventory of who all was there. "Stick around
if you saw something. Otherwise, you're being a
nuisance and should go home."

"You should go home," someone said.

Betty scanned the crowd, looking for whoever
dared to speak against her. "Whoever did this could
still be around. We might all be in danger."

She stepped aside just for a second. I moved
around a couple of people and craned my neck.

Inside the foyer was a pool of blood. Slumped over
the blood was a body. Wearing a sleeveless white
undershirt and jeans. With a brown ponytail and
beard.

I recognized the body. It was the man in Sherman Oaks who demanded money from Tony.

Doug.

CHAPTER 71

Doug was dead. Not Mikey. I had a ton of questions racing through my mind. What had happened? And when? I had heard nothing. Maybe it happened while I was out.

Doug was at Tony's house when I was there. And Doug was dead in Len's apartment where Mikey had been staying. That meant Doug and Mikey were connected. Did that also connect Tony to Mikey? Did that mean that Tony was A. Baker, the person Len was looking for? If so, why would Len give Tony money if he was involved with Mikey? It made no sense.

While I couldn't tell how Doug died, I knew the obvious. Someone murdered Doug. Was it Mikey? That was the most likely answer. Who else could have done it? Mikey was the only person I had seen in the apartment since Len went missing.

What did all this mean for Len? If Mikey killed Doug, had he also killed Len? It was getting harder to stay hopeful that Len was okay.

Where was Mikey? If he killed Doug, planned or

not, had he taken off? If he had been holding Len somewhere, had Mikey ditched him?

It felt like an imaginary clock had started. I had the overwhelming feeling that time was running out for Len. I had to find him before it was too late. But what should I do?

Considering the circumstances, I only had a brief time to figure it out. The police were on their way. Things were heating up and about to get even more chaotic.

But if the police would soon be here, why didn't I just wait to talk to them? Less than an hour ago, I was ready to file a missing person's report. And now the police were coming to me. I could explain how Len was missing, give details about Mikey, and then the police could find Len. Right? I wasn't so sure. I doubted they would begin an urgent search for an adult male, who may have left on his own volition.

A sense of urgency continued to plague me. I didn't want to wait while the police worked through the situation. I didn't doubt they could find Len, but how long would it take? Mikey might be tying up loose ends, which explained why Doug was dead. Len might be next. Len could be dead and Mikey in the wind before the police even started their search.

Of course, the cops might also consider Len a suspect in Doug's murder. Or at least a person of interest because a dead body was in his apartment. They would probably look for him either way. But again, how long would that take?

In no way could I sit around and wait for the cops

to find Len when he could be in imminent danger.

If I didn't wait and talk to the police, then what was my plan? Upstairs, I had a printed list with Len's properties. I could go to each one and see if I could find Len. I wasn't sure if this was the best idea, but it was my only idea. I could always call the police while I was out, or I could return at any time and talk to them.

I left the hectic scene downstairs and ran up to my apartment. I dashed to my bedroom, flung open my closet doors, and grabbed a tote bag. The day was growing chillier, and I didn't know when I would return, so I tossed my Stauffer sweatshirt and a black beanie into the bag. I went into my office and threw in a notebook and pen. Finally, I returned to the kitchen. I put my purse in the bag and stuck the list of addresses in my jeans.

I glanced around the apartment. I had everything I could think that I might need in the bag. I was all set. It was time to get going.

I exited my apartment and flew down the two flights of stairs to the first floor. The police hadn't arrived, and the crowd was still gathered. Betty was shouting, but I couldn't make out what she was saying. Her voice sounded like it was getting louder. The shriller she got, the less it seemed like anyone was listening.

I headed toward the back exit, on my way to the underground parking garage. I passed Tara's apartment. I didn't recall seeing her outside earlier.

Something caught my eye, and I stopped. Her

door was ajar. I knocked and waited, but Tara didn't answer. I rang the doorbell, but Tara didn't come to the door.

Inch by inch, I pushed the door open. I glanced back toward Len's apartment. The crowd paid no attention to me.

In one motion, I opened the door the rest of the way. Tara's apartment was empty. No furniture. No belongings. Nothing.

Tara was gone.

CHAPTER 72

I closed the door to Tara's apartment and continued to the back stairs, which would take me to the parking garage. When did Tara move out? I was sure I would've seen a moving truck out front at some point, but I'd seen nothing.

What was going on with her? Was it connected to Len? I didn't see how; it must be a coincidence. Just because I didn't see Tara move out didn't mean something weird was going on.

I arrived at my car, and as I did, indecision overwhelmed me. I simultaneously felt like I was doing something illegal while also wanting to get the hell away from here. I talked myself down. I wasn't fleeing the scene; I wasn't doing anything wrong.

If I didn't go now, I might not be allowed to leave later. The police might need me to wait around and answer questions. How long would that take? And what would I say? I could identify the body. I knew it was Doug. What would happen to me then? And while I was being questioned, what about Len?

Besides, I had little helpful information, except that I knew Mikey had been staying in Len's apartment. Other tenants, like Chris, knew that too. Plus, I didn't see or hear anything relating to the murder. But was that my call to make? Shouldn't I stay, just to be sure? I pulled the list of addresses from my pocket. Would this actually lead me to Len?

I bit my lip. Screw it. It was worth a shot. Maybe it was a mistake that I would later regret. But Len had saved me from Adam. With no questions asked. I had one last chance to help him, and I would do it.

I popped the trunk and tossed in the tote bag. I glanced at my storage unit. It was located directly above my parking spot. Len had labeled all of them by last name, so mine said Bennett. I stored little in it. Mostly my tennis racket and Christmas tree.

The lock looked funny, so I stepped closer. It was cut and now the lock was dangling. I removed it, and the creaky old door, made of plywood, popped open. I stood on my tiptoes and tried to look in. My racket and the empty tree box were still there.

I had a fairly good idea who cut the lock. Mikey. Was he looking for the same thing he had been looking for when he came into my apartment? What was it?

Since I kept nothing too valuable in it, I wouldn't worry about it for now. Just in case, I grabbed my tennis racket and tossed it into my trunk next to the tote bag.

Suddenly, I heard footsteps in the garage, which echoed off the walls. It startled me, and I turned around.

It was Tara.

I put a hand to my chest. "You scared me. Did you see what's going on upstairs?"

As Tara got closer, I noticed she looked rattled. Her eyes were bulging out of her skull, and I expected them to spin like a character in a science fiction movie. And she was chewing on a huge wad of gum. "I have to get out of here."

"What? Why?"

Tara pushed a white envelope into my hand. "Can you give this to Len?"

I held the envelope but didn't look at it. "I don't know where Len is."

"But you're looking for him. I know you'll find him. This explains everything."

"Explains what? Are you okay?"

She nodded. "I'm fine."

Tara looked anything but. "You don't look okay."

"I just need to get going, that's all."

"Did you move out?"

"Yes."

I shook my head. "But when?"

"Let's just say I didn't have much to take."

I tilted my head. "What does that mean?"

"My plans changed."

I was growing more confused by the second. And I was feeling like a parrot, repeating everything Tara said. "What plans?"

"For living here. It was never meant to be permanent. It was just supposed to be a brief stay."

I had no clue what Tara was talking about. "Why not?"

"I don't have time to explain. I've gotta go."

I wasn't sure I had much time either, but my gut was telling me to stay and get more information from Tara. "Why did your plans change? Are you talking about the dead body in Len's apartment?"

Her eyes fell to the floor, and I could see her jaw working on her gum. She looked at me. "Mikey killed Doug. I know nothing about that."

"Yes, you do. You know his name is Doug. And you're claiming Mikey did it."

Her eyes stayed glued to the floor. "I don't know anything."

"I don't believe you."

She lifted her head. Her eyes were open so wide that they looked too big for her face. "Please. You've always been nice to me. Will you help me? Will you give Len the letter?"

Tara was hiding something, and I felt it had to do with what was happening at our apartment complex: Len, Mikey, Doug, something. I had to get her to open up.

I could hear sirens, and I believed they were heading for our building.

Tara's eyes scanned the parking garage. "Are you going to help me or not? I don't have much time."

"I won't help you unless you tell me more. Come on, Tara. Something's very wrong here. I'm not accusing you of anything. But tell me what's going on."

She dropped her hands to her side. "Fine. My name's not Tara."

"What?"

"My real name is Corinne Reynolds."

CHAPTER 73

The sirens I heard earlier grew louder. Tara and I remained the only two people in the garage. I felt frozen in my spot.

I processed what Tara told me. "You were Mikey's hostage? From the Santa Monica robbery?"

Tara nodded.

I stared at her. Her bewildered expression had gone blank. Her eyes seemed to shrink back to their normal size. They no longer looked like they were about to spin out of her head and land on the concrete floor. "I don't understand what's going on."

"Tara's not my real name. My real name is Corinne."

"No. I know that. I mean, you're living in Len's building. He's Mikey's relative."

She nodded. "I know."

"But how did that happen? You must have ended up here on purpose."

She shrugged. "So what?"

"But why?"

She sighed. "I don't have time right now to get

into all of that. I just need to know if you'll give Len the letter."

I held up the envelope. "Yes, I'll give this to him, but I need to understand what's going on first. You can't just drop all this on me and then dip out."

Tara sighed. "Len called me after the robbery to check on me. Somehow, he found my number. He said he was sorry to hear about what Mikey did. He wanted to see me, but I was uncomfortable meeting him."

"But you moved into Len's building. All these years later. Why?"

Tara said nothing.

"Do you know where Len is?"

She crossed her arms like she was hugging herself. "No."

"Did you see Mikey do anything to Len?"

She shook her head. "No."

Tara had earlier said that Mikey killed Doug. "Did you see what Mikey did to Doug?

Her eyes grew enormous again. "No, I didn't. And I didn't kill Doug either, if that's what you're thinking."

The thought had crossed my mind. "Okay. But how do you know Mikey killed Doug?"

Tara tapped her foot. "I just know he did it. But I didn't see anything. I wish I did. Please, I have to go."

"Does Len know who you are?"

Tara smacked her gum. "No. I never met Len in person until I moved here. He doesn't know I'm Corinne. He thinks I'm Tara."

"Wasn't there ever a picture of you on the news? You know, after Mikey took you? So that people could find you?"

"Yes, but I look different now."

"How so?"

Tara stomped her foot. "It doesn't matter. Look, it'll take too long to get into all of this. I've been more than patient. Will you give Len the letter or not?"

"The police are on their way. Why don't you talk to them? Tell them what you know."

"I can't do that. Look, I gotta go. Please. Will you give the letter to Len?"

"Yes, I will, but can you tell me anything else? I don't want to jam you up. But please. I need to find Len, and I'm not sure what to do next."

Tara pulled a wrapper from her pocket and spit her wad of gum into it. She balled it up and stuck it in her pocket. "When I talked to Len all those years ago, he said that he would never be rid of Mikey. So I knew Mikey would show up wherever Len lived once he was out."

"I'm confused."

Tara stomped her foot again and crossed her arms. "Here's the short version. Mikey took me. He had two accomplices. Doug was one. I don't know the other dude's name. But I saw their faces, including Mikey's." She glanced to the floor. "Even though I said I didn't."

CHAPTER 74

I could no longer hear the sirens and wondered if they were headed elsewhere. A light breeze was wafting through the garage and the air was getting cooler.

I stared at Tara. "Why didn't you tell the police you saw Mikey's face?"

Tara sighed. "Mikey told me he would kill me if I tried to find him or do anything."

"Okay."

"I only saw his face, but I didn't know his name. Not until…"

"Until what?"

"Until Len called me. That's when I started following Mikey."

"Wait a second. When did Len call you? Before Mikey was arrested?"

"Yes. Mikey wasn't arrested until much later. But Len was sure Mikey robbed the Santa Monica bank. Right from the start, even when the police had no suspects. And he was right. Mikey must've done something around then that made Len suspicious, I don't know."

Something Tara said a few seconds ago hit me. "Hold on. Did you say you were following Mikey?"

She nodded. "I found out where he lived, and I would wait outside the place. Sometimes, I followed him."

I was having a tough time believing what she was telling me. But after everything I learned in the past few days, I shouldn't be surprised. "But not always?"

"No. Sometimes, I went into Mikey's apartment. But that's not important."

"Then what is?"

Tara's eyes had calmed down. "That Mikey was arrested. He may not have served time for Century City, but he was in jail, where he belonged. Len said that we had to be okay with that."

I wondered why Tara was concerned with the Century City robbery. "How often did you talk to Len?"

Tara lowered her head. "Well, Len called me that first time, the one I told you about. I would call him, occasionally, to see if he heard anything about Century City. I kind of got obsessed about the whole thing, even after Mikey was in prison."

I remembered what Mary Watts had told me about a rumor she heard. "Did Len ever tell you anything about a witness at the Century City bank?"

Tara stuffed her hands in her pockets. "He would always say that he didn't know anything. And then too much time passed. You know, the statute of limitations."

I thought about how Tara was following Mikey. Could she have been following him that day? "Was that you? Were you there?"

Tara glanced around the parking garage and then looked at me. "Where? In Century City?"

"Yes."

Tara looked panicked. "I didn't know what he would do that day, I swear, or I would've never gone there. It's a business park; I figured it was just offices. So yeah, I followed him there, stupid me. And then he robbed the place."

Pete and Mary had said that Mikey looked like a farmer that day. "Didn't you think his clothes were strange?"

"Whose, Mikey's?"

"Yeah, I heard he was wearing a costume."

"That was weird, but what does it matter?"

I wondered if perhaps Tara knew something was off about Mikey that day, but she followed him anyway. Did denying she knew Mikey was going to rob a bank make her feel better about not reporting it? "And you never said anything after the fact?"

"No. And I stopped following Mikey after that."

I didn't know what to think, and I didn't know if I believed her. "Someone was shot at that robbery."

Tara dropped her head. "I know. I felt awful about that. But he made it through okay."

What could I say? I wasn't in Tara's position. I wasn't judging; I just wanted to sort this out. But the more she told me, the less any of it made sense.

Tara sighed. "I wanted to tell someone, but I

freaked out. I was afraid I would get in trouble. I would be asked why I was there. What would I say? That I was stalking him? How could I admit that? I was this guy's hostage. And then I ended up at another of his bank robberies? Would you believe me? I just happened to be there? Or would you think I was involved?"

"What was your reason for following him in the first place? Were you trying to catch him committing a crime? To make sure he went to prison?"

"I don't know why I did what I did. I wasn't thinking straight at the time. I was confused."

I wasn't sure I believed Tara, but I didn't have time to argue. "You could have anonymously reported that you saw Mikey. No one would have to know your name."

"Yeah, right. I don't believe that for a second. Someone would've figured out I was the one who reported it. And then made me testify. And then it would've all come out. About me following Mikey. How would that make me look?"

"It would be understandable."

Tara laughed. "Yeah, right. Come on. You don't believe that."

I didn't know what I believed.

Tara shifted from one foot to the other. "Then Mikey was arrested and took a plea, and before I knew it, he went to prison. And there's no point in speaking up now. I had my chance, and that chance is gone."

After all this time had passed, why was Tara still so worried and scared? "Well, you said that Mikey killed Doug. I believe you. I think he did. If you saw something, then you can help put him away for murder. Then he'll be gone for good."

I heard sirens again. This time, they were closer, and I sensed these were headed for our building on Montana Avenue.

Tara pointed to the letter. "Give that to Len, please. And tell him to check my storage locker too."

"What's in the storage locker?"

"Just something to help him move on."

Tara walked away.

"Wait," I said.

Tara turned back to me and put up a hand. "I'm done talking."

"This is all so confusing."

Tara walked away again. She threw up her hands. "Sorry!"

A few seconds later, Tara was gone, leaving me holding her letter to Len.

PART 3

GOING THE EXTRA MILE

CHAPTER 75

Jared walked into the bank in Azusa, off the 210 freeway in the San Gabriel Valley. He came to Azusa often since he lived over in Glendora. But he'd never been inside this building.

Some of his shaggy, brown hair was in his eyes, so he pushed it away. He pulled up his pants, which hung loose around his narrow hips.

Jared glanced around. The bank wasn't too busy. Just a short line. Nothing too out of hand. It shouldn't take too long to do what he had come here to do.

He felt uncomfortable about the whole thing, but he had no one to blame but himself. He agreed to do the work, and he needed the money. Well, he wanted the money; he didn't need it. His parents gave him enough each week. But it barely covered meals out, and he wanted more. This seemed like an easy way.

He didn't expect to be here at the bank so soon. He figured there were other things they would need done first. Yet here he was.

Jared noticed a security guard in the lobby. The

dude looked jacked, like all he did was lift weights and pound energy drinks. Plus, he wore freaking combat gear. Lots of black and what looked like a bulletproof vest. He even had his pants tucked into his boots.

Jared made his way up the line. He had the phone in his pocket, ready to go. His employer hadn't been too specific about everything that was required. And things had already changed. The person he was supposed to call was unavailable, so they gave him a different number.

It was his turn. He stepped up to the counter.

Sue was the name on the teller's tag. She was a stern-looking older woman who didn't seem the type to take crap from anyone. She had gray hair that looked glued to her head like a helmet. Like a prison guard. His left eye twitched.

Perfect.

She leaned forward, her lips in a straight line. "How can I help you?"

Jared's hands were sweating, and he wiped them on his jeans. "Hi, yes, I'm here to make a withdrawal."

"Do you have an account with us?"

"No, ma'am. I'm withdrawing the money for someone else."

"All right, I'm going to need you to complete some things," she said.

"Well, he said to call him, and he could give you anything you need over the phone."

Sue tilted her head. "I don't think I've ever done

that before. You should fill out the forms."

Jared felt his stomach rumble. It was fifty-fifty whether he would throw up or crap his pants. Something was wrong; he knew this was a bad idea the minute he heard it.

He pulled out the cell phone. "Here, hold on for a second." He punched in the number; he had it memorized. A voice answered on the first ring.

He handed the phone to Sue. She listened. He saw her make a quick motion with her hand. She did it fast; he would have missed it if he had blinked.

Before he knew what was happening, someone slammed into his back. He flew across the room and landed on the hard marble floor.

Shit. The jacked security guard. Was he going to shoot him?

Jared threw his hands to his head and laced his fingers together. He hoped to show he wasn't a threat. "I don't have a weapon! Please, don't kill me!"

"Shut up, son," the guard said.

Sue must have run around the side because she was standing next to him. "You got him?"

The guard grunted. "Yeah, I got him. This little shit isn't going anywhere."

Jared didn't know what to do except to beg. "Please, what's this about? I didn't do anything!"

"I'm sure. That's what they all say," the guard said.

Jared didn't dare make a move, but his mind raced. How could he get them to listen to him? "I'm here to withdraw money for someone! I'm working for someone! I swear!"

"Likely story," Sue said. "Whoever was on the other end of that phone told me to take all the money from the drawers, put it in a bag, and give it to you. Or else you would put a bullet in my head."

"No! I don't know what you're talking about! I swear! I'm just here to withdraw money. I don't have a gun. Check me."

Jared knew he should've listened to his first instinct. That's what he got for answering Help Wanted ads online.

CHAPTER 76

I closed the trunk of my car and got in the driver's seat. I held the letter from Tara. I thought about reading it but was unsure what my responsibilities would be once I did.

Then again, I was already involved. And if I was that concerned about getting in trouble, then I would be upstairs right now waiting to talk to the police.

I opened the letter and read it. It ended up being anti-climactic, pretty much everything Tara had told me, including a mention of the present for Len in her storage locker.

Satisfied that the letter had nothing to help me find Len, I put it in my glove box. It was time to get going. I reversed out of my parking spot, and my tires squealed as they always did on the polished concrete. Today, however, the sound was deafening.

The sirens were growing louder. Even though I knew no one was looking for me, it felt like they were. My sense of urgency in finding Len was growing stronger.

Even though I could've walked to the Gorham, Darlington, and Mayfield addresses from my apartment, I needed my car to get to Long Beach and San Pedro.

I left the parking structure, and I didn't see the police. I drove around the block, found an open spot, and exited my car. The wind had picked up. It wasn't the warmer Santa Ana winds that Los Angeles got this time of year either. It was a cooler wind, just enough to put a chill in me.

I opened my trunk, grabbed my Stauffer sweatshirt, and put it on. I slipped the beanie on my head. The list of Len's properties was in my pocket.

I headed to Gorham Avenue, the first address on my list. The building looked a lot like mine. Then again, most apartments in this area had a similar style, because they were built around the same time. Not every building was decades old, however. Occasionally new apartments popped up.

As I stood on the sidewalk on Gorham, I looked around for the silver Porsche I had seen in Santa Monica outside Tina's condo. There were plenty of silver cars, just no silver sports cars.

The building had a locked gate, but I couldn't find a call box anywhere. I didn't see anyone coming or going into the building, and I decided not to waste time hanging around. I needed to move on to the other addresses. I could always come back. Strike one.

I walked over to Darlington Avenue. The building had a buzzer, identical to the one at my apartment complex. The first number on the call box said Frederick–Manager. I pushed it. An apartment door next to the entrance opened a few seconds later, and a short, balding man in khakis and a plaid button-down shirt walked over to me. He stood behind the gate, not opening it.

His face was serious, without a hint of a smile. "I'm Frederick. How can I help you?"

"I'm looking for Len Zobak. Have you seen him?"

Frederick slipped his hands behind his back. "Not lately, no. I've been away, traveling through Europe on an extended vacation. I've only just returned. Are you looking to rent? We have a two-bedroom, which will open in mid-January."

"No, I'm a tenant in another of Len's buildings and thought I might find him here."

"Well, I'm very sorry, but like I said, I haven't seen him."

The man returned to his apartment and closed the door.

Strike two.

CHAPTER 77

I picked up my pace and arrived at the Mayfield Avenue address a few minutes later. This apartment building was smaller and only one story.

The place had no security gate, and I found apartment number one, which I deduced was the manager's apartment.

I knocked on the door, which had a large green wreath with a massive red bow. A woman answered, and the smell of cinnamon and vanilla wafted out with her. She was petite with gray-blonde hair wrapped into a chignon. She wore dark jeans and a red sweater with a jeweled reindeer pin. The reindeer's nose was a giant ruby.

She smiled. "Hello, dear. We don't have any available units."

It looked like I had found the manager. "That's okay. I'm not looking to rent. My name is Jocelyn Bennett. I'm looking for Len Zobak."

She stuck out her hand to shake mine. Her nails were painted a deep red. "Nice to meet you, Jocelyn. I'm Babette. Len's gone for a while. I don't know when he'll be back."

"Did he tell you he was leaving?"

"Usually, he does. This time, his nephew came by to let me know. Seemed like a charming young man."

"Mikey?"

"Yes, Mikey. He was just wonderful. He told me about Len being gone and that he was here to do a few checks. He fiddled around the property a bit and made sure everything looked okay. He even checked the utility room."

I thought about what Babette was telling me. Was there any chance Len was being kept in this utility room? "Have you been in there lately?"

"Been in where?"

"The utility room."

Babette tilted her head. "That's a funny question. But yes, I was in there last night, getting out some Christmas decorations." She put a finger to her lips in a shushing gesture. "Don't tell Len. I'm not supposed to store things in there."

A small Bichon Frise huddled at the woman's feet. So quiet it hadn't even made a peep.

Babette pointed to the dog. "Mikey just loved Mitzy. He told me she was the cutest dog he'd ever seen."

Mitzy was cute. She resembled a fluffy, bright white cotton ball.

Babette stared at Mitzy, then looked back at me. "I invited Mikey in, and he told me all about how he was helping Len. You know, he really liked my apartment. Said I did a fabulous job decorating."

Babette winked. "I agree."

Jeez. Babette may be friendly, but she was oblivious and easily flattered. Mikey did not give off nice guy vibes. More like ex-con vibes. And Babette was inviting him into her apartment?

Babette adjusted the pin on her sweater. "What do you need to speak to Len about? Is it urgent?"

"No, I just had a question for him, is all. I live in one of his other buildings."

"Which one?"

"Montana."

"Oh, that's a lovely one. I would love to be the manager, but Len prefers to live there. Until Mikey told me, I didn't realize Len owned so many. I always thought it was mine and yours. Len doesn't talk much. I'm sure you already know that."

I wondered if I could get more information on the other properties from Babette. "Are all the other places in Brentwood?"

"Yes, several are in Brentwood. One is on Gorham, I think. Then maybe Dorothy. No, wait, that's not right. It starts with a D though."

"Darlington?"

Babette snapped her fingers. "Yes, that's it, Darlington. I should've remembered."

I wasn't sure if Babette knew anything else, but it was worth a try. "Besides those, does Len own any others?"

"Why do you ask, dear?"

"I'm just curious, is all."

"Oh, well, I don't know. Len used to live down in

San Pedro. Ages ago. Before he bought the places up here. So maybe he still has something down there?"

"What about Long Beach?"

Babette shook her head. "Not that I recall."

"Have you seen Mikey since he first came by?"

"No. Just the once. I'm sure he'll be by again. If only to see Mitzy."

I smiled. "Of course."

A timer went off. Babette's eyes got big. "Oh, my cookies. Gotta run, dear. Take care."

With that, Babette closed the door.

Len wasn't here. Strike three.

I walked the several blocks back to my car. The wind had picked up even more, gusting through the streets.

I had been to all three of Len's buildings in Brentwood with no luck. This was all so frustrating.

Could the address in San Pedro be the same place Len lived all those years ago? Could it be a house? That would mean fewer tenants than at Len's multi-unit buildings in Brentwood. A lot fewer people to deal with if you were hiding someone. So maybe Mikey was keeping Len there.

Babette had nothing on Long Beach, but I would still stop there, anyway.

After I checked out Long Beach and San Pedro, I would have exhausted all my leads. If I didn't track down Len, I would talk to the police. I would tell them what I could and file a missing person's report.

I crossed my fingers that I might find him yet. I wasn't optimistic, but I'd give it one last shot.

CHAPTER 78

I arrived in Long Beach. Len's property was a strip mall, not a residential dwelling like a house or an apartment complex. All the storefronts were occupied and included a salon, donut shop, laundromat, taco place, and mail store.

I even saw a tax company. It was almost Busy Season, and I pictured what the place would be like in just about a month. Lots of people coming in trying to figure out what, if anything, they got for refunds. When I told people I was a CPA, most assumed I did taxes. But I had actually started my career in auditing. Like tax accounting, financial auditing also had a busy season that typically ran from January through April.

I diverted my eyes from the tax company and continued scanning the mall. I didn't see a potential space where Mikey might keep Len.

I kept looking, to be extra sure that I missed nothing in a property this big. I paced the parking lot, even making my way around the back. All the parking spaces behind the building had signs that showed they were reserved for employees of the various businesses. Next to the building, near a retaining wall, were a couple of dumpsters. They were empty. I peered in. Just to be sure. No Len.

I went around to the front of the strip mall and back toward my car. Even though the mall's parking lot was almost filled up, no one was out. I pulled out my list of addresses. I was down to my last one. San Pedro was my last hope. I slipped the paper back into my pocket, arrived at my car, and pushed the key fob to unlock the doors.

I heard footsteps behind me. I whipped around, gripping my car keys. A man walked up to me. I recognized him. He was at Main Street Burgers earlier today. He was still wearing the Stauffer Law sweatshirt. But he had ditched the baseball hat. His curly blonde hair blew around in the wind.

He smiled. "Hey there, Jocelyn. Fancy meeting you here."

Startled, I looked at where I could run to but realized maybe that was premature. Still, my eyes scanned the parking lot for an exit strategy.

"Do I know you?" I asked.

He walked closer to me. "Not officially."

Was this the person in the silver car who followed me from Hermosa Beach? Did that explain why he was at the burger place and now in Long Beach? I didn't see any silver sports cars, but that meant nothing. He could've parked out of sight.

"But you know my name."

In one move, the man was on top of me. He

pushed me into the rearview mirror, pinning me to my vehicle. "Yep. I know your name, Jocelyn."

I needed to run. I used all my force to push him away, to get some space that I could slip through. But he was too strong. He yanked my arms and slammed me back against the car.

Then, he pulled a gun from his waistband. "Let's talk. In your car. I'm Barry Corcoran, by the way."

CHAPTER 79

I didn't know who Barry Corcoran was or what he wanted from me. I looked around the strip mall. No one was around. It wasn't a good idea to follow Barry's orders, but I also didn't want to get shot in broad daylight. "Why are you doing this?"

Barry stuck the gun into my ribs. "Get in the driver's seat."

I took one last look around and then got into my car.

Barry slipped into the passenger seat and stuck out a hand. "Where's that paper you had?"

"Huh?"

He made a grabbing motion with his hand. "The paper you were holding in the parking lot."

"It's in my pocket."

"Well, get it."

I pulled out the paper. Barry snatched it from me.

"What do you want?"

"You know."

I shook my head. "No. I don't."

"Well, you noticed me following you, right?"

"Maybe."

Barry smiled. "Yeah, you did. Went to the police and everything, huh?"

I frowned. "What would you do if someone was following you?"

"Hey, it's a great idea. But it was my bad for getting too close on your way back from Hermosa Beach. What did you tell the cops?"

"Nothing."

"All right. Don't tell me. But nobody goes into a police station and tells them nothing."

"Just that a silver car was following me, that's all. I didn't have anything else."

"Until Santa Monica."

"What?"

"Yeah, you walked up to that silver car in Santa Monica. Took down the plate number and everything, right?"

My skin tingled. Barry had been close enough to see what I was doing.

Barry laughed. "Too bad for you that wasn't my car."

Barry kept the gun on me while looking at my list of addresses. "What is all this?"

I didn't respond

He tapped the paper with his gun. "You're here. In Long Beach."

I scanned the parking lot. No one was out. Not one patron. Someone had to come out at some point, right?

"Answer me."

I turned to him, but I didn't know what he had asked. "Huh?"

"The addresses. What's up with them?"

What should I say? I pleaded ignorance. "I don't know."

"You don't know? You're going to tell me you don't know?" He pushed the gun into my shoulder. "Tell me what's up."

"I'm searching for someone."

Barry pulled the gun from my shoulder. "Len?"

"Yes."

"Well, I don't give a shit about him. But I am looking for something. And it's related. Where are you going next? San Pedro?"

What should I say? I needed to buy myself some time to find a way out of this. Maybe continuing my conversation with Barry was the way to do that. "Yes."

"Then we'll go there together."

I didn't want to go anywhere with Barry. "Just tell me what you want."

"None of your business."

"Then how can I help you?"

"You can't."

None of this made any sense. I felt like I had lapsed into my recurring Adam Davis nightmare. "Then why bring me along?"

"You're going to lead me to it."

"To what?"

"Stop asking questions. Let's roll."

I made one final furtive look around the strip

mall. I still didn't see anyone. Just a lot of empty cars. Even if someone came out right now, would anyone know I was in distress? Who was I kidding? Barry had moved the gun lower, pointing it at my hip. The gun wasn't visible to anyone outside. From the looks of things, Barry and I were a couple in a car. No one was going to help. I was on my own.

Barry rapped his knuckles on the dashboard. "Let's get a move on."

"To San Pedro?"

Barry let out an exasperated sigh. "Yes, ma'am, that's what I've been saying."

I didn't know what to do. At a loss for a clever escape plan, I put the San Pedro address into my GPS and reversed. A black car zoomed up behind me, probably hoping to take my space. But the car had come so close, it was basically riding my ass, barely giving me enough space to get out.

Barry turned to me. "Let's go. We don't have all day."

"I'm trying. There's a car behind me."

Barry twisted to look behind us. He flipped the person off.

Before I knew it, Barry and I were heading to the 710 freeway, which would take us to San Pedro.

CHAPTER 80

We drove for about five minutes. In that time, Barry appeared to relax a bit, so I asked a couple of questions. "How did you find me, and why did you decide to follow me?"

"You were at Tony's house when Doug was there. I was hanging back, seeing what Doug could find out. I've been following you ever since. You're going to take me where I need to be."

"Where's that? And how do you know I can lead you there?"

Barry lifted himself in his seat and pulled out his cell phone. "Just drive, will you? Oh yeah, how was your burger today? Mine was awesome. I didn't know that place existed. Nice choice."

He punched in a number. I could hear it ringing, but no one answered. Then, an automated voicemail picked up. Barry closed the phone. "Where is he?"

According to my GPS, we didn't have far to go. And, even though it was getting close to rush hour, traffic wasn't bad. We cruised at a pace that was too fast to allow me to try anything to escape. Once we exited the freeway, I had to figure something out. For now, there were no good options.

Barry shifted in his seat. "You know who Mikey is, right? He's been staying at his uncle's place, where you live. Well, Mikey and I go way back."

I focused on driving. A red truck was weaving in and out of lanes, nearly sideswiping other cars as it sped past. I kept my foot hovering over the brake in case the erratic driver caused an accident.

Barry tapped a hand on the dashboard. "What? You have nothing to say."

I had been concentrating so much on the red truck that I had spaced out whatever Barry had just said. Had he asked me a question? Made a statement?

"Yeah," I said, though I wasn't sure the response would work.

"Yeah, what?"

"Whatever."

"I was telling you how Mikey and I go way back."

The red truck was still bobbing and weaving, but so far, all the other drivers had avoided getting hit. The car was distracting me, and I wondered how Barry hadn't noticed it. "What do you want me to say?"

"Okay, my bad. That's more of a statement. You know Mikey Miles, right?"

"Yes."

"Well, we're friends. Or we were before he did his stint. But now he's out, and he's being a real dick; I don't even know how I was ever friends with him.

He seems to have forgotten that I helped him out all those years ago."

"What'd you help him with?"

"That's not important. And you know what the worst part is? Mikey tried to murder my ass. In my own garage. Have you ever heard of such a thing?"

I thought about what Barry was telling me, and an uneasy feeling grew in my stomach. Doug was dead. Mikey tried to kill Barry. So what hope was there for Len? Was he already gone? Had he been dead since Sunday?

Barry grabbed his phone again and made another call. It seemed to be the same number, as I heard the same voicemail pick up. This time, he left a message. "Yo, Doug, it's me. I'm with the solution to our problem. Hit me back."

"You're looking for Doug?" I asked.

"Yeah, what about him?"

I ran my hands around the steering wheel. "Doug's dead."

Barry shook his head. "No, he's not."

"Yes, he is."

I could feel Barry staring at me, trying to decide if I was messing with him and this was all some sort of ploy.

"He can't be. I just talked to him."

"When?"

"Yesterday."

"Well, he's dead. In Len's apartment. I'm sure the cops are there by now."

Barry tossed the cell phone like it was hot. It

landed on the floor. He laughed, a nervous laugh. "Dead? Doug? And I'm calling his phone? Shit."

"Yep."

Barry leaned down and grabbed the phone. "I gotta turn this fucker off. They can't trace this thing if it's off, right?

"I don't know."

"Man, I didn't think Mikey'd try that with Doug. Me, yeah, I get it. He thinks I'm weak. But Doug? That son of a bitch. Well, I'm definitely gonna get my share. And I'm getting Doug's share too."

"Share of what?"

"Scrilla."

The red truck was now gone. We had made it through unscathed. "Huh?"

"That means cash."

Was it possible that Barry was Mikey's other accomplice? "Like from a bank robbery?"

"Great guess. Are you psychic or what?"

CHAPTER 81

We continued our drive to San Pedro and my mind raced. I had a zillion different thoughts, and I still didn't know how to get out of this situation.

Barry had been relaxed earlier, but that was long gone. Ever since he found out Doug was dead, he had been agitated.

I wasn't a person who could sweet talk my way out of things, especially not sticky situations. But I figured it was worth a try. Maybe Barry was prone to flattery. "Nice sweatshirt."

He snapped his head toward me. "What?"

"Your Stauffer sweatshirt. I'm wearing one too. Did you go there?"

Barry tilted his head, but he said nothing. I didn't think what I was saying was confusing, but I would try to clarify. "Did you go to Stauffer Law School?"

Barry laughed. "I went there."

"That must've been difficult."

"Slow your roll. It was only for a year."

"What happened?"

"You want me to be honest? It was hard as shit.

But do you know what I told everyone? My real passion was to work in finance."

"You can always go back. I'm sure you're smart enough—"

Barry put up a hand and laughed again. "Don't even finish that thought. You were going to say 'if I put my mind to it,' right? That's a good one."

Obviously, Barry wasn't easily flattered. But as long as he was talking, I would try to keep the conversation going. In the least, he wasn't shooting at me. At most, it was an opportunity to see if I could find out more about his plan. "How did someone who went to law school get mixed up with someone like Mikey?"

"Please, stop, seriously. I see what you're doing. I'll humor you anyway. Mikey was fun to hang out with, you know? Different from most people I grew up with. I don't know how he talked me into helping rob those banks. I didn't care about the money. I still don't. But Mikey tried to kill me, so you know what, fuck him. I'm taking my cut."

"Sounds like you have it all figured out. You don't need me."

"Well, you're trying to find Len."

"How do you know that?"

"Excuse me, I was talking." Barry sighed. "Where was I? Oh yeah, so I figured that Mikey wasn't keeping the money at the old man's place, because that would be too obvious. I just didn't know where. I knew you'd get me there."

I noticed that traffic was slowing down a little.

There were more cars, and my speedometer said we were going around forty miles per hour. "You couldn't have possibly known I would take you to the money. Wouldn't it have been easier just to follow Mikey?"

Barry shook his head. "Too big of a risk. Mikey thinks I'm dead, and I want to keep it that way. He knows my car and would recognize me right away, which would spoil the surprise. You'll be a nice diversion while I get the drop on him."

"I still don't get why you'd follow me. You said you saw me at Tony's house? You could've followed either of them. Tony or Doug."

"Well, Doug and I have the same goal and are working together, so that would be silly. As far as Tony goes, Doug went to Tony's house to get him to tell us where Mikey was keeping the money. When Doug caught up to him, he roughed him up a bit and searched his van, but he found nothing. He even went to Tony's house before the kid got back and tore the place apart. Still nothing. Doug decided it was best to go straight to Mikey. While he did that, I figured it didn't hurt to see if you, or that guy you were with, might know something."

I figured Barry was talking about Jeff. "You mean the friend I was with at Tony's?"

"Yeah. I wasn't sure who to follow, but I stayed on you, after you dropped the guy off. I saw you lived in Len's building. Bingo. I knew you were the one."

"I still don't understand. Why me?"

"Huh?"

None of this made much sense. "I mean, there must be more to it than that. What is it?"

My GPS alerted me we had reached our exit off the 710 freeway, and my stomach filled with butterflies.

Barry leaned forward to look at the GPS. "We're almost there."

I glanced in the rearview mirror as though I expected to see someone behind me who would save me from this mess. But I was out of luck.

I took the exit and made a left, as the GPS instructed. After a while, it told me to turn again. Before I knew it, we were in a residential area.

We approached the house. The address in San Pedro was a one-story duplex with a fresh coat of dark blue paint, a green, cut lawn, and a smoothly paved driveway. A For Lease sign was in the yard.

Barry waved his gun, using it as a pointer to show where he wanted me to go. "Park on the left side."

I pulled into the driveway and put the car in park. I looked up and down the street, thinking about how I might run for it. That's when a red Jeep pulled up next to me.

Jessica Cecil hopped out of the driver's seat a few seconds later.

CHAPTER 82

Jessica had a large purse and carried several brown bags with cartoon tacos all over them. She wore low-slung jeans, a black tube top, large silver hoop earrings and tall wedge sandals. Her hair was pulled high and tight into a ponytail.

Mary Watts was correct; Jessica was involved somehow.

"Come on," Barry said. "Get out of the car. Let's get inside."

We exited the car, and Barry ran to the driver's side and grabbed my arm. Barry was wearing what looked like bright white designer court shoes.

Barry kept his gun directed at me. But he didn't ask me for my keys. I slipped them into my front pocket without him noticing.

Jessica pointed at me. "What's she doing here? She's a cop, you know. She came to my house and asked about Len. Got my mom on my case."

I wanted to tell Jessica that I wasn't a cop, and her mom knew that because I had given Candy my business card. Oh well, what did it matter? Let her think I was a cop for all I cared.

Barry laughed. "She's not a cop."

Jessica adjusted her ponytail. "How do you know?"

"Give me a break. While you're at it, open the door."

Jessica stared at Barry, and then she looked at the gun. She froze.

Barry jerked his head toward the house. "Let's go. I mean, like five minutes ago. We need to get inside, not stand around looking like jackasses."

Jessica pointed to the gun and gripped the paper bags in her hand. "Why do you have that?"

Barry exhaled and shook his head. "Is Mikey here?"

Jessica adjusted the purse on her shoulder. "He's running errands. But he'll be back soon. He won't like this."

She said it in a tone that implied Barry shouldn't try anything. Well, too late for that.

Jessica put a key in the lock and then turned around and pointed at me. "But why is she here?"

"Get inside."

Jessica shook her head and her ponytail swished. "Mikey won't like this."

"You already said that. And for what it's worth, I don't give a shit."

Jessica looked like she knew something was wrong. Yet she unlocked the door.

Barry squeezed my arm tighter. "Let's go."

Jessica looked at Barry. "But…"

Barry jutted out his chin. "What?"

Jessica lowered her head. "Nothing."

Barry nodded and smiled. "That's what I thought."

Jessica pushed open the door. We entered a furnished, renovated half of a duplex. The entryway opened to an expansive living room with an overstuffed L-shaped sofa, a coffee table, and a large TV. The dining room had a four-seater table. The kitchen was off to the left and was open and airy.

The place was clean, and almost nothing was on the counters or tables. The floors were polished hardwood, and I could swear I smelled fresh paint.

By the living room's window was a Christmas tree. A real one. It had all white lights and red bows. I wondered who had bought and decorated it.

"Yo, we're here," Barry said. "Come out, come out, wherever you are."

Who was Barry calling to? His voice was light like we were all friends gathered to hang out and eat the tacos Jessica had picked up.

The TV was playing a dating reality show. It was one I recognized, but the name eluded me.

"Yo," Barry said. "We're here."

A shaggy blonde head popped up from the sofa. It was Tony from Sherman Oaks.

CHAPTER 83

Tony got up from the couch and shuffled toward us. He looked like a deer caught in headlights. One thing that was new was a large green bruise under his left eye.

The last time I saw Tony, Doug was in hot pursuit, chasing Tony down a residential street in Sherman Oaks. Now Tony was here. In San Pedro. And Doug was dead in Len's apartment.

Tony was wearing a black hooded sweatshirt, baggy jeans, and Adidas sneakers.

Barry pointed to me. "Tie her up, Tony."

Tony's eyes flashed between Barry and the front door. He looked like he wanted to bolt, but he didn't. He turned to Jessica and stared daggers at her. "Why'd you let them in?"

She looked embarrassed. "Barry made me."

Tony looked like he still didn't know what to think of this whole situation.

"I told you to tie her up," Barry said.

Tony threw up his hands. "With what, dude? We got nothing."

"There's got to be something."

Tony sighed and stomped down the hall. I stood frozen next to Barry, while he gripped my arm. I had to figure a way out of here.

Tony returned, carrying thick twine. He marched into the kitchen and came back with a pair of scissors. He grabbed a chair from the kitchen and put it next to the sofa. The chair was solid wood with a high, tall back.

Barry walked me over to the chair and pushed me into it. I was facing the television. Tony grabbed my hands, pulled them behind the back of the chair, and tied them.

Barry inspected Tony's work. "Not too bad for having nothing around."

Tony rolled his eyes. "What's up, dude. Why are you here?"

Barry squinted. "I'm here for my cut. Then I'm gone. *Hasta luego*."

Tony pointed to me. "I know her. Why's she here?"

"She helped me find the place."

"She your girlfriend or something?"

"No, man. If Jocelyn was my girlfriend, I wouldn't tie her up, would I?"

"I don't know. You guys look like twins in those sweatshirts."

Barry laughed. "I guess we are."

Tony's shaggy hair fell into his eyes. "Look, I don't wanna be involved with any of your weird shit."

"Don't worry about it."

Tony frowned. "Mikey'll be back soon."

"Yeah, I know. Jessica already told me."

"Well, he's not going to like this."

"I'll tell you the same thing I said to Jessica. I don't give a shit. I want my share. You got that?"

I thought Tony's eyes might spring from his head. "From Century City? What are you on? We don't have that here."

"I'm dead fucking serious, man. You've got to have something around, even if it isn't from Century City. I'm entitled to my share. Where is it? And don't make me beat it out of you."

Tony nodded at Jessica. "Go ahead."

Jessica shook her head. "No. We should wait until Mikey gets here."

Barry looked at Jessica. "No, ma'am. No can do. I know you've got cash. Where is it?"

Jessica had a defiant look on her face. "In my car. What's it matter?"

Barry's eyes got big. "You've been driving around L.A. with a bunch of cash in your car? Do you have a death wish or what? Someone will jack you for that, and you'll be lucky if they don't kill you."

Jessica huffed. "Mikey asked me to. After what happened."

Barry glanced from Tony to Jessica. He looked confused. "What happened?"

Tony looked at Barry. "After Doug came to my house."

Barry waved his hand at Jessica like he was a teacher dismissing a pupil from class. "Go get it. Now."

Jessica clomped out of the house. Her wedge shoes on the hardwood floor made her sound like a Clydesdale. A minute later, she came back inside with a duffel bag.

Jessica slung the bag onto the kitchen table and glanced in my direction. She looked at me like she didn't want me to see what was in the bag, even though I already knew it was money.

"What about her?" Jessica asked and nodded in my direction.

"Don't worry about her. How much is there?" Barry asked.

Jessica's mouth fell open. "It's been like thirty seconds. I haven't even started counting. Jeez."

Tony plopped onto the couch, ran a hand through his unruly hair, and crossed his arms.

Jessica took her hands off the bag. "Can we eat first?"

Barry shook his head. "Count first. Eat later."

Jessica exhaled noisily.

Barry came over to the table and grabbed the bag. "You see this? This is all I want you to worry about. Count. The. Dough. And you better not even think about holding out on me."

Jessica unzipped the bag and started pulling out stacks of cash. "We're done with this, right? After what happened?"

Barry frowned. "Done with what?"

"Shut up, Jessica," Tony said.

Barry turned to Jessica. "What happened?"

Jessica's cheeks flushed pink. "Nothing."

Barry walked over to the couch, blocking Tony's TV view. "What's she talking about?"

Tony leaned to the side, trying to look around Barry. "Nothing."

Barry shifted, continuing to block Tony's view. "You better tell me."

Tony looked up at him. "Or what?"

Barry stooped down. "Or I'll kick your ass."

"Whatever," Tony said. His voice lacked enthusiasm.

Barry stepped back and kept his eyes on Tony. "What's Jessica talking about?"

Tony's hair fell into his eyes. "Just this thing that we're doing with Mikey."

"What thing?"

"A bank thing."

Barry frowned. "Are you guys crazy?"

Jessica threw her hands on her hips. "It's not a bad idea."

Barry spun around. "Robbing banks is not a bad idea? Mikey didn't even lay low for a month?"

"We don't rob the banks," Jessica said. "We get some idiot to do it for us. Except this last guy, he just got popped by the police."

CHAPTER 84

Barry paced the living room. He gripped his gun but kept it at his side. "What guy got popped?"

Tony sat forward on the sofa and slapped his hands on his thighs. "First off, dude, why do you have a gun out?"

"Tell me about this guy at the bank."

Tony folded his arms. "Mikey puts an ad online. He gets someone to go to the bank for him. This person thinks he's just withdrawing money for some old geezer. Then, Mikey gets on the phone with the teller and demands all the money. It worked the first time. The second time, not so much."

"And this guy got arrested?" Barry asked.

"Yeah, we heard the whole thing," Jessica said.

Barry turned to Jessica. "How did you hear it?"

Jessica continued pulling cash from the bag. "Mikey got tied up with some stuff, so he had the guy call Tony instead. Well, he got arrested. He never disconnected the call and we heard everything."

"And this guy who got arrested, he knows who you are?"

She shook her head. "No."

"But he has Tony's number?"

Jessica paused, cash in hand. "It was a disposable. A burner. You know, the kind you throw away when you don't want it anymore."

"Did you get rid of it?"

Tony rubbed his face. "Duh, we're not stupid."

Barry started pacing again. "All right, well, you need to hurry the fuck up and get me my money."

Jessica pointed to the bags of food sitting on the table next to the duffel bag. "But I'm hungry. And our food is getting cold. I don't want to eat soggy tacos."

Jessica, Tony, and Barry weren't paying attention to me, so I began working to loosen my hands. So far, it didn't feel like the ties had much give. It was going to be more difficult than I thought.

Barry walked over to the table. "You need to be told a million times? Count the money. Then you can eat. I need to get out of here. The police may end up finding you two here. And I'm not getting caught up in this."

Jessica looked scared. "What do you mean? Do you think we'll get in trouble?"

"What did you think?" Barry asked. "That you wouldn't get arrested because you weren't at the bank?"

Jessica's eyes filled with tears. "We just helped. You helped Mikey before. And you never went to jail."

Barry shook his head. "That was different."

Jessica blinked several times. Two tears escaped.

"How so?"

Barry waved his hand around. "Just count it. Get a move on. Now."

Jessica flipped through the bag, and she stopped crying. "Seriously, let's wait for Mikey. He can tell you how much you're supposed to get. He'll be mad if I don't do it right."

"I'll tell you what I'm owed. But I want to know how much you have first."

Tony looked up from the couch. "You know Doug's been asking for his money too."

Barry laughed. "You're behind on the news, man. Doug's dead. Murdered. I'm taking his cut too."

Jessica froze. "What?"

Barry pointed at me. "That's what Jocelyn said."

Jessica whipped her head to look at me. She narrowed her eyes. "I don't believe you."

I looked at Jessica. "It's true."

Jessica ran over to the couch, plopped down next to Tony, and tugged on his sweatshirt sleeve. "Did you hear that? Doug's dead."

"I heard, I heard. I'm in the same room, for crying out loud. He's not dead."

Barry again pointed at me. "You heard her."

Jessica popped off the couch and stood next to me, her hands on her hips. "Is it true?"

I nodded. "Doug was killed in my apartment building." While I had Jessica's attention, I figured I'd ask the most important question. "Is Len here?"

Jessica froze. "What did you say?"

"Len Zobak. Is he here?"

Jessica's mouth dropped open, and she looked at Tony. "Did you hear what she asked?"

The front door opened. Mikey walked into the house.

CHAPTER 85

Mikey closed the door, looking confused. He wore his lumberjack flannel, unbuttoned, with a white T-shirt, jeans, and the same worn-out work boots. His right sleeve was rolled up, and there was a cast on his wrist.

Barry raised his gun to Mikey. Mikey held up his hands. His eyes were wide and glued to Barry.

Barry alternated the gun among the three. "Jessica and Tony, you guys get on the couch. Mikey, stay where you are."

Jessica scurried to sit on the couch next to Tony.

Barry stood a few feet back from the sofa. He smiled a big smile, one that looked like he was relishing this moment. He turned toward Mikey. "Nice chokehold, bitch. I see your dumbass found your keys. I guess you didn't take five seconds to check that I was dead, huh?"

Mikey lowered his hands. "Put the gun down, would you?"

Barry looked incredulous. "You're just gonna ignore the fact that I'm standing in front of you?

Alive. After you tried to kill me?"

Mikey shrugged. "What do you want from me?"

Barry stepped closer to Mikey. "It'd be nice to have an explanation as to why my old friend tried to strangle me in my garage."

Mikey had no expression on his face. "You might've talked."

"Fuck you. I kept quiet all these years. Why would I talk now?"

"It wasn't personal, man."

Barry smirked. "Yeah, okay, sure."

"How did you find this place?"

"Let's just say it was a person in this room."

Tony jumped up from the couch. "It wasn't me. I never told anyone where we were!"

Barry kept the gun on Mikey but turned to Tony. "Sit down."

Tony crossed his arms and did as he was told. "It's true. Even after that fucker Doug chased me all the way to Tarzana. Gave me this bruise on my face that keeps getting bigger! Went through my car. Accused me of having money in my backpack. It was just clothes! I still didn't say anything, I swear!"

Mikey looked at Tony. "You're not helping."

Barry aimed the gun at Mikey. "Enough reminiscing. Time to pay up."

Mikey looked confused. "What are you talking about?"

"My money. I want it."

Mikey rubbed his eyes. "I thought you had some sweet finance job. Why do you give a shit about the money?"

Barry smiled. "It's the principle of the matter. You understand. It's not personal."

"I don't have it."

"You have money." Barry pointed to the table. "See that bag there?"

Mikey glared at Jessica.

Jessica spoke up. "Did you know Doug is dead?"

Barry looked at Jessica and when he did, Mikey inched closer to Barry. It was so subtle I almost didn't notice it.

Jessica frowned. "Hello? Earth to Mikey. I said Doug's dead."

Mikey nodded. "I already know."

Even though Barry had the gun aimed at Mikey, he was staring at Jessica and Tony. Mikey crept closer to Barry, but Barry still didn't notice.

Barry looked back at Mikey and smiled. "And you killed him, right?"

Jessica and Tony stared at Mikey, waiting for his response.

Mikey lifted his hands. "Come on, Barry. Can we talk about this? I'll get you your money. You're right. You're owed that. For your silence and all."

Barry looked like he was considering Mikey's proposal.

Mikey lunged forward and grabbed Barry's wrist, the one that held the gun. Barry let out a surprised yell and yanked his arm back. Mikey brought his arm with the cast down *hard* on Barry's hand. Barry released the gun, and it landed with a thud. It skidded across the floor and came to rest under the couch.

Mikey yanked his head in Tony's direction. "Tony, get that! Don't let him get it back."

Barry charged Mikey, pushing him into the Christmas tree. Barry shoved Mikey until he tackled him to the ground. The Christmas tree fell over, branches swishing.

Jessica screamed, scrambled up from the couch, and sprinted out the back door.

Barry was on top of Mikey, slamming the injured wrist onto the floor. I could hear a loud thumping each time the cast landed on the ground.

Mikey yelled in pain. With his good arm, he grabbed Barry's throat.

Tony stared at what was happening, then ducked to the floor, reached under the couch, and grabbed Barry's gun. He held it, looking uncertain about what to do.

Mikey yelled at Tony. "Shoot the fucker, what are you waiting for?"

Tony's body flinched. "No dude, that's crazy!"

"Then give it to me. I'll do it."

Tony shook his head. "I'm not doing that."

Tony set the gun on the coffee table, pushed up his sleeves, and dashed over to Barry and Mikey. Tony put his arm around Barry's neck in a chokehold. Mikey took his good hand off Barry's throat and began punching him in the face. I watched the mix of arms and legs of Mikey, Barry, and Tony. All three scrambled to secure a dominant position.

Suddenly, Barry groaned and stopped moving. That's when I saw it. Blood. A lot of blood.

CHAPTER 86

I closed my eyes and tried to forget what I had just seen. But it was too late; I felt like I might faint in my chair. I took a few deep breaths, calming myself. I did not want to pass out. I had to stay alert and figure a way out of this.

I opened my eyes. Mikey rocked back on his heels and rubbed his forehead. His face was streaked with blood, and so were his clothes. He held a knife in his hand. It was covered in blood.

Barry twitched and blood pooled around him. He wasn't dead, but he was on his way. This time, I felt Mikey would leave nothing to chance.

Jessica was still outside somewhere. She had escaped before the bleeding started.

Tony looked dazed. He stood, staring at Barry, bobbing like he was trying to keep his balance.

Mikey stood up and slugged Tony in the shoulder. "Hey."

Tony stayed frozen, just staring at Barry, his head still bobbing.

Mikey punched Tony again. "Do you hear me or

what?"

This time, Tony jerked. He grabbed his arm and then snapped his head toward Mikey. "Why'd you do that, dude?"

"You wanna go to prison?"

"What? Barry just wanted money. You could've just given it to him."

"Nope."

Tony was shaking. He had blood spots on his face and jeans. Because he wore a black sweatshirt, I couldn't see blood on it, although I presumed there was.

Mikey threw the knife toward the ground. It landed and stuck into the wood floor. "We gotta get rid of him."

Tony wiped his hands on his jeans. "Huh?"

"We can't leave him here."

"Where are you going to put him?"

Mikey jerked his head toward the back of the house. "Out there."

"How are we going to do that?"

Mikey looked at him like it was the most obvious thing in the world. "Carry him outside. How else?"

"No way. I'm not doing that."

Mikey kneeled to Barry's now-still body and grabbed Barry's ankle with his one working hand. The designer shoes were no longer bright white. "Shut up and grab his arms."

Tony shook his head. "No way. I didn't sign up for this."

"What did you think, it would all be puppies and

rainbows?"

Tony continued shaking his head, this time harder. "Damn it."

Tony grabbed Barry's arms. He and Mikey yanked and pushed Barry across the hardwood floors toward the back door. It was slow going, with Mikey only able to use one arm. Barry's body created a streak of blood as they towed it out of the living room.

The realization of just how terrible of a situation I was in slammed into me. I had witnessed Barry's murder. I could identify all of them: Mikey, Jessica, and Tony. And I knew Mikey would not let me leave here alive. If I didn't do something, I would end up like Barry, my lifeless body being dragged across the floor.

Jessica peeked into the house, saw Barry and the blood, and screamed. She ran back outside. Tony and Mikey shoved Barry over the back threshold.

It was just me. Alone in the house. I had to get out of here.

CHAPTER 87

I assessed the situation. I was tied up in the living room. My car was in the driveway. My keys were in my pocket. If I could make it to the front door, I would have a chance to escape.

Despite my hands being tied tight behind my back, I could tilt forward in the chair and walk with baby steps. The front door seemed miles away. But I had to try. I had a small window of time while Tony and Mikey dealt with Barry. Every second counted.

With the chair stuck on my back, I started moving. I inched my way across the floor. The chair wasn't that heavy, but it was solid and had no give. The wood dug into my spine, making each step painful. The twine was rough and tied so tight that it cut into my skin. But those were the least of my worries.

Slow and steady, I was making progress. I was halfway across the living room. The TV was still on, and although the volume wasn't high, it sounded loud. Two people on the show were arguing, and it was grating on my nerves. Overall, the sound was a good thing. It helped muffle any noise I was making.

Before I knew it, I had made it past the sofa. Barry's blood was on the floor, making me queasy. My mouth watered like it did right before throwing up. I swallowed several times, trying to focus on the front door and pushing the image of Barry's lifeless, bloody body out of my mind.

I twisted my head as far as I could turn, to check behind me to see if anyone had entered the house. Neither Mikey, Jessica, nor Tony had come back inside. Despite the TV muffling the noise I made while huffing it across the room, the closer I got to the front door, the more thunderous each step sounded. Like I was a five-ton elephant clambering through the Serengeti. Yet I continued.

I passed the kitchen and was almost to the entryway. I hoped I could make it there, but I didn't know how to open the door. The ties were still tight.

After a few more steps, I was at the front door. My heart raced. I was close to being free. My car was just steps away.

I turned the chair to the side and tried to lift it, so my hands were at the same level as the door. I leaned toward the door and tried to grab the knob with my hands.

I heard the back door open. *Shit.*

Then, a voice and shoes stomping toward me. "Hey!"

It was Jessica. But not Mikey or Tony. I figured I could escape if it was just her, so I needed to keep trying. I leaned into the door again, but this time, I missed the knob and all I did was bump into it.

Jessica's wedges pounded on the floor as she ran toward the back door. I heard it open. "Help! Jocelyn's getting away!"

The back door slammed shut, then a few seconds later, opened again. Heavy footsteps ran toward me. I knew I wouldn't make it, but I tried one last time to reach the knob.

Tony tackled me. We crashed to the ground, my shoulder slamming hard into the floor.

A second later, Mikey pulled me up. "Not so fast, Jocelyn."

Tony and Mikey lifted me, chair and all, and placed me in the same spot in the living room.

I was back to where I'd started from and no closer to escaping.

CHAPTER 88

Mikey's cheeks were streaked red, like he'd tried to wipe his face but only smeared everything around. He stripped off the lumberjack shirt, and his white T-shirt had a massive bloom of wet blood. His jeans were spotted with blood too, and his cast was streaked, making it look like an abstract painting.

Because he had carried me over to the living room, his chest had pressed against my shoulder. I turned to look. Barry's blood was smeared all over my Stauffer sweatshirt. It was my favorite sweatshirt but one that had seen better days.

The sight of the blood made my mouth water all over again. I could feel the vomit wanting to come up, so I closed my eyes and took several deep breaths. I pushed the sensation away, but I wondered how many more times I could do that.

Mikey walked over to me, and my stomach flipped. "Well, Jocelyn, here we are again. Are you going to tell me where it is?"

"Where's what?"

"You know. It's not in your apartment. Or your

storage unit. I checked. Tell me where it is."

I was right; Mikey was the one who was in my apartment, and he was also the one who cut the lock on my storage unit. But what did confirmation of this matter? I was tied up in San Pedro, and my chances of getting away were looking slim. "Maybe tell me what you're looking for."

He laughed. "Like you don't know. My money. Just give it up. This will go a lot easier on you."

"Money? I don't have your money. Seriously. I have no clue what you're talking about."

Mikey tilted his head. "This isn't over." Then he looked at Jessica and Tony. "You guys watch her. Make sure she doesn't get away. And clean up this mess. I need to shower. When I'm done, we're out of here."

Jessica and Tony fired off a series of questions to Mikey.

What about Barry?

You're just going to leave his body out back?

And what about Jocelyn?

What do we do with her?

Where will we go?

What do we do?

What do we take?

Do you have a plan?

Mikey threw up his good hand. "Enough! I'm taking a shower. When I get out, I want this mess cleaned up. Thirty minutes. We're gone. You got that?"

Mikey walked into the kitchen. Seconds later,

he held a black garbage bag and a smaller plastic grocery bag. "We got any rubber bands?"

Tony stared at him like it was a strange request. "I don't know, why?"

Mikey held up his cast, which was streaked with Barry's blood. "Because I can't get this wet is why." He shook his head. "Ahh, fuck it."

Jessica stared at the blood trail on the hardwood floor. "This is disgusting. I'm not cleaning this up."

Mikey glared at her. "Everyone has to do their fair share. Get to it."

Then, Mikey walked down the hall. A door slammed.

Jessica stood with her hands behind her back, looking at Tony. "Well?"

Tony diverted his eyes from her. "Well, what?"

"You're going to listen to him?"

Tony sighed. "Just do it."

Jessica shook her head. "No way, are you kidding me? This will take hours, if not days. He said we're leaving in thirty minutes. Why even try?"

"Because he asked us to."

"Why are we taking orders from Mikey? The guy's been gone for ten years. He comes back and bosses us around like we're his servants. Who put him in charge?"

Tony sighed again. "You have a better plan?"

Jessica walked closer to Tony. "You can see that Mikey's losing it, right?"

Tony still didn't look at her. "He's just stressed out."

"Are you serious? He killed Barry like it was no big deal. And then he told us to clean up all the blood like it was our turn to do dishes after dinner or something. What the hell?"

"He had to do that."

Jessica grabbed Tony's shoulders and turned him to face her. "Kill Barry? Umm, no. He didn't. He could've given Barry the money. You know that's true."

"I dunno. Barry might've talked."

Jessica shook him. "No way, Tony. It's been forever. That was never going to happen. I'm telling you, he's losing it."

"Whatever."

Jessica stepped back. "We haven't even told him about Jared getting caught yet. He's really going to flip out then."

"What are you saying?"

"Isn't it obvious? He's going to try to kill us. Maybe we should kill him first."

CHAPTER 89

Tony went into the kitchen and returned with a roll of paper towels. "You're the one who's losing it now."

Jessica put her hands on her hips. "Why? You know I'm right. We need to kill him before he kills us."

Tony ripped off several sheets of paper towels and handed them to Jessica. "You couldn't even stand to look at Barry's body. How are you going to kill Mikey? We gotta start cleaning."

Jessica turned up her nose. "I'm not touching someone else's blood. Do you have any gloves?"

"You know we don't have any."

Jessica threw her hands in the air. "Then I'm not doing shit."

Tony threw the roll on the floor, stomped over to the couch, and sat down. Jessica frowned and sat next to Tony.

I didn't know how long it had been since Mikey went into the shower. I couldn't hear any water running, so there was no way to tell. Tony and Jessica were living dangerously. I wondered how to get out of this before their inevitable double murder.

Jessica looked relaxed, like she was just hanging out without a care in the world. "I just want to be done with this. I'm turning thirty next year, after all."

Tony looked at her. "We'll be okay. No matter what happens, I'll never rat you out. We're family. Okay?"

Were Tony and Jessica somehow related?

Jessica smiled. "I know. I won't rat you out either. We should've never gotten involved in all of this."

Tony rolled his eyes. "It's a little late now, don't you think?"

"I knew that guy was trouble the first time we met him."

"Yeah, right. You liked Mikey back then. Even had a crush on him. I know it."

Jessica blushed. "No, I didn't. But seriously, I don't want to go to jail."

"We're cool. Don't worry about it."

Jessica pushed herself up on the couch. "Maybe for the stuff in ninety-five, but what about this recent bank stuff with Mikey?" Jessica waved her hand. "Or, you know, like what just happened here. What about that?"

Tony seemed to shrink beneath his baggy sweatshirt. "I don't know."

"Barry said we could be in trouble."

"Knock it off, would you?"

Jessica turned to face Tony, putting a knee on the couch. "You've seen all the stuff Mikey has done since he's been here. I mean, this is now totally out of control. We should at least leave." She pointed to the duffel bag on the kitchen table. "We have money. My Jeep's in the driveway."

"We can't leave. We have to stay here," Tony said.

"But why?" Jessica asked.

In all this time, I hadn't spoken. It was like I was invisible, and Jessica and Tony were in their own world, reminiscing and rehashing their regrets.

What had Jessica been talking about? All the things Mikey had done? What else was there, and did any of it have to do with Len? More than ever, I needed to escape before I became the next corpse they dragged out back.

I cleared my throat. "Jessica's right, you know. You guys can just leave."

Jessica whipped her head around like I was a ghost who had just appeared. "What do you mean?"

I nodded toward the front door. "Like you already said. You can take the money. Your car's here. Why not just go?"

Tony shook his head. "Mikey'll find us."

"Not if you go somewhere he doesn't know about."

Jessica looked like she was considering it. She had already expressed an interest in bugging out. I was just giving her the nudge she needed.

But it was too late.

Mikey lumbered down the hall.

CHAPTER 90

Mikey came back into the room. His face was clean, but his cast looked like melting raspberry swirl ice cream. He was wearing a gray sweatshirt and sweatpants, and a pair of beat-up running shoes.

He held a black garbage bag. I wondered if it contained his bloody clothes. He threw the bag by the entryway, and it landed with a thud.

I sat back, defeated. Now what?

"Tony, I need your help," Mikey said. Then he looked around the house. "You guys haven't even started cleaning up this mess."

Jessica stood up from the couch. "It's unsafe to touch bodily fluids without gloves. And we don't have any. So I'm not doing it."

Mikey rolled his eyes. "Screw it." He went down the hall and came back with his arms filled with sheets. "At least set these on the floor. Otherwise, we're going to track blood all over the place."

Jessica grinned and crossed her arms like she had scored a victory. She walked over to Mikey and grabbed the sheets. She started laying them down where Barry had been killed and worked her way along the path that Mikey and Tony had dragged the body.

"Come on, Tony. Jessica, you watch Jocelyn and make sure she doesn't get loose."

Mikey and Tony went out the back door.

Jessica finished placing the sheets on the floor, then sat back on the couch and adjusted her ponytail. She grabbed the remote and flipped through the channels. She ended up right back on the reality TV show.

The sun was going down, and it was getting dark inside the house. Given the time of year, it had to be around five.

Was Mikey going to be out of here in less than thirty minutes? That meant time was running out for me.

"Jessica, did you consider what I said?"

Jessica swiveled her head like she had once again forgotten I was there. "You mean leaving?"

"Yeah, getting out of here before Mikey comes back. You have time."

"I don't know."

"You were considering it before."

Jessica played with her ponytail. "Yeah, well, where am I supposed to go?"

"There are lots of places."

"But I've only lived here. I don't know anyone anywhere else."

"You can always meet new people."

"I don't know."

I wasn't getting anywhere. Jessica seemed far more relaxed than before. I needed to bring her back to her earlier state of fear. "You don't think Mikey's going to kill you?"

"I'm not so sure anymore. I mean, we helped Mikey."

"What about Doug and Barry?"

Jessica waved her hand. "Those guys were loose ends. They were the lookouts in Mikey's other robberies. Doug was hounding Mikey for his money. Barry's dad's a lawyer, so Mikey was afraid of him."

"But he's not worried about you or Tony?"

"No, we were there for him while he was in prison."

"And you were a teller at the bank? In Century City?"

She looked at me. "How did you know that?"

"I just do."

Jessica leaped from the sofa. "I knew it. I knew you were a cop!"

CHAPTER 91

This again? I couldn't believe it. I shook my head. "I'm not. Ask your mom. She has my business card."

Jessica sat back down, almost instantly calm after her outburst. "I know. You say you're an accountant or something. That's what my mom said. But that doesn't mean you're not a cop. Undercover."

I did a little shrug, as best as I could, being tied up. "Fine, don't believe me. But what do you think about leaving? Think of the money. And you have your car. You're home free."

Jessica narrowed her eyes. "I don't know."

Maybe I could convince her she wasn't out of the woods, and it was in her best interest to leave and bring me along. "You don't want to go to jail, do you?"

"I'm not going to jail."

"You're an accessory to murder."

Jessica scrunched up her nose. "What? No, I'm not."

At last, it looked like I had said something that concerned her. "Yes, you are."

"But how? I didn't kill him."

"Well, that's why you're an accessory."

Jessica rubbed her face. "What do you mean?"

"You know Mikey murdered Barry. You saw him and Tony get rid of the body. Did you do anything? Did you try to help Barry? Did you call the police?"

"No."

"There you go. Accessory to murder. I think that will get you some heavy prison time."

Jessica's eyes widened as she processed what I was saying. She bit her nail. "They can put me in jail for that? For how long?"

I didn't know how long, but neither did Jessica and that was all that mattered. "I'd say twenty years."

She looked like she might cry. "Twenty years? Are you frigging serious? For not even doing anything?"

"And that doesn't even take into account the stuff you've just been doing with Mikey. Getting the people to rob the banks for you."

"What? That? No, they won't find us."

"If they do, that's more time. And of course…"

I trailed off, hoping she'd take the bait.

"And of course what?"

I knew that what I would tell her might be nonsense. But I was in a life-or-death situation, so I didn't give a crap if I gave her the wrong info. "Well, there's always a chance you could get in trouble for the robbery in ninety-five."

She shook her head. "No, too much time has passed. That I'm sure of."

"Well, either way, twenty years is no joke."

"You think that would happen? I would get that much time?"

"Oh yeah, at least. That's why you should leave. While you have the chance. Either that or call the cops."

Jessica rubbed her face again. "Where would I go? This is turning into such a nightmare."

"Well, your car's in the driveway. So is mine. We could leave. We can go anywhere. But we have to go now. Before Mikey and Tony get back."

"I can't leave Tony."

"You can always contact him later. And help him then."

"No, you don't understand. Tony's my cousin. His dad is my mom's brother. We're close. I can't do that to him."

"You're better off helping yourself and then coming back and helping Tony."

Jessica munched on her lips. She was thinking about it. "I don't know."

"Tony might not even want to leave, have you thought about that?"

She frowned. "He's just loyal to Mikey for some weird reason."

"Then you have to think about yourself right now."

She looked at me and nodded. Then, she stood up. "Okay."

I felt relieved. I just had to hope she'd untie me and take me with her.

She ran to the kitchen table and snatched the bag of cash.

That's when the back door opened.

Mikey and Tony entered the house. They were holding onto someone.

It was Len.

He was alive.

CHAPTER 92

Mikey walked Len the rest of the way into the living room. Tony grabbed another chair from the kitchen and placed it next to mine. He went down the hallway and returned with more twine.

Tony tied up Len in the same way he had tied me. Len and I were sitting next to each other. Len looked okay for having been in captivity for several days. A bit rumpled but uninjured, as far as I could tell.

I felt an enormous sense of relief. Len was alive. I almost couldn't believe it. Sure, I was tied up in this house in San Pedro, and I didn't know how I was getting out of here. But I had found Len.

Len and I turned our heads at the same time and looked at each other. Len smiled. Then, he rolled his eyes. I expected a more significant reaction, but maybe he already knew I was here. Or perhaps nothing surprised him anymore.

Mikey paced the room. "We need to make sure these two don't get away."

"Or you could let us go," Len said. "And end all this craziness."

"Shut up," Mikey said. "You keep saying that, but you haven't figured out that I'm not going to do that, right? I mean, you're still here, aren't you? Forget about it."

"There's no reason to involve Jocelyn. Let her go."

"For your information, I didn't bring her here. Barry did. But now that she's here, I can't just let her go."

"Mikey, Jocelyn's not involved."

"Yeah, right. You hid my money with her. That's what you were doing during your so-called business meeting. I want my money."

"I don't have your money," Len said.

Mikey scowled. "What about what you said in your letter? How money can't buy happiness."

"It's just an expression. I didn't mean anything by that."

Mikey ran a hand along his head. "Sure you didn't. Either way, I need that money. Just tell me where it is."

"I don't have it. Don't you think I would have given it to you by now? I've been here since Sunday. What would be the point of holding out?"

"You were writing checks to people. Handing out money like it's candy. I know where you got it."

"That's my money."

"Sure," Mikey said. "I left my money in the utility room at your Mayfield place. It's not there. Your dingbat of a manager let me in so I could check."

"Babette?"

"Yeah. And it's not there. I know that imbecile

didn't take it."

Len shook his head. "I've never found any money there. Why would I lie?"

"Because you're stubborn. Or maybe because you think I deserve to be in prison."

"I would still give you the money."

Jessica turned to Mikey, her eyes big. "Am I an accomplice? To Barry's murder?"

Mikey looked at Jessica. "Of course not."

Jessica looked at me and then at Mikey. "Jocelyn said I am."

My heart skipped a beat at Jessica's mention of my name.

"You're not."

"But how can you know for sure? Does that mean I could get arrested?"

Mikey scowled. "What are you talking about?"

Jessica pointed to me. "She said I could get twenty years. At least."

Mikey walked over to me. I felt a hot flash all over my body. The sudden attention from Mikey made my chest feel tight and restricted. I couldn't breathe.

He crouched down, so that his eyes were level with mine. His mouth was formed into a sneer. "What kind of nonsense are you telling her?"

My heart was racing. "It's nothing."

Mikey turned away, like he couldn't stand looking at me. He pushed himself up and glanced at Jessica. "There was always a chance you could get arrested. You knew that."

Jessica looked like this was the first time she had

heard any such thing. "No, you said we were in the clear."

"Yeah, for the stuff a long time ago."

"But for the stuff now? You said they couldn't touch us."

"I never told you that."

"Enough, Mikey," Len said. "What do you want? I don't have your money, but I will give you whatever you want to allow you to leave. Then you can let us go, and you can start a new life."

"Yeah, I'm getting out of here. But you're not."

"Whatever you want, Mikey, it's yours. I mean it."

Len spoke without a hint of desperation in his voice.

Mikey walked to the kitchen table, where the duffel bag of money was. "It's too late."

My heart was still racing. I tried to take deep breaths, but it wasn't helping. My chest still felt tight. But Len's relaxed demeanor, along with the fact that he wasn't panicking, gave me hope. Maybe he had a plan. Or an idea. *Something.*

Then again, he had been kidnapped since Sunday. If he had a plan, he had so far not executed it.

Mikey cracked his knuckles. "I'm getting packed. I'm leaving in fifteen minutes."

"But where will we go?" Jessica asked. "I don't want to leave Los Angeles."

"You can go wherever you want, but I'm not staying here. You remember that I'll find you if you snitch on me."

Tears slipped down Jessica's cheeks, but she said

nothing.

CHAPTER 93

Mikey left us tied to our chairs while he walked back down the hallway on his way to pack. Tony and Jessica were in the kitchen.

I could hear them grabbing items from the pantry. Possibly stocking up on food to take to their yet-unknown destination. If they were talking, I couldn't hear it.

I wanted to speak with Len, but I didn't want Jessica and Tony to overhear. The TV was still on, and I figured it was loud enough to muffle our voices so long as we whispered.

"I'm glad you're all right, Len."

"I'm sorry I brought you into this. How did you end up here?"

"It's a long story, but I was looking for you."

Len raised his eyebrows. "You've been trying to find me?"

"Yes, since you didn't make our meeting on Sunday."

"That's kind of you. Too much."

"You helped me."

"Mikey called me on Friday. I had a feeling he would try something like this once he was out of prison. You know…"

"That Mikey would kidnap you?"

"Yes. Or worse. And I wanted to make sure the checks got delivered, which was why I asked you to do that. Then I realized I couldn't ask such a thing of you. So I took them back. But Mikey, well, he showed up on Sunday. And he saw the checks and the letter to you. He believes I hid his money with you. I'm very sorry."

"It's okay. Do you know who Doug is?"

Len nodded. "One of Mikey's friends. He is also an accomplice, although he's never been caught."

"He's dead. In your apartment. Betty found him."

Len shook his head. "I can just imagine what's going on right now."

"The checks. You were going to give Tony and Jessica each one. Did you know they were involved?"

Len sighed. "No, I wish I had."

"Your check was for Tony, not his dad, Andy?"

"Yes, it was for Anthony Baker, so Tony. I wanted to help those wronged by Mikey. With Mikey getting out of jail and it being the holidays, I decided it was the right time to give some restitution."

"And you thought Jessica and Tony were victims?"

"Yes. But I was wrong. They were very much involved. I thought Jessica was an innocent bank teller and Tony was just some poor guy that Mikey forced to fill the bags with the stolen cash."

I nodded.

"I knew Mikey was in cahoots with Doug, the man you said is dead in my apartment. There was also Barry, who is now dead in a storage shed behind this house. But I never suspected Mikey had roped these young people into it too."

"You know Tara, right? She lives in your building?"

Len nodded. "Her name is actually Corinne."

"How did you know?"

"I recognized her. Almost right away."

I wondered what Tara would say if she knew she hadn't fooled Len. "She said she changed her appearance."

"Not much. But it doesn't matter."

"She's gone now. She asked me to give you a letter. And she said to search her storage locker."

Len smiled but said nothing.

"Mikey thinks you have his money?"

"I don't have it. I don't know where it is. It's not at my Mayfield property. I'm sure of that."

"He's not going to let us go."

"We'll see about that."

"I met your friend Jan," I said.

Len twisted toward me as much as his ties allowed. "You met Jan?"

"He was looking for you. You're supposed to give him a ride to the airport."

Len nodded. "Tonight. What did you tell him?"

"I told him that I was trying to find you."

"Jan knows I'm missing? Well, yes, of course, he

would know. Or he will when I never show up to take him to the airport."

"I told him about Mikey," I said.

Len's expression changed. It wasn't a smile, but something came over him, and his face relaxed even more. "You told Jan that Mikey had been to my apartment?"

"Yes."

"I think it's all going to be okay, Jocelyn. Wait and see."

I wished I could share Len's optimism. But I was worried that Mikey was going to kill us before he left. "We're running out of time. We need to do something."

"It'll be okay."

"How can you be sure?"

Just then, someone knocked on the front door.

CHAPTER 94

Tony popped his head out of the kitchen and yelled. "Yo, Mikey, you expecting someone?"

Mikey walked down the hallway. "What do you think, numbnuts?"

"Screw you, dude. I'm just trying to help," Tony said.

Mikey shook his head. "Turn that fuckin' TV off, would you? We don't need to advertise that we're here."

Jessica emerged from the kitchen. "Won't that make it even more obvious? They hear the TV, and then they don't?"

Mikey mimed pressing a remote. "Shut it off."

Jessica rolled her eyes but walked over and turned off the TV. Then, she sat down on the couch.

"What do we do?" Tony asked.

"Well, we don't answer the door, do we?" Jessica asked. "What if it's the cops? Will they break the door down?"

I looked at Len, but he stayed facing forward, so I couldn't see his expression. The shades in the house were all closed. No one could see in. But we also couldn't see out.

Mikey walked up to the door and pressed his face to the peephole. "Well, no one's there. Tony, make sure that the back door is locked."

Tony ran to the rear of the duplex and checked the door. "We're good."

"Thank goodness," Jessica said. "That freaked me out."

Tony was still standing by the back door when someone knocked on it. He froze.

Mikey glared at Len and me. "Both of you keep your mouths shut, you hear?"

Mikey stormed to the back of the house and peered out a nearby window.

Jessica flipped around on the sofa, her knees on the cushions and her elbows on the sofa's back. She peered expectantly at Mikey. "Who is it?"

"I don't know. I can't see."

Her eyes got big. She turned pale, and her skin looked slick with sweat. "What's going on?"

Mikey walked over to Len and me. "What's up?"

I didn't move or even look at Mikey.

Len cleared his throat. "Seems like you have a visitor."

"Yeah, no shit. But who is it?"

"How would I know, Mikey? I've been here since Sunday."

Mikey narrowed his eyes. Then, he looked at me. "Jocelyn, you know anything?"

"No," I said.

He grabbed my shoulders and shook me. "You sure?"

"Lay off, Mikey," Len said.

Mikey stepped back and stared at us for a while. But then he seemed to realize the knocking had stopped, and so he relaxed.

Jessica looked like a tiny, nervous dog. "What do we do?"

"We keep going as planned," Mikey said.

Tony frowned. "We don't have a plan. Except to leave. And you still haven't told us where we should go."

"Do I have to do everything for you? You can't think of a plan for yourself? Because prison will be your plan if you don't start using your brain."

Tony slid onto the couch and crossed his arms.

I heard another knock on the front door.

Mikey's eyes grew wide. "All right, I've had enough!"

He stomped to the front door and yanked it open.

CHAPTER 95

No one was on the other side of the door, and for whatever reason, I wasn't surprised. For a minute, I thought that maybe some teenagers were pulling a prank. Like playing ding dong ditch, if that was still a thing kids these days did.

I knew that was unlikely, if only because it would be an enormous coincidence to prank the one house on the street that had two people tied up inside and a dead body out back.

No, something was going on. I just didn't know what, but I wondered if Len did. Was that why he had stayed so calm?

Mikey was still outside, and it stunned me he was so brazen. He hadn't even taken a gun with him. I wished that whoever was out there would clobber Mikey over the head and drag him away. Never to return. Then, Tony would get curious about why Mikey never came back. He'd go outside to check. The same thing would happen to him. Jessica wouldn't want to go out. She would know something was wrong, but her curiosity would overwhelm her, and she would meet the same fate.

That's how it went in horror movies. Why couldn't that happen now?

I glanced at Len. He was still silent. Sitting in his chair like a statue, like nothing was out of the ordinary, except his hands were tied behind his back. He must somehow have an idea about what was happening. But how was that possible, considering he had been here since Sunday?

Mikey came back inside, and my dreams of the horror movie scenario playing out collapsed.

He slammed and locked the door. "We're getting out of here."

Tony and Jessica perked up, but neither said a word.

Mikey pointed at Len. "You know something."

Len didn't move. It didn't even look like he was breathing. That was how motionless he was. I followed his lead and remained as still as I could.

Mikey stormed up to Len. "All right, what's up?"

Len still ignored Mikey.

Mikey rubbed his head. "Just tell me what you know!"

Someone tapped on the front window. Mikey, Tony, and Jessica froze.

Then, the tapping stopped.

Jessica was the first to move. She opened her mouth, but Mikey held up a hand toward her. She said nothing.

Then, there was tapping on another window. And then another. Mikey, Jessica, and Tony remained still as the tapping continued around the house. On one side and then the back. Finally, it stopped.

Jessica started crying, and Tony looked like he might cry any second.

Mikey stayed silent but ran his hands around his head several times. He grabbed Barry's gun, which was still on the coffee table.

"Mikey, what do we do?" Jessica asked.

"We get out of here."

Jessica ran over to Mikey and grabbed his arm. "We have nowhere to go."

Mikey pulled away. "We have plenty of cash. That gives us options. Five minutes. Pack your shit and be ready, or I'm leaving without you."

Mikey went down the hallway. Jessica and Tony followed him.

I glanced toward the front door. It was then that I saw it.

The deadbolt lock began to turn.

CHAPTER 96

I glanced at the front door, doing my best not to draw attention to what I was looking at. The deadbolt lock had turned. The door was now unlocked.

I wondered who was on the other side. I felt lightheaded like I might faint.

Was it help that was on the way or more trouble? Did Mikey have other associates out there that were coming to collect? I had no way of knowing. Despite the chaos, Len remained composed. It gave me hope.

Mikey came down the hall about a minute later. He was still carrying the gun and had a duffel bag slung over his shoulder. Mikey went to the kitchen table. He zipped up the bag of cash.

Ever so slightly, the door knob turned.

Mikey grabbed the two bags, strode over to the entryway, and threw them down.

The front door swung open. A man wearing all black, a ski mask, and leather gloves burst in. The man raised his left hand, which held a gun.

Mikey saw it but said nothing. Just threw his

hands in the air.

"Down," the masked man said. "Put the gun down. Put your face on the floor."

Mikey obeyed, setting the gun on the floor, and lying down next to it. The man kicked the gun away from Mikey and picked it up. He stuck it in the back of his pants.

Suddenly, Mikey popped up and lunged at the man. But the masked man was too quick. He sprung back in one smooth motion and put distance between him and Mikey. Enough space to allow him to draw down the gun on Mikey with both hands. "Don't move."

Mikey froze.

Tony and Jessica came down the hallway, each carrying a bag. They paused at the sight of the masked intruder.

The man waved his gun at them. "You two, stand by Mikey."

I wondered if Tony and Jessica would listen. They did; they fell in line behind Mikey.

Mikey remained motionless. He had a scowl on his face, but he didn't try anything.

The man kept his gun on Mikey. "Nobody tries anything, got that?"

Then, the man inched over to Len, slipping a knife from his pocket. Using one hand, he flipped it open in one smooth motion. He cut Len's ties. Len rubbed his wrists and stood up.

The man pulled Mikey's gun from his back and handed it to Len.

"I'll get the skinny one," Len said. "You deal with Mikey."

Jessica stood behind Tony. She tugged on his sweatshirt pulling him close to her like a shield. I noticed her slipping off her sandals.

Out of nowhere, Mikey lunged at the masked man. The man fired off one round, striking Mikey in the shoulder of his good arm. My eyes shut at the sight. I took a deep breath and forced my eyes back open.

Mikey grabbed his shoulder and fell to his knees, trying to hold his shoulder with his cast.

Jessica and Tony looked like they were in shock. Neither moved. They stood just like two statues while Mikey cursed and writhed in pain on the ground.

Len grabbed the knife from the masked man and dashed over to me. Holding a gun in one hand and the knife in the other, he cut my ties. He looked me directly in the eyes. "Jocelyn, do you think you can take Jessica?"

Jessica was skinny and looked like she lacked any muscle, but that might be deceiving. "I'll try."

Jessica whispered something in Tony's ear. Tony looked around the room and then darted down the hallway. Jessica sprinted in the opposite direction toward the back door.

"Get back here!" Len yelled to Tony.

I took off after Jessica.

CHAPTER 97

Jessica threw open the back door and raced into the backyard. Adrenaline kicked in, and my legs seemed to move like they were motorized. A blast of chilly air hit me.

Just as I thought I was closing in on her, she glided away from me, her legs moving just as smoothly as mine. She was barefoot but was running with ease. Her massive ponytail swished around like the mane of a thoroughbred in the Preakness Stakes. I reached out to grab it, but I missed.

Jessica ran around the side of the house and then into the street. I could hear nothing except for our feet on the pavement and my heavy breathing. The streetlights were on, and more cars were parked on the street than when Barry brought me here earlier.

I was a runner in high school, but always long-distance, never sprinting, and my running days felt like a million years ago. I wasn't sure how long I could keep up this pace.

We passed house after house, and she didn't slow down at all. My lungs and chest burned. My hair flowed around me, but my beanie kept it out of my eyes. My Converse sneakers held their own.

After what felt like a marathon, we reached the end of the street, which was a cul-de-sac. Jessica halted, just for a second, looking unsure about what to do. She turned, ran around the circle, and doubled back to where I was.

This allowed me to gain on her, but as before, every time I got close, she pulled away. She seemed to be heading back toward the duplex. I wondered what her plan was. She ran back along the side of the house. I followed her into the backyard. My lungs burned as I inhaled the cool night air.

I made another attempt at her ponytail. This time, I got close enough. My fingers grazed the very ends of her hair. I pushed myself for one last burst. I grabbed more of her hair. I yanked. Hard. She jerked back.

I kicked her right ankle. She screamed as she lurched forward and tumbled to the ground. I dropped to my knees to subdue her, but by that time, she had flipped on her back.

Jessica clawed and kicked me. Her nails tore at my arms, but my long sleeves protected me. She swung for my face, but I dodged her attempts. Even though Jessica was skinny, she was stronger than she looked.

She continued squirming and screaming. She stopped resembling a racehorse and reminded me of a fish being pulled up by the line.

Just then, I heard a gunshot. Then another.

Startled, I loosened my grip. Who had been shot?

Jessica pushed out from underneath me, crawled away, and sprung to her feet. I scrambled up and lunged at her, wrapping my arms around her.

She pushed against me, then kicked me in the shins. Her arms were flailing, and she was trying to scratch my face. I ducked while still trying to hold on to her, but eventually she got away. She raced back toward the side of the house.

But she was too late. Len and the masked man materialized out of nowhere. Each grabbed one of her arms, held her up against the house, and then Len threw zip ties on her wrists.

CHAPTER 98

I watched the masked man grab Jessica and drag her back toward the duplex.

She was staring up at him. "Please don't hurt me. I'll help you however you need, I promise."

The masked man didn't speak.

"He won't hurt you," Len said. "Just follow his instructions."

The masked man took Jessica inside, and the neighborhood fell silent.

I bent over, my hands on my knees. My face was flushed, and I was out of breath. I inhaled, but each breath of the cool night air still burned.

Len stayed quiet, standing in the darkness. I felt like he was waiting for me to catch my breath. Finally, I felt well enough to stand up straight.

"Good work," Len said.

I laughed, but it was a nervous laugh, like I wasn't in reality any longer. What was happening right now?

Len walked over to me. "Are you okay?"

"I'm all right. Just out of shape."

"You did well."

I smiled. "She can run."

"You got her; that's all that matters. Listen, I need you to stay out here, do you understand?"

I wasn't sure I understood. In fact, I was confused. "Don't you need help?"

"No," Len said. His voice was gentle. "Can you do that for me? Stay here until I come back?"

"Sure."

"You're safe as long as you stay here."

What did that mean? I felt uncomfortable with his plans. "Should I call the police?"

Len shook his head. "No. Don't do anything. Just stay here."

While Len was still speaking calmly, my voice had become high-pitched, almost shrill.

"You're sure you don't need me to do something?"

"We'll handle it. Stay here. I'll come back for you. I promise."

I bounced around, and my legs were feeling like Jell-O. But overall, I was okay; I wasn't hurt. "All right, I'll stay here."

Len walked away from me and went back into the house. The back door and all the shades were closed; I could see nothing. I strained my ears but didn't hear anything; there was just silence.

The place looked like every other house on the street. Just another weeknight.

A small concrete slab was in the backyard with a table and two chairs. I sat down and the chair squeaked when I did.

A few seconds later, I stood. I was antsy, and my legs felt like they were cramping up. I paced around the backyard and then walked to the side of the house. My car was in the driveway; my keys were still in my jeans.

I returned to the backyard and sat back in the chair. My mind felt like it had been racing for days. But after my sprint through the neighborhood, endorphins flooded my body and my mind felt almost blank. I should have had even more questions, but I only had an odd sense of calm.

I was no longer tied up in the chair. Len was alive. Everything was going to be okay. I could feel it.

After an eternity, Len opened the back door of that little duplex in San Pedro. "It's time, Jocelyn. You can come back in."

Just as he promised.

ONE WEEK LATER

It was December 20. It had only been a week, but things were already returning to normal. For a while there, I was sure I would have to move. I liked where I lived and was happy it didn't come to that.

I thought about everything that had happened. Mikey, just out of prison, was already back to his old ways, this time robbing banks by proxy. It was a unique way of doing it; I'd give him that. Less violent, and less of a chance for Mikey to get caught. As far as the poor person who answered the ad and found him or herself at the bank? The same could not be said.

Despite the gunshots I heard when I was outside, no one had been killed. Mikey, however, had been hit twice. The first time was when I was still inside, and he went for the masked man's gun. He had been hit a second time when he tried yet another escape. That time, I was outside.

Mikey, Tony, and Jessica were all arrested that night. I knew that each was looking at a lengthy prison sentence for their involvement in Len's kidnapping, my being held hostage, and Barry's murder. Then, of course, there was Doug's murder. I figured I might have to testify at some point.

When everything happened at ADWR, the thought of going to court terrified me. I had been spared then. But if I had to testify this time, I felt prepared. Like I could do it.

Mikey was sure that Len had his money from the Century City heist. Yet Len insisted he didn't have it. And I believed Len was telling the truth. So far, the money had never been found. Well, not officially.

I was glad that Len was back. He kept referring to Mikey as a bum and thanked me for trying to find him. I told Len to forget about it. He had helped me, and I had helped him.

The masked man was gone when Len brought me back into the house, but I knew it was Jan. I owed him for saving us. But Len and Jan didn't want to discuss it. Or anything about it. Including Len's kidnapping. I still had many unanswered questions. But I followed their lead and kept quiet. Maybe Len would tell me about it later. Maybe not. Either way was fine with me. I was just glad we were all okay.

I was heading out for an afternoon walk. I locked my apartment and went toward the front gate. Len and Jan were sitting on Len's patio. The two looked like they could be brothers.

As I came down the stairs, Betty's door opened. "Look who it is, The Number's Gal. Len, have you told Jocelyn about the murder yet?"

"What about it?" I asked.

"We found out how Doug died," Betty said.

Len raised a finger. "We think we found out. That's just what's in the paper."

"Well, I believe it," Betty said. "Why would they lie?"

Len rolled his eyes.

"How did Doug die?" I asked.

Betty stuck her hands on her hips. "Mikey gave him a sedative. And then…"

"And then what?" I asked.

Betty made a slashing motion across her throat. "You know."

I wondered why Mikey would have drugged Doug before killing him. I looked at Len and Jan, but neither had any expression I could read. "A sedative?"

Betty walked over to Len's patio. "There were two glasses on Len's kitchen table. One with Mikey's fingerprints and the other with Doug's. Mikey's glass was still full. Doug's was almost empty. Both had sedatives. Since Mikey never drank his, it's obvious he put in the sedatives."

I nodded, but something felt off about the story. "Okay."

Betty stepped closer to me. "That's not the weirdest part. One of Len's glasses is missing."

Len frowned. "No, it's not, Betty. I wish you'd stop saying that."

"You had four cocktail glasses. Two were on the table. There's only one left in the cupboard. What happened to the fourth?"

Len stood from his chair. "Who knows, Betty? It could've been gone for years, for all I know."

Betty shrugged. "Suit yourself, but I swear you had four."

Jan stood up. "What are your Christmas plans, Jocelyn?"

"I'm going to Palm Springs."

Jan smiled. "That will be very nice for you."

I had canceled my trip to Omaha. My Aunt Pauline lived in Nebraska and was traveling to Palm Springs for Christmas. She was single and had no children. Every year, Aunt Pauline spent Christmas in a warm climate. This year, she had rented a house in Palm Springs and invited me down. I wondered if she felt sorry for me, with my mom and dad's separation, and had chosen Palm Springs because of its proximity to Los Angeles.

As the expression goes, it was best not to look a gift horse in the mouth. We planned to shop, make delicious food, and spend time in the sun.

"Jan, I thought you were going to Poland," I said.

Jan winked at me. "I had to change my flight because something came up. I've rescheduled it for tomorrow."

"Well, have a good time."

"Thank you."

I nodded. "No, thank you."

Jan's blue eyes seemed to sparkle. "I told Len how you don't know much about him. How that should change."

Len waved and laughed. "Don't listen to him."

Jan continued, "Get him to tell you about the old days!"

Len waved again like he was swatting flies. "No one wants to hear about that, Jan. Besides, you're holding Jocelyn up. Let her go on her walk."

Jan shook his head. "Fine, fine. I can tell you, Jocelyn, any time you want to know."

I exited the gate. As I did, I bumped into Tara, walking up the sidewalk. She was carrying a box. Gone was her light brown hair; she was a blonde now. I was surprised to see her here.

"Hey, Jocelyn."

"Hi, Tara. Or should I call you Corinne?"

She set the box on the brick wall outside the gate. "Tara's my middle name. Either is fine with me."

"What do you prefer?"

She smiled. "Corinne."

"Okay, great," I said. "Are you moving back in?"

She nodded. "Len asked me if I'd still like to live here, and I said yes. And it looks like Mikey's going away."

"That's good news, huh?"

Corinne beamed. "Yes! It's such a relief. And this time, Mikey should be gone for good."

"I'm glad you're back," I said.

"Thanks, me too. I'll see you around."

Corinne picked up the box from the ledge and approached the gate. I turned to walk down Montana toward Bundy.

"Oh, hey," Corinne called after me. "Thanks for giving my letter to Len. I appreciate it."

I read Corinne's letter to Len, but it didn't mention Doug or why Corinne had moved out in such a hurry. I had lingering questions about what happened to Doug in Len's apartment and what made Corinne want to flee. I kept my questions to myself for now. "No problem."

"Did you read it?"

I figured there was no point in lying to her. "Yes."

"I assumed you would."

I smiled. "I'm not planning to tell anyone."

"I know. Even if you do, it's okay."

"I won't."

I meant what I said to Corinne. I read the letter because I was trying to find Len. I had no intention of blabbing about what was a private communication. But Corinne's mention of the letter made me remember something. Corinne had said she left something in her storage unit for Len.

I had a general idea of what it was and wanted to find out if I was right. "Did you know the money from the Century City robbery has never been found?"

Corinne shifted the box in her hands. "No kidding?"

"Mikey stashed it at one of Len's properties. The one on Mayfield. But it's not there."

She smiled. "That's interesting."

"Hopefully, someone found it and is using it well."

Corinne winked at me; I chuckled to myself. For the second time today, someone had winked at me.

I gave Corinne a slight wave and then put in my

headphones.

The sun was out, the sky was clear, and the temperature was in the seventies. I couldn't ask for a more beautiful December 20.

My mind went to my new career. I wanted to make a go of it working on my own. I didn't feel destined to spend my life working in a cubicle all day. But after everything that had happened, I was wary.

Yet I still felt optimistic. My future projects couldn't all turn out this bad, could they?

AUTHOR'S NOTE

Thanks for reading! If you enjoyed *The Missing Client*, would you consider leaving a review? The following link takes you directly to the review page for the book: https://amzn.to/4eldq41.

For periodic updates, including notification when the next installment in the Jocelyn Bennett series is released, subscribe to my newsletter here: sendfox.com/krystalpowersauthor.

ABOUT KRYSTAL

In another life, Krystal was an accountant who dreamed of writing thrillers. Now she's writing thrillers about accountants. She lives in California and is working on her next book.

Visit krystalpowers.com.

Made in the USA
Monee, IL
12 August 2024

63679952R10217